ALIEN WIFE

When Abby trapped Luke Jordan into marrying her, her motive was revenge—on Luke's girl-friend, Abby's glamorous aunt Ella, who had wrecked her parents' marriage. But Abby wasn't yet twenty, while Luke was a thirty-eight-year-old man of the world. Hadn't she got herself into rather too deep water?

ALIEN WIFE

BY

ANNE MATHER

MILLS & BOON LIMITED
17–19 FOLEY STREET
LONDON W1A 1DR

First published 1976
This edition 1977

© Anne Mather 1976

ISBN 0 263 72368 2

*Made and Printed in Great Britain by
Richard Clay (The Chaucer Press), Ltd, Bungay, Suffolk*

CHAPTER ONE

LUKE pushed the Lamborghini up to a hundred on the brief straight, impatience making him grind the gears as yet another corner confronted him, forcing him to slow to a saner sixty. Since leaving Fort Augustus, the scenery had grown progressively more rugged and wilder, the road narrow and winding between reed-edged lochs and purple banks of heather. After the motorways of the south, the powerful car baulked at these primitive highways where long-horned Highland cattle seemed to have right of way. He had already had to make one detour to avoid a lumbering stock wagon, and wondered how long it took to develop the kind of temperament that took all these obstacles in its stride.

Glancing at the plain gold watch on his wrist, he saw that it was only a little after three o'clock, and taking into account the fact that he had stopped for a superb lunch of locally caught salmon and out-of-season strawberries, rounded off by strong black coffee and brandy, he was making quite good time. Ardnalui should not be much further and with luck he would have time before dusk to study the general layout of the place so that when he rang Scott later, he could give him an honest opinion.

A few spots of rain landed on the windscreen, as if to mock his intentions, and he looked up at the low clouds hanging over the mountains that had dogged his progress. It was so remote, thought Luke irritably. How could they possibly bring a film crew out here? And not even an airstrip within fifty miles.

The road swung round a steep curve and there ahead of him lay the village, a cluster of whitewashed dwellings bordering the shores of the loch. A long narrow inlet of water, Loch Ifor ran into the Sound of Sleat, and a collection of fishing vessels nudging a stone jetty indicated the livelihood of many of the villagers. As he drove slowly between the cottages, he had to concede that Scott had been right in his belief that Ardnalui was the ideal setting for Luke's novel. But then Scott had been born here. Luke, born and bred in Liverpool, had seldom been far from the concrete trappings of his kind of civilisation.

He wondered what his host, Daniel McGregor, would be like. The fact that Scott had been closely acquainted with the parish priest did nothing for Luke himself, who on the whole preferred to make his own arrangements. But Ardnalui did not possess a hotel, and the inn he passed on his way through the village did not look as if it had room for boarders. Besides, Scott had arranged that he should stay with McGregor, and it was only for a couple of nights anyway. It would be amusing to tell Ella he had been to her birthplace when she got back from Rome. Somehow he sensed she would not altogether approve. She was not proud of her humble beginnings, while he had no compunction about telling people how his mother had struggled to bring up his three sisters, four brothers and himself after their father lost his life in an engine explosion at sea.

Several children turned to stare at the car, and Luke felt his normally good humour returning. He liked children, and had several nephews and nieces who benefited from his weakness. Now that he was here, he could forget about the tortuous journey, and concentrate on the job in hand.

He passed the grey stone church of St Cecilia and there, exactly as Scott had described it, was the presbytery. Grey stone, like the church it served, with small leaded panes and a sturdy wooden door. A cobbled yard fronted the building, and Luke parked the Lamborghini here before sliding out to stretch his legs.

He was a tall man, easily six feet, with a lean muscular frame. Used to an active life, since his writing success, he had kept himself fit with a twice weekly workout at a gym not far away from his London apartment, playing squash and badminton whenever he had the time. He was tanned, from a recent holiday in the Bahamas, and his hair was silvery fair, bleached even whiter by the sun. It was smooth, thick hair, overlapping his collar at the back, but it needed no hairdressing and always looked clean and vital to the touch. He was not a handsome man, but he was attractive

6

to women, a fact he had not lived until thirty-eight years without appreciating.

The air was sharp for April, or perhaps he was soft from the milder London climate, he thought dryly, breathing deeply. And it was so quiet here. He doubted he'd be able to sleep. Looking about him, he wondered where Ella used to live. One of these cottages? Some transition to a Mayfair apartment and a villa in the South of France. What a pity she had no relatives to share her success.

A huge lion's head knocker resounded noisily throughout the presbytery, and he stood, his hands in the pockets of his black leather jacket, waiting to be admitted. He had never expected to stay at a priest's house, but at least he had been baptised into the Faith.

The door was opened by an elderly woman in a long black dress and a white apron, a lace mob cap set on her grey hair. Good God, thought Luke in astonishment, do servants like this really exist outside of novels?

Smiling disarmingly, however, he said: 'I'm Luke Jordan. I believe Father McGregor is expecting me.'

'That he is,' agreed the woman politely. 'Will you come in, sir?'

Luke stepped inside, his eyes taking in the polished floor with its single rug, the dark wood panelling and angled staircase. The doors opening into the hall were all closed, but even as he registered this, one of them opened to an elderly man, leaning on a cane, whose sharply alert eyes belied any diminishing faculties of his advanced years.

'Is it Mr Jordan?' he asked, staring at Luke appraisingly.

'That's right, sir,' Luke nodded. 'How do you do?'

'I'm well.' The man smiled and held out his hand. 'I'm pleased to make your acquaintance, Mr Jordan.'

'Luke will do,' responded the younger man easily, taking an immediate liking to his host.

'You're not a Scotsman, Luke,' observed the priest, leading the way back into the room he had just left.

'No,' Luke agreed. 'I came from Liverpool, actually, although I live in London now.'

'Ah!' McGregor nodded. 'Well, let us make ourselves comfortable, shall we? It's a chill day, and you're no doubt

7

feeling the cold after all that central heating you have in the south. No such refinements here, I'm afraid. A fire is all we have. But it's cosy, and it keeps you warm.'

The room they entered was a comfortable study, pleasantly illuminated by the fire burning in the grate, and lined with shelves of books. There was the scent of pine logs and pipe tobacco, and indicating that Luke should take the armchair at the opposite side of the fire from his own, McGregor issued the hovering housekeeper with orders for afternoon tea.

'Unless you'd like something stronger?' he queried, raising his eyebrows, but Luke said tea would be fine.

After they were seated, Luke added: 'It's very good of you to accommodate me like this. I mean, Scott tends to expect everyone to jump to his bidding at the studio, and I guess he lets the feeling carry him away.'

'Any friend of Scott Anderson's is a friend of mine,' McGregor assured him warmly. 'And you're welcome to stay as long as you like. I enjoy a bit of company, and there's a little enough goes on here at the best of times. Tell me, do you play chess, by any chance?'

Luke looked apologetic. 'Not very well, I'm afraid.'

'Ah, well. That's a pity.' McGregor reached for his pipe. 'And you're here to consider making a film of Ardnalui?' He lit a spill from the fire. 'Scott told me that you are a writer. Should I know your name?'

Luke grinned. 'It's possible. It depends what kind of literature you read. My books are not masterpieces, but I've been lucky enough to have a couple of them filmed, and now they're wanting to make a television series about the third. That's why I'm here. Scott commissioned the book, you see.'

McGregor chewed thoughtfully away at his pipe. 'Do you know Scotland at all?'

'No.' Luke was honest. 'This is my first visit.'

'And yet you wrote about it.'

'It's not difficult, sir. I have been to Austria, and the scenery is not too dissimilar. And people are people, the world over.'

'I doubt the people here would agree with you,' remarked McGregor dryly. 'But I know what you're trying to say.'

'Inverleven—the imaginary place in my book—isn't intended to be Ardnalui,' Luke explained quietly. 'But I used Scott's descriptions of the place, and it was his idea that I should come to see it for myself.'

'With a view to filming here.'

Luke shook his head. 'Somehow I doubt it. It's too far off the beaten track, I'm afraid. I think Scott just wanted me to see this place—where he was born.'

The priest nodded. 'I can't deny you've somewhat reassured me. I don't know that I like the idea of Ardnalui being overrun with film people.'

He made them sound like a different species, and Luke smiled. He had had similar reservations when his first book was bought for the screen. But he had met a lot of decent people in his association with the industry, and they offset the seamier side.

'Are you a married man, Luke?'

McGregor had a priest's healthy interest in the personal lives of his acquaintances, and Luke shook his head. 'Not now. I was. I got married when I was about—eighteen. It didn't work. We were divorced twelve years ago.'

'Divorced!' The priest looked regretful. 'There is no divorce in the eyes of God, my son.'

Luke shrugged. He had expected that. 'Jennifer's dead now,' he said flatly. 'She married again, but she and her husband were killed in a car crash five years ago.'

The housekeeper returned with a tray of tea and some delicious-smelling scones and sandwiches. While McGregor took charge of the teacups, Luke looked round the room with interest. His host's interest in chess was evident in the exquisite set of chessmen, set upon a board table to one side of the fireplace, but he obviously enjoyed fishing, too, for there were rods and a creel basket, and several boxes of flies.

While they ate, McGregor described the village. He was interested in its history, and mentioned how the Jacobite cause had been strongly supported in these parts. He talked about Prestonpans and the bloody defeat of Culloden, and it was with reluctance that Luke eventually pulled himself up out of his chair and explained his desire to take a walk around the village before supper.

'Can it not wait till the morning?' suggested McGregor hopefully, and Luke guessed the old priest was trying to prolong his stay. After the lazy relaxation of the last hour, Luke was not so averse to that as he might have been. His life in London was inclined to be hectic, and it had been good to loosen up and let time take care of itself for a change. And after all, he had nothing to hurry back to town for.

'Well . . .' he began, and guessing he was weakening, McGregor added: 'You could take a walk down to the loch. Then tomorrow, I'll accompany you on a tour of Ardnalui.'

'All right,' Luke nodded. 'But I promised to phone Scott later.'

'You can use the phone in here,' said McGregor at once. 'Now, I expect you'd like to see your room before you take your walk. I'll have Mrs Tully show you.'

Luke collected his overnight case from the car, secured its doors and windows, and then followed the ample proportions of the housekeeper upstairs. The panelling of the staircase was continued along the landing. There were several doors, and a half frosted glass one which Mrs Tully explained was the bathroom.

'There's a wash basin in your room, sir,' she said, opening one of the bedroom doors and preceding him inside, 'but I'm afraid we only have the one bath.'

Luke assured her that he didn't mind, and after she had departed, he walked to the low windows which overlooked the loch. It was quite a view, and he turned back to face the room with resignation. It was reasonably large, but chilly after the warmth of his apartment, and although the bedroom suite was large and old-fashioned, the bed was a modern divan, and singularly ungenerous in its proportions.

He left his room and used the bathroom, amused at its antiquated fitments. The bath had claw feet, and the cistern made peculiar noises when one turned on the taps. Back in his room again, he washed his face and hands, ran a rueful finger over his roughening jawline, and then de-

10

ciding that shaving could wait until later, he went downstairs.

He let himself out of the house, and stood for a moment, bracing himself against the cold evening air. Perhaps he should have put on his overcoat. The leather jacket was little protection against the mist that was now rising from the loch. Still, he wouldn't stay out long, he decided briskly, and ran lightly down the steps.

As he did so, a figure straightened from the far side of the Lamborghini, and used to the ever-present menace of car thieves in London, Luke checked and turned about, reaching the youth before he could get away. 'What do you think you—— Good God! Ella!'

The girl turned to face him and he saw at once he had made a mistake. This girl was tall but slimmer than Ella, and her long silky black hair had none of the chestnut lights he was used to. Her eyes were different, too—dark, instead of blue, her mouth wider and more generous. Besides, she was casually dressed in tight-fitting jeans and a red wool sweater, the kind of attire Ella would never dream of assuming. Nevertheless, there was more than a resemblance.

She frowned at his recognition, and said flatly: 'My name is Abby Rodriguez. Should I know you?'

Luke stared at her helplessly, and then shook his head. 'I'm—sorry. I thought you were someone else. You have a definite—look of someone I know. But I realise now, you're younger than she is.'

And more attractive, he realised incredulously, his senses stirring. How Ella would dislike the knowledge that there was someone else with her particular brand of beauty, someone with youth and innocence on her side.

The girl's face cleared. 'Of course.' She smiled. 'You must be Mr Jordan. You—know my aunt.'

'Your—aunt?' Luke was confused.

'Yes. Aunt Ella—Ella McKay.'

'Ella McKay is your aunt?'

'Yes. Didn't you know she had a niece?'

'I—why, no.' Luke could not have been more astounded. Why hadn't Ella ever mentioned the girl?

'I was admiring your car,' she said enthusiastically. 'It's

11

beautiful! How fast can it go? Over a hundred?'

Luke endeavoured to grasp his thoughts. 'Well over a hundred,' he agreed dryly. 'Do you drive, Miss Rodriguez?'

'Call me Abby, everyone does. And yes, I can drive. Uncle Daniel taught me.' Her expression was rueful. 'You look as if you could do with a drink. I think Uncle Daniel has some fire-water, as well as the sherry he keeps for his parishioners. Shall we go inside?'

Luke was perplexed. 'Daniel McGregor is your uncle?'

'My adopted uncle,' she amended quietly. 'My parents are—dead. Uncle Daniel made himself responsible for me.' She paused. 'Aunt Ella didn't tell you, did she?' Luke shook his head, and she went on: 'I'm not really surprised. A film star with a sex image doesn't want a twenty-year-old niece hanging around, does she?'

Luke supported himself against the bonnet of the car. 'I didn't even know Ella had a sister.'

Abby shrugged her slim shoulders. 'Oh, well...' She smiled again. 'I must say, you're not what I expected either. Uncle Daniel told me you were coming, but I expected someone old—forty-five or fifty, at least.'

'Thank you.' Luke half smiled. 'I am nearing forty, and strange as it may seem to you, I don't consider that old!'

She laughed, revealing even white teeth. 'Well, you don't look it,' she conceded lightly. 'Are you staying long?'

'Two—maybe three days.'

'Is that all? Uncle Daniel will be disappointed. He expected you to stay a week, at least.'

Luke straightened. 'We'll see.'

She put her foot on the bottom step. 'Are you coming in?'

'Actually, I was going to walk down to the loch,' he replied, although that idea was not so attractive as it had been.

'Shall I come with you?' she suggested. 'I can point out our famous landmarks.'

'All right.'

Luke was willing, although he wondered that she didn't feel the cold in her thin sweater. She walked easily beside him, matching her steps to his long strides, exchanging a smile of shared enjoyment.

'Do you live in London, Mr Jordan?' she asked, as they climbed over a low wooden fence and crunched across the shingle to the water's edge.

Luke nodded. 'Have you been there?'

Abby shook her head. 'I've only been away from Ardnalui once, and that was on a holiday to Madrid. My grandparents used to live there, but they're dead now, too.'

Luke was amazed. 'So you're half Spanish?'

'Mmm.' She laughed softly. 'Not so like Aunt Ella after all.'

'But how did your parents meet?'

'My father was working in a hotel in Glasgow. He used to come up here for holidays.'

'I see.' But Luke was curious. She was very young to be an orphan. 'Did your parents have an accident?'

A flicker of pain crossed her face and he realised how tactless he had been. 'I'm sorry,' he apologised. 'Don't answer that. I had no right to ask. It's nothing to do with me.'

'That's all right.' She had herself in control again. 'No, they didn't die together, if that's what you mean. My father —went away with another woman. It broke my mother's heart. Later, when she learned he had died, she just didn't want to go on living.'

From anyone else, the words might have sounded over-dramatic, but she spoke quietly, without emphasis, relating the events as they had happened.

'I'm sorry,' he said again, his hands deep in the pockets of his leather jacket. 'It must be very painful for you to talk about it.'

'It used to be. But it's five years since my mother died. I've got over the worst.'

'And now you—live with Daniel McGregor?'

She nodded. 'He's been like a second father to me.'

Luke wondered how much of this Scott Anderson had known. He must have known Ella had a sister, of course, yet he had never mentioned it. Why? And even when he had arranged for Luke to stay at the presbytery, he had not said a word about its other occupant. Scott and Ella only tolerated one another, Luke knew that, but had it some other deeper significance that the conflict of artistic temperaments Luke had imagined?

'Do you see that mountain across the loch—the one that's almost obscured by the mist? That's our most famous landmark—Ben Lui. And the one beside it, the smaller peak—that's Ben Ifor.'

Realising that Abby was speaking again, Luke tried to pick up the threads of her conversation. But it was difficult when his mind was filled with questions he was reluctant to voice, and presently she shivered, and suggested they walked back.

On their way up to the house, he said: 'What do you do all day? There can't be much work for a girl like you here.'

'You'd be surprised,' she smiled. 'I work at the inn.'

'The inn!' Luke was surprised.

'Why?' she teased him. 'You're not teetotal, are you?'

'No, but . . .'

Luke made a helpless gesture, and she chuckled. 'But you don't think it's a suitable occupation for someone who lives in the presbytery, is that it?'

'I suppose so,' he agreed ruefully.

She shook her head. 'You don't have to concern yourself. I'm not the local barmaid. I look after the Dalrymples' three children. The Dalrymples keep the inn,' she explained.

Luke nodded. 'I see.'

The wind was beginning to rise as they entered the house, and Abby hunched her shoulders expressively. Mrs Tully was in the hall, and she viewed the girl with impatience.

'You'll be having pneumonia, miss,' she announced, with a sharp familiarity. 'Away upstairs and take a bath before supper.'

The girl took her scolding with an affectionate grimace, and Mrs Tully shook her head at Luke as she ran upstairs. 'I never thought,' she exclaimed. 'Perhaps you would have liked a bath, sir.'

'A shave will do,' remarked Luke easily. 'Er—Father McGregor said I might use his phone . . .'

'Yes, sir. The study's free now. Father Daniel has gone over to the church.'

'Thank you.'

When Scott came through, his voice was faint and barely distinguishable, and it was impossible for Luke to speak as forcefully as he would have liked.

'I've met the girl,' he said without preamble. 'I gather that was why you sent me up here.'

'Now why should you think that?'

There was faint amusement in Scott's voice, but Luke found he was not amused. 'It's obvious, isn't it? Arranging for me to stay here! You knew I couldn't avoid meeting her.'

'So what did you think of her?' Scott asked. 'She's a beautiful creature, isn't she?'

'Why didn't you tell me Ella had a niece?'

'Why didn't *I*? Why didn't she?'

'I don't know.' Luke was impatient. 'Some idea of protecting her image, perhaps. What the hell! The girl's only her niece. She could have told *me*.'

'But she didn't.'

'What's that supposed to mean?'

'Nothing.' Scott was annoyingly guileless. 'Anyway, what of it? Abby isn't the reason you went up there.'

'Isn't she?'

'What do you think of the place? What do you think of Ardnalui?'

Luke sighed. 'Exactly what you'd expect me to think, I suppose. You're right, it is the ideal setting for the series. But something tells me we won't be filming here.'

Scott laughed. 'Remote, eh? Yes, I knew that. As a matter of fact, someone's put forward a suggestion that we should do the filming in Cornwall. There's a village there that——'

'And you let me come up here!' Luke was getting angry, resentment at the feeling of being manipulated destroying all his earlier enjoyment of the place.

'You needed the break, Luke. And I'd hazard a guess that Dan made you welcome.'

'He did. But that's not the point——'

'Cool it, Luke. Okay, I guess I did think it would be amusing for you to meet Abby——'

'*Amusing!*'

15

'—but I wasn't trying to take a rise out of you. You have to believe that, Luke. Abby's a nice kid. Why should Ella have it all her our way?'

'All her own way? What're you talking about?'

'Well, Ella could have—helped the girl, contributed to her upbringing. But has she? Not one blind cent!'

Belatedly, Luke remembered what Abby had told him about her parents being dead and Daniel McGregor making himself responsible for her. It hadn't registered at the time, but now he did wonder why Ella had never cared sufficiently to send money for her own niece's welfare.

'Are you sure about that?' he asked now, loath to relinquish the image he had always held of Ella—as someone warm and generous, someone who cared about people more than possessions. She could be arrogant, he knew that, but then so could he, and he knew the feelings she had for him were not counterfeit. His feelings towards her were less easy to analyse. Since his disastrous first marriage, he had avoided that kind of commitment, and although he liked Ella very much, and was fond of her, he was not yet convinced that their temperaments were compatible to that extent.

'Ask me that question when you get back to town,' Scott told him blandly. 'Now, how long are you staying?'

'I don't know yet.' Luke wanted to go on talking about Ella, but obviously Scott had said as much as he was going to for the moment. 'The whole trip seems to have been pointless. Have you heard from Ella?'

'There was a cable for you, so I took the liberty of opening it——'

'Thanks.'

'—and in it she mentions she'll be back by the end of next week. I have her phone number ...'

'So do I,' retorted Luke shortly. 'Okay, Scott. I'll see you in a few days.'

'My pleasure.'

The phone went dead as Scott hung up and Luke replace his receiver with suppressed frustration. Why should Scott do this to him? Why send him up here on a wild goose chase? His excuse about him needing a break was not enough. Ella was away, finishing the film in Rome; the

16

coincidence was too great, the opportunity too good to miss. And why? To meet a girl who resembled Ella to the extent that there could be no doubt about their relationship. If only Ella had told him herself. The fact that she hadn't made the situation that much more difficult, putting an entirely different light on the quality of their relationship. He had been completely honest about the facts of his divorce. Why couldn't Ella have been the same?

CHAPTER TWO

WHEN Abby came down to breakfast next morning, Daniel McGregor was alone at the table. Noticing the way she raised her eyebrows at the empty place, he smiled.

'Mr Jordan is not, I think, an early riser, my dear,' he remarked, helping himself to more toast.

Abby seated herself at the table and reached for the coffee pot. 'I don't consider eight o'clock is early,' she pointed out.

'No, not for us, perhaps. But we don't keep the hours they keep in London.' McGregor paused. 'Well? What did you think of him?'

'What did I think of him?' Abby played for time. 'That's an odd question.'

'But apt, don't you think?' The old man shook his head. 'I'm not a fool, Abby. I know you wanted to meet him.'

Abby's cheeks burned. 'Well, that's not unnatural, is it?'

'No.' McGregor shook his head. 'I understand your feelings. But don't be bitter, child. Life is too short for that.'

Abby bent over her toast, her long dark hair successfully concealing her features from her adopted uncle. Bitter? Yes, she supposed, she was bitter. But it wasn't that that had made her want to meet Luke Jordan. Other emotions had long since taken over from bitterness, emotions far more destructive if she allowed them free rein.

'So?' McGregor was speaking again. 'What was your impression?'

Abby frowned. What had been her impression of the

man her aunt was reputed to be going to marry? Yesterday afternoon he had seemed amiable enough, and certainly attractive in a hard, masculine kind of way, but during and after dinner he had been broodingly morose, only speaking when spoken to and contributing nothing of his own experiences to the conversation. She had hoped he would talk, perhaps about her aunt, but instead he had concentrated on the food on his plate, and only occasionally had she encountered his gaze upon her in frowning meditation.

Now she shrugged her slim shoulders, and said: 'He—he seemed withdrawn.'

'Last evening, you mean?' McGregor nodded. 'Yes, I noticed that. Perhaps the man was tired.'

'He didn't seem so in the afternoon.'

'Until after he had met you...' murmured her adopted uncle thoughtfully.

Abby looked up. 'What do you mean?'

'Well, you know he didn't know of your existence, don't you?'

'I—yes.'

'Mmm.' The priest wiped his mouth with his napkin. 'I wonder why Scott refrained from telling him.'

'You might say the same of Aunt Ella,' Abby interposed quickly, before she could stop herself.

McGregor sighed. 'You are bitter, Abby. I was afraid you might be.' He leant across the table to imprison one of her hands beneath his gnarled one. 'My dear, Ella has her own reasons for eschewing her responsibilities towards you, and we both know what they are. Who knows? Perhaps she regrets what happened as much as we do——'

'I don't believe that.'

Abby's tone was flat, and the priest released her hand and rested back in his chair regarding her disappointedly. 'Abby, Abby! Things haven't been so bad for you, have they?'

Abby felt a twinge of shame. 'Of course not, Uncle Daniel. But—without you...'

'But there was me,' he replied quietly. 'And believe me, Ella will have suffered for her thoughtlessness.'

'Thoughtlessness!' Abby pressed her lips tightly together. She could think of other words more apt.

'Well...' McGregor pushed back his chair and got to his feet, 'I must go. Mrs Lewis was taken ill again in the night, and I promised I'd go over this morning. If you see our guest, will you tell him I will have to postpone our tour of the village?'

Abby replaced her coffee cup in its saucer. 'I—er—I have the morning off,' she volunteered. 'I could—show Mr Jordan the village.'

McGregor hesitated. Then he shook his head as if dismissing the problem. 'Why not?' he agreed. 'I'm sure the choice of courier will not cause any dissension.'

Abby felt a momentary pang of remorse, and reached for his hand. 'You've always been like a father to me, Uncle Daniel,' she mumbled unhappily.

The priest patted her head reassuringly, but there was an anxious expression in his eyes. 'You said that as if you regretted it, Abby,' he protested, and she forced a smile and lifted her head.

'I—as if I could!' she exclaimed, and then coloured anew as a tall figure darkened the doorway.

'I'm sorry. Am I late for breakfast?'

Luke Jordan stood regarding them both apologetically, lean and disturbing in black suede pants which hugged the bulging muscles of his thighs and emphasised the length of his legs. A black roll-necked sweater completed the ensemble, throwing the lightness of his hair into sharp relief, a startling contrast to his tanned skin. Tall and powerful, he emanated a sexual attraction that was both unconscious and disruptive.

McGregor released Abby's hand, and greeted his guest warmly. 'Of course not, my son,' he told him firmly. 'Mrs Tully will provide you with whatever you wish. And...' he paused, glancing at Abby half doubtfully, '... as I have parish matters to attend to this morning, Abby has offered her services as your guide.'

'Abby?' Luke's green eyes turned in her direction, and she could see the guarded expression in their depths. 'That's—very kind of her, but it's not necessary. I can make my own way.'

Abby's smile felt fixed and artificial, but she insisted she

19

had nothing else to do. This was too good an opportunity to miss.

'But I understood you looked after some children,' he interposed smoothly, and she had to compel herself to go on with the charade.

'I'm free this morning,' she explained, aware of the old priest's eyes upon her. She forced a light laugh. 'If you say much more, I shall think you don't want my company!'

Luke recognised defeat, but there was a grimness about his mouth which belied her victory. Mrs Tully appeared to see whether their guest required breakfast, and McGregor took his leave, mentioning he would see them both at lunchtime.

Abby finished her meal quickly, and went to change her shoes while Mrs Tully attended to Luke Jordan. She guessed he was not pleased with her offer of companionship, but if she was to go through with this she must not be put off at the first obstacle. Besides, he was aware of her —how could he not be?—and once they got to know one another ... She refused to consider her own feelings.

She zipped her slender legs into long boots and added a crimson windcheater to her attire of jeans and denim shirt. Her hair she left loose for once, aware that its silky strands looked well against the brilliant colour of her jacket.

Luke Jordan was still at the breakfast table when she returned, reading the morning newspaper and apparently in no hurry to begin his sightseeing. But he was polite enough to get to his feet when she entered the room, and his gaze flickered briefly over the attractive picture she made.

'I'm ready,' she said unnecessarily, and he inclined his head.

'So I see.'

'Have you finished breakfast?'

He indicated his empty plate, the dregs in the bottom of his coffee cup. 'It would appear so.'

Abby sighed. 'But you don't want to come out with me?'

Luke regarded her dourly for a few moments, and then he folded his newspaper and laid it beside his plate. 'I— there's no urgency, is there?'

'No.' Abby wished she could control her colour, but

right now she didn't seem to be having much success at controlling anything.

Luke frowned. 'Tell me something—how well do you know Scott Anderson?'

'Scott?' Abby was glad she was red now. It disguised any further embarrassment she might have exhibited.

'Yes, Scott. You do know him, don't you?'

'Of course.' Abby lifted her shoulders awkwardly. 'He—well, he used to live in the village.'

'I know that.'

'He was—a friend of my mother's.'

'Was he? How close a friend?'

Abby's eyes sparkled angrily now. 'What do you mean?'

Luke made a gesture of innocence. 'Nothing detrimental, I assure you. I'm merely trying to ascertain Scott's relationship to you.'

'Well...' Abby sought for words. 'When—when my father first left my mother, Scott's father was still alive and living in Ardnalui. He used to come up to see him, and he used to visit my mother at the same time.'

'So he and your mother—and your aunt—were much of an age?'

'No.' Abby shook her head. 'Aunt Ella was younger.'

Luke nodded. 'But Ella—your aunt—she had left the village by this time.'

'Oh, yes. She went away before I was born.'

'And she never came back?'

Abby half turned away. 'To begin with, she used to.' She shrugged. 'Do you want to see the village or don't you?'

'Do you know why Ella never mentions you?'

His question was direct, and Abby raised her dark eyebrows. 'Like I told you, I suppose I might have ruined her image.'

Luke regarded her steadily for several seconds, and she was made intensely aware of the strength of her adversary. This was no easy task she had set herself, but already she had made some headway. All she needed was time, and an ability to act, almost as great as Ella's.

The air was sharp, and the mist still lingered beside the loch. But it was going to be a fine day, and Luke breathed deeply of the clear northern air.

'Where do you want to begin?' asked Abby, as they walked away from the presbytery, and Luke glanced down at her wryly.

'You tell me,' he suggested, his hands deep in the pockets of his leather jacket, and she smiled.

'All right. We'll walk to the harbour. It's small, but you might find it interesting.'

They walked in single file along the narrow village street which the Lamborghini had negotiated the day before, and Abby had a greeting for everyone who passed. Some of the villagers stared openly at Luke, but she failed to satisfy their curiosity. She walked with an easy casual grace that gave elegance to the most informal attire, her long hair clinging in strands to the crimson windcheater, like ropes of black silk.

The jetty was almost deserted, the fishing boats which had nudged its sides the afternoon before all gone. A few old men sat together mending nets and smoking their pipes, and one or two of them called to Abby and she answered them.

'Do you know everyone in this village?' Luke asked, as they leaned together on the wall, looking out over the choppy waters of the loch, and she smiled.

'Of course. I've lived here all my life—I told you.'

'Except for a trip to Madrid. Yes, I know.' Luke turned to look at her, and she had to look away from the penetration in his eyes. 'That's why your hair is so much darker than——' He broke off. 'Don't you have any relations in Spain?'

She shook her head, and a strand of her hair blew into his face. He put up a hand to brush it away, and his fingers lingered on the silky threads.

'My father's two brothers were killed in the civil war,' she explained. 'When my grandparents died, there was no one else.'

'I'm sorry.'

'Yes. So am I.'

Luke frowned. 'Would you like me to speak to Ella——'

'No!'

The vehemence of her denial brought a hardness to his

22

jawline, and his mouth, with its full lower lip, became a thin line.

'Why not?'

Realising she had been careless, Abby twisted her hands together and turned away. 'You don't understand, Mr Jordan,' she said, in a choked voice. 'After all these years, I—I couldn't accept...'

Luke's expression softened slightly. 'People change, you know, Abby. And sometimes it's difficult to show one's feelings, sometimes one's afraid they'll be rebuffed.'

He put a hand on her arm, and beneath that persistent pressure she turned to face him. Deliberately, she looked up into his face, and as she did so she saw his instinctive withdrawal. For some reason, he resented her, and only time would prove whether it was on Ella's behalf—or his own.

'Do you know my aunt very well, Mr Jordan?' she asked innocently, and his hand fell away from her.

'Reasonably,' he returned, straightening. 'Shall we go on?'

As they passed the bakers, the smell of newly baked bread and pastry was irresistible. Abby gave Luke a rather speculative glance before disappearing inside, emerging a few minutes later with a paper bag containing two hot meat pasties. She offered him one, and after a moment's hesitation he took it, biting into the crumbling pastry as she was doing and savouring the juicy filling.

'I've just had breakfast,' he protested, when she suggested they seated themselves on the low wall surrounding the church yard to eat them.

'So have I,' she replied easily. 'But I'm sure a man of your size doesn't need to watch his weight.'

Luke's eyes narrowed. 'Is that a compliment?' he inquired dryly, and she coloured, unable to meet his gaze.

'Naturally,' she murmured, looking down at the pastry in her hands. 'Don't you think this pastry is delicious?'

Luke conceded that it was, and they sat in silence until they were finished. The sun was gaining strength, and its rays beat warmly upon their backs.

Afterwards they walked down to the shore of the loch,

and Abby pointed to a small rowing boat pulled high up on the shingle.

'That's Uncle Daniel's,' she said. 'Would you like to go out on the loch? You can see the whole village from there.'

Luke was obviously torn between a desire to do as she suggested, and his desire to get this outing over. His reluctance for her company had not diminished, and she wondered what had made him so wary of her. Unless, somehow, he had spoken to her aunt...

That telephone call he had made the previous evening. He had told her uncle that he had spoken to Scott. What if he had spoken to Ella as well? But she was in Rome, Scott had told Abby so. And Luke would have told her uncle if he had made a call to Rome.

Now Luke said: 'I should very much like to row out on to the loch. But there's no need for you to come with me. I'm sure you must have better things to do than keeping me company.'

Abby took a deep breath. There it was again—that aloofness, that withdrawal. This wasn't at all how she had planned it. But how could she penetrate that mask of politeness he was wearing?

She gambled, knowing that if it didn't come off, she might have destroyed any chance of success. 'What's the matter?' she asked. 'Don't you like me?'

Luke sighed then. 'That's not the point, is it? Good God, I'm old enough to be your father! You can't possibly enjoy being with me.'

Abby held up her head. 'And if I do?'

Luke shook his head. 'I'd rather go alone.'

Abby's confidence crumbled. 'Why?' she demanded, childishly. 'Because I remind you of my aunt?'

Luke's brows drew together. 'That would be silly, wouldn't it?'

'Would it?' Abby knew she had to make a stand. 'I don't think you like being reminded of the kind of woman she is!'

That was unforgivable. She knew, as soon as the words were uttered, and Luke looked justifiably furious.

'What the hell do you mean?' he snapped, forcing her to go on.

'I—I know about you—and her.' Abby fumbled the words. 'I—I know about your—your relationship . . .'

'Indeed?' His tone was grim.

'Y—yes.' Abby swallowed convulsively. 'I—I know that she—she's your mistress, that—that you've been living to-gether——'

'What?' Luke's green eyes blazed into hers. 'Where the hell have you got that from? What do you know about my affairs? What can you know, living here, miles from any-where, out of touch——'

'I can read,' she reminded him unsteadily. 'We get news-papers——'

'*Newspapers!*' Luke's denigration of the word made her flinch. 'Don't you know better than to believe what you read in newspapers!'

Abby's shoulders quivered. Well, she had certainly suc-ceeded in breaking his politeness, but any association they might have had must surely be doomed from this moment on. With a little gulp she turned away, and walked up the slope towards the road on trembling legs.

'Abby!'

She heard him call her name, and although she would have preferred to ignore him until she had herself in con-trol again, instinctively she slowed and glanced back. He was still standing near the rowing boat, his hands pushed into his pockets, the breeze from the loch stirring the sil-very thickness of his hair. He looked so big and powerful somehow, so remote. She must have been out of her mind to imagine she might be able to influence a man like him, she thought bitterly. Her methods were so gauche, so un-sophisticated, so amateurish! Ella would have known how to go about it. She *had* known. But Abby's experience of men was limited to the boys from the village and Uncle Daniel.

'Come back here!' Luke called to her, but she could sense the irritation still in his voice and remained where she was.

'What's the point?' she called in answer. 'I'll—see you later.'

'Abby!' Frustration hardening his tone, he strode up the shingle towards her where she stood, shifting her weight

25

from one foot to the other, poised for flight. 'Abby, you can't expect to say something like that without arousing some reaction!' He sighed, his anger controlled. 'All right, so I do find your resemblance to your aunt—disturbing. But not for the reasons you think.'

'I was rude,' she said stiffly. After all, this man was a guest in her uncle's house and old habits die hard. 'I'm sorry.'

'Are you?' Almost against his will it seemed, his hand came out and lifted her chin so that she was forced to look into his face. His fingers were cool against her heated skin, and his thumb probed her jawline involuntarily. 'Don't pay lip service to me. I get enough of that back home.'

'I'm sorry,' she said again, shivering, and he let her go.

'Come on,' he said, as if coming to a decision. 'We'll take the boat out.'

Abby caught her breath. 'But you said you didn't want me to come with you.'

'Perhaps I was being unselfish,' he remarked enigmatically. Then, still unsmiling, he added: 'If you're prepared to waste your time with a middle-aged contemporary of your aunt's, why should I object? Do you want to come or don't you?'

'Oh, yes,' she nodded.

'All right, let's go.'

It was cooler on the loch, but she insisted on taking a turn at the oars and kept warm that way. He leaned back lazily as she rowed, his long legs stretched at either side of hers, and it was difficult for Abby to prevent herself from staring at his lean muscular body. It was true, she thought, she had never met anyone like him before, but she could quite see why her aunt—or *any* woman for that matter—would find him attractive. But *she* had to be objective about it . . .

Surprisingly, once the first few moments of awkwardness were over, they talked together easily. When he put aside the guard he had adopted, he became an amusing companion, telling her about his family—his brothers and sisters, and the struggle his mother had had to support the children after his father was killed.

'It was one of those quirks of fate,' he said with a shake

of his head. 'He was in the Merchant Navy and went right through the war without even an injury. He was killed in 1952 when the engine of his coaster exploded on a trip from Liverpool to Newcastle.'

'How awful!' Abby's eyes were wide and sympathetic. 'Your mother must have been frantic. With eight children to support.' Eight children, she thought incredulously. She couldn't imagine what it must be like to have seven brothers and sisters. Would Luke want a large family? she wondered, and trembled at the thought.

'I was fourteen at the time,' he recalled now. 'I have two brothers older than me, but the rest of the family are younger.'

'All the same, it must be nice for you belonging to a large family,' she murmured, half enviously, and he smiled ruefully.

'It's expensive,' he conceded with a dry inflection. 'So many birthdays.'

'And—and yet you've never had a family of your own?' she probed, amazed at her own temerity.

Luke shrugged. 'I was married once. But it didn't work out. We were divorced twelve years ago.'

Abby hadn't known that. It surprised her. Although as it was twelve years since his divorce, he must have been very young when he got married. Not so easy now to bring a man like him to the altar.

'What about you?' he asked, his eyes narrowed and questioning. 'Do you want to get married?'

Abby bent over the oars to hide her flushed cheeks. 'I—I suppose so. When—when the right man asks me.'

Luke drew out a case of cheroots and placed one between his teeth. 'Ardnalui's not a big place. If the right man hasn't asked you yet, surely he can't be here. Or are you waiting, as your mother did, for someone up from Glas——"

'No!'

Abby shipped the oars and let the small boat drift with the current, staring out blindly across the loch. She had no intention of marrying a man like her father—a charming man, but weak, drifting as this boat was doing with the

27

current, only struggling for survival when it was too late . . .

'So what will you do?'

Luke's voice was soft as he applied the flame of his lighter to the cheroot, and she turned to look squarely at him. 'I don't know,' she answered, pushing her hair back from her face with both hands, drawing his eyes to the pointed swell of her breasts surging against the thin nylon material of the windcheater. 'You tell me.'

CHAPTER THREE

For several minutes Luke looked at her, and even in her innocence, she knew he was enjoying the experience. Her heart pounded heavily, the blood thundering in her head, and her palms moistened where they rested against the sides of her neck. Then her pulses steadied when he looked away, taking the cheroot out of his mouth and saying in a curiously flat voice: 'What do you mean?'

She took a couple of quick breaths. 'Perhaps—perhaps *I* should leave Ardnalui. Aunt Ella did, and look how successful she's been. I could go to London. Maybe I could become an actress.'

Luke's eyes turned back to her, cooler now and more penetrating. 'I shouldn't advise it,' he told her harshly.

'Why not?'

Luke shifted restlessly, putting the cheroot back between his teeth, reaching forward to take the oars. 'It's time we were getting back.'

Abby stared at him frustratedly. 'Aren't you going to answer me?'

Luke dipped the oars into the water. 'What time is lunch?'

She clenched her fists. 'I shall do it, you know. Whatever you say.'

Luke heaved a sigh, regarded her tense expression for a moment, and then shipped the oars again. 'All right, all right. If you want it bluntly, I don't think you stand a chance of doing what Ella has done.'

'Why not?'

'Because you're not like her. You need to be a certain sort of person to become a successful actress. You have to be—hard, if you like. Dedicated, ambitious! I don't think you have that kind of ambition. If you had, you'd have done something about it before now.'

'What could I have done?'

'Left Ardnalui, for a start. Pushed yourself into Ella's life, whether she liked it or not.'

Abby bent her head. 'I don't think she would have let me.'

'How could she have stopped you? You're sufficiently like her to cause quite a bit of an upset, one way and another.'

'Do you think so?' Abby hunched her shoulders. 'Well, there's still time.'

Luke regarded her compassionately. 'I don't think so.'

'So what am I to do? Look after the Dalrymples' children until I'm an old maid?'

Luke half smiled. 'You've a long way to go before that happens.'

'Have I?'

His eyes narrowed. 'I really think it's time we were going back,' he said. 'It must be the air here. I'm feeling decidedly hungry.'

And with that, Abby had to be content. As Luke rowed them back to the shore, she reflected that the morning had proved much more productive than the previous evening, in spite of its doubtful beginnings...

That evening, Abby had a telephone call from Scott Anderson.

Fortunately, Luke and her uncle were out at the time. Daniel McGregor was showing Luke over his church, St Cecilia's, and Abby had been amusing herself setting out the chess pieces in the study when the phone rang.

Abby lifted the receiver tentatively. She was not wholly convinced that her aunt would not discover where Luke was and try to contact him here, and she had no desire to speak to her—yet. But it was Scott, and Abby sank down

29

weakly into her uncle's chair, cradling the receiver against her shoulder.

'Now then, young Abby,' Scott sounded amused. 'What have you been getting up to?'

Abby shook her head, realised he couldn't see her, and said: 'I don't know what you mean.'

'Don't you?' Even faraway, the disbelief in Scott's voice was unmistakable. 'Did you know I had Luke on the phone again this afternoon? What have you been saying to him?'

Abby straightened her spine. 'What did he tell you?'

Scott laughed. 'I'm asking the questions.'

'Oh, come on, Scott. Why did he ring you?' She paused. 'Did he tell you he was coming back?'

'N—o, I don't think that was mentioned.'

Abby didn't realise she had been holding her breath until at his words she felt the tension go out of her. 'So?'

'He thinks I sent him up there because you have some latent desire to go on the stage.'

'And what did you say?' Abby pressed her lips together.

Scott snorted. 'What was I supposed to say? You didn't tell me you were going to use those tactics.'

'I'm only playing the cards as they're dealt to me.'

'Really?' Scott sounded sceptical. 'Don't you think you've bitten off more than you can comfortably chew, Abby?'

'No!' She was vehement. Then: 'You didn't—you didn't——'

'—let you down? No, I won't do that, honey. But if I think this thing's getting out of hand, I'll get Luke back here so fast, you won't feel the passing.'

Abby's fingers tightened round the receiver. 'Don't be silly, Scott. What could get out of hand?'

'Luke could!' retorted Scott dryly. 'Look, Abby, he's not like your regular Scottish gentleman, nor is he like those boys you play around with in the village. They have respect for you—and for Dan. You can trust them. Don't trust Luke Jordan.'

'I've told you, Scott, I—I can handle it.'

'Can you?' He sounded less than convinced. 'Well, I just thought I'd warn you.'

'Thank you.'

'Huh? Don't thank me. I'm not at all sure I did the right thing in letting you persuade me to send Luke up there.'

Abby's teeth caught at the soft inner flesh of her lower lip. 'I think you owed me a favour, Scott,' she reminded him quietly, and heard his impatient exclamation.

'Well, you take care, d'you hear?' he told her severely, and she assured him she would before replacing the receiver.

When Luke and her uncle came back she learned that they planned to play chess together. Daniel McGregor was going to teach his guest the finer points of the game and her presence was superfluous. With a sense of impotence, she went up to her room, wondering how much longer she had before Luke decided to pack his case literally and return to London.

The following day was Saturday. It meant that Abby was free for two whole days and she wondered if it would be enough. She doubted it. She doubted it very much.

To her surprise, Luke was at the table when she went down for breakfast, and for an awful moment she thought he intended leaving that morning. But Uncle Daniel reassured her.

'Mr Jordan has decided to stay on for a few more days, Abby,' he told her. 'He's never seen anything of this part of the country, and I've persuaded him to do a little sightseeing while he's here. I've suggested he ought to drive up to Keilaig, and Achnaluin Forest. Then there's Loch Keil, and Lucifer's Bowl, and the Kyle of Storfar. Any number of places he should visit. Don't you agree?'

Abby could not bring herself to meet the old priest's eyes. Why was he doing this? she asked herself in confusion. Did he suspect? No, he couldn't, or knowing Uncle Daniel as she did, she knew he would never countenance her plans. And yet he had told her he knew that she had wanted to meet Luke Jordan, and he must also know how Ella would feel about that ...

She risked a brief glance in Luke's direction and was disconcerted to find him watching her. His eyes were thickly lashed and enigmatic, and she had no way of knowing what he was thinking.

31

'Well, Abby?'

Uncle Daniel was waiting for her reply and she moved her shoulders in a careless, dismissing gesture. 'It's a good time of year for driving on these roads,' she agreed off-handedly. 'Before they become jammed with holiday traffic.'

'I don't believe your—niece—is too enthusiastic about my staying on,' remarked Luke mildly, and Abby found herself glaring resentfully at him.

'That's not true,' she protested, conscious of Uncle Daniel's interest. 'I—maybe you would like me to come with you. To be your—guide.'

Luke regarded her steadily for several seconds and then he inclined his head. 'Why not?'

Ridiculously, a wave of panic swept over her. 'It could only be over the weekend,' she said hurriedly. 'I have to go back to work on Monday.'

'I'm sure Mr Jordan appreciates that you have a job of work to do, Abby,' Daniel McGregor assured her quietly. 'As for you acting as his guide, I venture to suggest that he might prefer to make his own way to our local beauty spots. They're not difficult to find. And besides, didn't you promise to help Mrs Jameson this morning?'

Mrs Jameson was the local police sergeant's wife, as well as being a keen horsewoman. Abby had completely forgotten her promise to go up to the stables and help Mrs Jameson whitewash the stalls. Panic gave way to irritation at the realisation that she was committed. Without doubt, Uncle Daniel had taken *this* into consideration.

Luke, who had finished his breakfast, pushed back his chair. 'Now that's a shame,' he observed wryly, and Abby looked infuriatedly up at him.

'I could ring Mrs Jameson,' she exclaimed. 'Explain the situation...'

'Oh, don't do that on my account,' Luke objected calmly. 'Perhaps tomorrow, hmm?'

'Mrs Tully will prepare you a picnic lunch, Luke,' put in Daniel. 'There are few eating places where you're going.'

'Thank you,' Luke nodded. 'I'll have a word with her. See you—both—later.'

The door closed behind him and Abby looked fretfully

32

down at the toast on her plate. Her appetite had evaporated and she could have cried with frustration. It didn't help when Daniel said: 'Cheer up, Abby. Think of the horses. You know how much pleasure you get out of exercising them. Mrs Jameson has always been very generous with you. Don't begrudge the chance to help her when it comes your way.'

Abby hunched her shoulders. 'I'm not, but——'

'—but you'd rather go with Luke. I know.' For a moment she tensed, expecting a lecture, but it didn't come. Instead, he said: 'I have to go. Mrs Lewis is worse. I'll give her your good wishes, shall I?'

'Oh, yes. Please.' Abby felt ungrateful. 'I'm—I'm sorry if you thought I was selfish.'

The priest shook his head, his eyes gentle. 'You're young, Abby, that's all.'

After he had gone, Abby drank a second cup of coffee before leaving the table. As she opened the dining room door she came face to face with Luke, and she stepped back in surprise.

'Where does this Mrs Jameson live?' he asked, and her lips parted in astonishment.

'Er—at Dun Ifor.' She made a futile gesture. 'It's a tiny village two miles round the loch.'

'And how do you propose to get there?'

Abby had no time to question this catechism, and she answered automatically: 'On my bicycle.'

'A bicycle!' Luke stared at her, half amused.

'Yes.' A trace of resentment coloured her tone now. 'Why not? Cycling is very good for you.'

'I'm sure it is. But I was going to suggest I took you— in my car.'

Abby gasped. 'Why should you do that?'

Luke hesitated. 'Shall we say I'm prepared to wait until this afternoon to go—sightseeing?'

Abby coloured then. She couldn't help it. Success was intoxicating. 'I—but—I might be hours at the Jamesons'.' She had to say something.

'Perhaps I can give a hand,' remarked Luke, and she stared disbelievingly at his cream corded pants and heavy cashmere sweater.

'In those clothes!'

'I can change,' he replied steadily. 'Well?'

Abby's hand involuntarily sought the open vee of her cotton shirt. 'All right,' she agreed. 'If that's what you really want to do. Only——'

'Only?'

'——I don't know what Uncle Daniel would say.'

'Uncle Daniel won't know, until it's too late,' Luke returned dryly, and Abby felt a tremor of apprehension sweep over her as she turned away.

By the time she had paid an unexpectedly urgent visit to the bathroom, and pulled on the crimson windcheater and wellington boots, Luke was waiting for her in the hall, lean and workmanlike in faded denims and a waist-length leather battle jacket. He held open the door for her and they emerged into the brisk air, overlaid this morning with the threat of rain. The dark green racing lines of the Lamborghini rested on broad tyres on the cobbled forecourt, much like some hungry predator waiting to spring. Even the prospect of riding in such a monster filled Abby with excitement which intensified when he swung open the door beside the wheel, and said: 'Would you like to drive?'

'Me?' Abby stared into his dark face disbelievingly. 'I—I couldn't.'

'Why not? You have a licence, don't you?'

'Well, yes, but ...'

'Don't you want to drive?'

Abby wrapped her arms around herself. 'I'd love to.'

'Come on, then. I'll show you how it works.'

Behind the wheel, with a seat belt securing her in place, Abby's hands trembled as they clasped the wheel. Luke walked round the bonnet and levered himself in beside her, smiling at her tense face.

'Relax. It's as simple as learning your alphabet. All you've got to remember is that you've got five forward gears instead of four.'

'It's air-conditioned!' she exclaimed.

'Yes. And the windows are electrically operated, if you should wish to open them.'

Abby looked at the comprehensive dashboard. 'It's like flying an aircraft.'

'I can assure you it's much simpler.'

She turned to look at him with wide eyes. 'Can you fly?'

'Not without a plane,' he conceded derisorily, directing her attention back to the dashboard. 'Now, it's power steering. Probably lighter than what you're used to.'

Abby looked at the milometer and caught her breath. 'That says two hundred and——'

'They're kilometres,' he corrected her dryly.

'Even so——'

'You're not likely to take off along two miles of the lake shore.'

'The loch! The loch shore.'

'All right, the loch shore, then. Right. Can you get us off this forecourt?'

The powerful engine roared to life, and Abby unknowingly had her tongue jammed between her teeth as she found bottom gear and the car crept forward. Driving through the village, she was intensely conscious of the curious glances cast her way, but she had no time to acknowledge anyone's greeting this morning. Instead, she concentrated on avoiding the bicycles they passed, and the butcher's van as it swung carelessly away from the kerb.

At last they emerged on to the open road, and she breathed a sigh of relief, taking the opportunity to rub first one palm and then the other over the knees of her pants.

'You're doing fine,' observed Luke beside her, and she stole a glance at him.

'Am I?' she asked breathlessly. 'Am I really? Oh, I nearly died when Mr Smith pulled out in front of us like that.'

Luke relaxed against the curving headrest. 'Open her up a bit,' he advised. 'She's baulking at this speed. You haven't even reached top yet.'

Abby depressed the accelerator and allowed the needle on the speedometer to creep upward. The road beside the loch would not allow for much more than fifty, but even at that speed the sensation of latent power was exhilarating. All too soon the gates of the Jamesons' property came into view, and she had to change down rapidly to negotiate the cattle grid.

Pauline Jameson was a woman in her late forties, whose family had owned this stretch of land for generations. Tall and rangily built, she had been brought up with horses and they were her passion. When she had first met and married Robert Jameson, a Glaswegian police constable, and gone to live in the city, no one had expected the marriage to last. But they had not taken Pauline's determination into account, and soon she had persuaded her husband to leave the city force and return with her to the Highlands of her birth. Now everyone knew Robert Jameson almost as well as his wife. Their only regret was that they had had no children to carry on the tradition, and consequently Abby, orphaned at quite a young age, had always been welcome there. In the summer months, Pauline hired out ponies for trekking, and Abby had always enjoyed going over there to exercise the animals through the off-season months.

If Pauline considered there was anything unusual in a man of Luke's evident wealth and ability desiring to help her part-time stable hand in cleaning out the stables, she succeeded in hiding her feelings admirably. Soon they were all wielding brushes of one kind or another while the Jamesons' two retrievers bounded about excitedly, jumping up and barking, and generally making nuisances of themselves.

The horses had been turned into the field behind the Jamesons' bungalow and when, halfway through the morning, Pauline called a halt while she went to make some coffee, Abby and Luke strolled over to the fence and leaned on it, talking to the animals. Luke had shed his jacket and with his denim shirt sleeves rolled back to his elbows, and the neck open to reveal the light mat of gold-flecked hair which covered his chest, he looked more disturbingly attractive than she had ever seen him. For the first time, she wondered what it would be like being married to such a man, and something inside her palpitated at the thought. But then, she told herself severely, situations altered cases.

Luke's bare arm brushed against hers as he reached out to offer a handful of straw to a chestnut gelding and his eyes switched sharply to hers as she flinched away from him.

'What's wrong?' he frowned, and quickly she shook her head.

'Nothing,' she denied, and then hurried on 'That's Paris, by the way. Mrs Jameson calls all the horses by legendary Greek names. Paris—and Athena, and Clytemnestra. Oh, and that's Agamemnon over there. Isn't that a terrible name for a horse?'

Luke was watching her confusion closely and she guessed that her attempt at diversion had not succeeded.

'Why did you jerk away from me like that when I touched you?' he demanded harshly. 'Haven't you ever touched a man before?'

'Don't be silly!' She refused to argue with him, turning aside to fondle Paris's muzzle. 'You're beautiful, aren't you?' she murmured to the animal, but Luke would not let it go.

'Correct me if I'm wrong, but I understood you were not averse to my company,' he snapped, and she turned reluctantly to face his annoyance, aware that she was in danger of losing all the ground she had made.

'I'm sorry,' she said uncomfortably. 'You—startled me, that's all.'

'Did I?' He sounded unconvinced. 'So come on—show me you don't object to touching me.'

Abby's breathing had quickened. 'How do you mean?'

'Like this!' He grasped her wrist and brought her hand up to his forearm. 'Go ahead. Take my arm.'

Abby looked up at him a little wildly. 'I—this *is* silly,' she protested, but he was uncompromising, and with a sigh she allowed her fingers to close round the hard muscle.

It was a peculiar sensation, particularly as in grasping her wrist he had brought her closer to him than she had been even in the car. She could smell the heat of his body after the hour of exertion, and the clean male scent of him was disturbing. Her eyes were on a level with the opened buttons of his shirt, and when she dared to look up, she found he was looking down at her. At once, she was conscious of the unbuttoned neckline of her shirt, and the way his eyes left her face to linger on the shadowy hollow just visible between her breasts. She shivered uncontrollably when his free hand slid up over her hip to her waist, his fingers probing the bones of her rib cage. She could feel herself stiffening, but before he could become aware of her resistance, he uttered an oath of self-disgust and turned away, long strides putting some distance between them.

Weakness enveloped her—weakness, and a clammy moistness all over her body which owed nothing to the effort she had expended. Oh God, she thought unsteadily, she had almost ruined everything. If only she had more experience! If only every time he came near her she wasn't so overwhelmingly aware of his strength and her immaturity. He had been married, and latterly his relationship with Ella left little to the imagination. How could she expect him to understand the fears she nurtured?

Running her hands over the seat of her pants, she saw to her relief that Mrs Jameson had emerged from the bungalow carrying a tray which Luke had gone to take from her. She watched him through averted eyes. Would it have been easier if he had been a less attractive man? Undoubtedly, from her point of view—although the prospect of sleeping with any man would be equally terrifying.

'You're looking rather pale, Abby.'

Mrs Jameson voiced an opinion which Abby had no doubt was an honest one. She felt pale—*drained*! A trembling facsimile of her normal self. But she knew Luke was looking at her, and with admirable nonchalance she indicated the overcast sky.

'It's this heavy atmosphere,' she claimed, accepting the cup of coffee Mrs Jameson handed her. She took a quick sip. 'Mmm, this is good.'

Mrs Jameson gave Luke a cup and then turned her attention back to Abby. 'Are you sure, my dear? You haven't got a headache, or anything? If you have, just say the word——'

'I haven't! Honestly!' Abby took a deep breath. 'We're making quite good progress, aren't we?'

'Very good progress,' Mrs Jameson agreed, smiling at Luke. 'With your help, Mr Jordan.'

'Please—call me Luke.' Luke was perfectly controlled, and Abby wondered if she had imagined his momentary weakness. But then he looked at her, and she knew she had not as the hot colour flamed up her throat to her cheeks.

'You're a writer—Luke.' Pauline Jameson rested against the stable wall. 'I do very little reading, I'm afraid, but I should like to read one of your books.'

'I'll send you one,' Luke told her easily. 'If you really mean it.'

'Oh, I do.' Pauline laughed. 'And how do you know Father McGregor?'

Luke finished his coffee and replaced his cup on the tray. 'I didn't,' he amended. 'But I work with Scott Anderson.'

'Oh, I see.' Pauline's expression grew speculative as it shifted to Abby. 'So you must know Abby's aunt—Ella Mackay.'

'Yes,' Luke spoke flatly, 'I know her.'

And how well! thought Abby fiercely.

'It's strange.' Pauline was thoughtful. 'That two sisters should be so totally different from one another. Abby's mother seldom if ever left the village, while Ella——'

'Oughtn't we to be getting on, Mrs Jameson?'

Abby didn't care that she was being rude, or that Luke was staring frowningly at her. She had no desire to get into conversation about her parents, wading into waters that were both treacherous and forbidden.

'Of course.' Pauline straightened away from the wall, regarding her sympathetically for a moment. 'That's all old history, isn't it, Abby? Now, where did I leave that broom?'

It was after twelve when Abby and Luke left the Jamesons'. Pauline had invited them to stay for lunch, but Abby insisted that Uncle Daniel would be expecting them back. This time Luke took the wheel, and there was a tension between them that had not been there before.

Daniel McGregor was surprised to see Luke at the table. He glanced round at Mrs Tully bringing in a tureen of Scotch broth and exclaimed: 'I thought you were having a picnic lunch today, Luke.'

Luke gave a faint smile. 'I decided to wait until Abby could accompany me,' he remarked levelly. 'I took her over to the Jamesons' myself.'

39

'Indeed?' Abby sensed that her uncle was not best pleased. 'And where do you plan to go this afternoon?'

'Where would you suggest?'

Daniel shrugged his narrow shoulders. 'Well, Keilaig is nearest, I suppose.'

'Keilaig?' Luke frowned.

'There's an old castle there,' put in Abby, needing to dispel the strained atmosphere between them. 'It's not much more than a ruin now, but it gives a magnificent view over Loch Keil.'

'You know it well,' said Luke. 'Are you sure you still want to come?'

Abby looked down at her plate. 'I should like to,' she answered quietly, and sensed that he was no more pleased with her than her uncle.

Luke had changed back into his former attire before lunch, and after the meal was over, Abby hurried upstairs to put on a fresh shirt. She didn't have a lot of clothes and her jeans would have to do, but at least she could wear a different top. Deciding it might be cold at Keilaig, she wore a somewhat faded purple sweater with a roll neck, which nevertheless was warm and serviceable. Its ribbed lines drew attention to her swelling breasts, and she thought impatiently that it was really too small for her now. Still, her windcheater hid its more obvious limitations.

Mrs Tully encountered her in the hall. 'Mr Jordan said to tell you he's waiting in the car,' she said half disapprovingly. Then: 'Ach, I don't know what the Father's thinking of—letting you go off with a man like that!' jerking her thumb towards the door.

Abby made an indignant sound. 'I'm not a child, Mrs Tully. I can go out with whoever I like.'

'Well, I'd have thought after what your mother suffered, poor thing, and him a friend of your aunt——'

Abby turned towards the door. 'I'll see you later, Mrs Tully.'

'Well, you watch yourself, miss, that's what I say,' Mrs Tully was saying as Abby closed the door with suppressed irritation behind her. As if it wasn't hard enough, without other people reminding her!

Luke was sitting behind the wheel, and he leant across

and pushed open the door from inside for her to climb in. Abby subsided on to the hide upholstery thankfully, glad the uncertainty in her legs was not having to be put to the test.

'I'm sorry if I've kept you waiting,' she murmured, folding her hands in her lap.

Luke made no comment and started the car, driving away from the presbytery with careful deliberation. Then he paused. 'Right or left?'

'Oh—right.' She spoke jerkily. 'The—the opposite way from the way we went this morning.'

Luke acknowledged this with a slight raising of his eyebrows, and they turned away from the village on the steep incline out of the valley. At the junction with the Achnaluin road, they turned west, following the single-laned track which petered out at Keilaig. A few specks of rain landed on the windscreen and the wipers quickly flicked them away. But they were followed by others that soon had the wipers working full-time.

'It would rain, wouldn't it?' she exclaimed, with enforced casualness, intensely conscious of the limited proportions of their surroundings. With the rain driving relentlessly against the vehicle on all sides, they were entrapped in a square of what seemed to Abby, in her nervous state, almost claustrophobic intimacy. 'Perhaps it will clear by the time we reach the castle.'

'Do you really expect it to?' Luke sounded bored.

'It might. We get these freak storms in the mountains. In half an hour the sun could be shining.'

Luke cast a disbelieving look her way. 'Not after the sky has been overcast all morning. I guessed it would rain.'

'Then why did you come, then?' Abby sounded a little distraite.

Luke shrugged. 'It seemed to be expected.'

Abby sighed. 'Uncle Daniel wouldn't have minded if you had wanted to stay at the house.'

'Now that I am sure of.'

Abby frowned. 'Why?'

Luke made a dry grimace. 'You know that as well as I do.'

'Do I?'

41

'Abby, don't play games with me. I'm too old for those kind of tricks. You must know your uncle doesn't approve of your spending too much time alone with me. No'—this as she would have interrupted him—'let me finish. I'm not saying he doesn't—well, like me. He tolerates me, at least. And he has no objections to my staying in his house. But I don't think he bargained for you wanting to come out with me, do you?'

Abby absorbed this mutinously. 'Are you saying you agree with him?'

Luke sighed. 'Not exactly.'

'Then what are you saying?'

'What is it with you, Abby? Why *did* you want to come with me? What is it that attracts you? Me—or the Lamborghini?'

Abby pursed her lips. 'That's a rotten thing to suggest!'

'Why is it? I've known women go out with men for the most peculiar reasons. And liking them isn't always high on the list.'

Abby expelled her breath noisily. 'Well, I do happen to —to like you.'

'I see.' Luke's acceptance of her statement was ominous. 'How well do you like me?'

Abby stared out at the driving force of the storm. 'I don't know what you mean.' And she didn't.

'You didn't like me touching you this morning.'

'Oh, for heaven's sake!' Abby pushed back her hair with a nervous hand. 'Must you keep going on about that?. I've told you, you startled me.'

'All right.' To her horror, the car appeared to be slowing, and after a moment he brought it to a standstill, the wipers stilling on the windscreen, completing the illusion of limbo-like isolation. Then he half turned in his seat toward her. 'Now, tell me again.'

Abby's throat felt so tight, every breath was an effort. 'Please,' she appealed, 'can't we go on? Or go back, if you'd rather.'

'There's no going back, Abby. Didn't you know that?' His arm was resting along the back of her seat. 'Aren't you hot wearing a thick sweater and a jacket?'

'No!' She shifted jerkily. 'I—you're wearing a jacket.'

'This?' He fingered the leather battle jacket he had worn that morning. 'You know, you could be right.' And withdrawing his arm for a moment, he struggled out of the jerkin, tossing it carelessly into the back of the car.

Abby did feel hot—but it was not just the weight of her clothing. She had the sensation of a non-swimmer thrown into the deep end of a swimming bath. Luke in this mood was wholly unpredictable, and not even the knowledge that she had, inadvertently, subtly altered their relationship could prevent her knees from shaking and panic from rearing its ugly head once more.

'Come on, Abby,' he said softly, and taking hold of the zipper of her jacket, he propelled it steadily downwards.

'Oh, please...'

Eyes mirroring fear stared into his, and he shook his head cynically. 'Don't worry,' he told her, continuing to slide the windcheater from her shoulders. 'Even I would find it difficult to rape you in this vehicle!'

Her cheeks burned. 'You shouldn't say things like that!'

'Why not? That is what you're afraid of, isn't it?'

'No.' She pulled her arms free of the jacket and he cast it into the back along with his own. She pressed the balled fist of one hand into the palm of the other. 'I—I don't think you would do a thing like that.'

'Don't you?' His expression was wry. 'I'm not sure I like that.'

'Please! Stop baiting me.'

Driven beyond reason, her eyes were desperate, and his features hardened. 'What would you have me do with you, then?'

She shook her head, staring down helplessly at her knees, and with a tremor of apprehension she felt his hand slide over and grip her nape under the silky curtain of her hair.

'You know, I should have had more sense!' he muttered, and she looped back her hair behind one ear to look at him.

'Wh-why?'

He regarded her for a long disturbing minute. Then, before she could offer any resistance, he leant forward and kissed the down-soft curve of her cheek. His mouth was warmly compelling, and for an instant she had the craziest urge to tilt back her head so that his lips would encounter hers. It was not a calculated reaction, and its urgency left her strangely weak.

'Oh, Abby,' he said, resting his head back against the soft leather. 'Someone should have warned me about you!'

'Wh-what about me?'

He chewed impatiently at the inner skin of his lower lip. 'How old did you say you were? Seventeen? Eighteen?'

'I'm twenty,' she asserted hotly. 'At least, I shall be next month.'

'Twenty!' He shook his head, moving it from side to side against the headrest. 'And did no one ever teach you the facts of life?'

'Of course!' She tried to shrug his hand away from her nape, but he didn't let her go. 'I don't know what you're talking about.'

He flexed his back muscles. 'I don't believe you do.' He straightened, looking at her through narrowed lids. 'You know what I think?' He raised his eyebrows, but she made no reply, so he went on: 'I think you should try your claws on someone else—someone less likely to take advantage of you.'

'You're not—taking advantage of me ...'

Luke's lips twisted. 'And you don't think I would?'

'Would you?'

He flung himself back in his seat, his hands seeking the case of cheroots he always kept in the car. When he had one between his teeth, he nodded savagely. 'You're a beautiful girl, Abby. If no one's ever told you that, let me be the first to reassure you. And I am only human! You've been throwing yourself at my head ever since you laid eyes on me, and while I'm perfectly willing to oblige, something tells me that that's not what you want ...'

'And if it was?'

She spoke breathily, and he took the unlighted cheroot out of his mouth to stare at her disbelievingly. 'Abby, if it's a film star you want to be, it's Scott you should be talking to.'

'It's not.'

Unknowingly provocative, her tongue appeared to wet her upper lip, and with a muffled oath he dropped the cheroot on the floor, his hands sliding possessively over her shoulders, compelling her towards him. His mouth on hers moved back and forward insistently, warm and probing, and disruptively sensual. Did he know she had never been kissed before? she fretted anxiously. Did he realise all the knowledge she possessed came from books like his own?

'Stop fighting me, Abby,' he spoke against the corner of her mouth, and she moved her head confusedly.

'I'm not fighting you,' she protested, the words dying on a gulp when his hand slid beneath her sweater to grip her bare midriff.

'Come on,' he breathed, his tongue tracing the curve of her lips. 'Open your mouth . . .'

'Open—*oh*!'

Her puzzled objection was stifled by the pressure of his mouth, forcing her lips apart to admit the searching penetration of his. No amount of reading, however adult, could have prepared her for the sensations he was arousing inside her, sensations that left her weak and submissive, neither seeking nor repelling the demands he was making on her. She didn't resist when his hand probed further beneath her sweater, cupping one rounded breast and stroking the nipple with his thumb, but Luke could feel the thrusting urgency of his own body and he could no longer ignore it. For long, lingering seconds, his mouth continued to possess hers, and then he pushed her away from him, shoving open his door violently and getting out, heedless of the falling rain.

CHAPTER FOUR

The draught of cold air was sobering and Abby caught an incredulous breath, pressing her palms to her burning cheeks, scarcely daring to believe what had occurred. She fumbled her sweater down over the waistband of her jeans and in doing so her wrist accidentally brushed her breast, still tender from the pressure of his fingers. She licked lips gone suddenly dry, and twisted the driving mirror round so that she could examine her face. Her pupils were wide and dilated, her cheeks splashed with hectic colour, her mouth bruised and bare of any make-up. It had happened, it had really happened! Somehow—she didn't quite know how she had done it—she had aroused Luke Jordan's interest!

She took a deep breath. He had kissed her. And not in any casual way. He had held her and kissed her until her head swam with the memory of it. She swallowed hard. It hadn't been so bad, after all. And she hadn't frozen up on him as she had been afraid she might do. She had let him do what he wanted, and not tried to stop him.

Then she remembered. Luke was outside now, in the pouring rain. She adjusted the mirror and leaned across his seat and said softly: 'Won't you come in, Luke? You're getting soaked to the skin!'

Luke looked down at her broodingly, his face wet, his hair plastered to his head and neck. Then, without comment, he got back inside the vehicle, reaching for his cheroots again and lighting one, still without speaking. His sweater steamed, and the odour of damp wool mingled with the scent of his tobacco. When he stretched out a hand to start the engine, however, she put restraining fingers on his sleeve.

'I think you ought to take off this—this wet jumper,' she murmured awkwardly.

'Do you?'

His voice was cold and cynical as before, and Abby looked at him reluctantly. 'Yes. Yes, I do.'

'You care about me?' His lips twisted mockingly.

'It's not a question of caring,' she exclaimed. 'It's common sense. You're wet through.'

'Perhaps I don't care,' he remarked.

Abby made an exasperated sound. 'Don't say things like that! It's stupid to risk pneumonia for the sake of a little forethought.'

Luke stared at her grimly for a few moments, and then jabbing his cheroot into the ashtray, he lifted his arms and hauled the sweater over his head. He wore nothing beneath it, and the tanned brown flesh rippled with goosebumps. With his chest bare, he looked younger, more vulnerable, and Abby was not unaware of the sexual attraction he possessed.

46

'Here,' she said, reaching determinedly into the back of the car, 'put on your jacket. It's better than nothing.'

'Thanks.' He slid his arms into the sleeves of the battle jacket and fastened the studs. If he was still shivering, she could not see it, his features taut and unyielding in the grey light.

'I think we ought to go back,' she ventured, and he cast a scathing look in her direction.

'You *think*!' he echoed. 'We're going back, Abby. Whatever you think!'

She regarded him anxiously. 'Why are you so angry?'

'For God's sake!' He started the engine savagely. 'After what you just did, how the hell do you expect me to be?'

'What—what did I do?'

'Oh, God!' He swore as in trying to turn on the narrow road, his tyres spun uselessly over the rim of a ditch. 'I don't believe even you are that naïve!'

Abby's lips trembled. 'You—wanted to make love to me?'

He glared at her. 'Yes,' he said aggressively, nodding his head. 'That's one way of putting it.'

Abby's tongue clove to the roof of her mouth. 'I—well, I didn't—stop you . . .'

'No,' he agreed grimly, grinding his gears as he sought to bring the wheels back on to the track. 'You didn't do that.'

'Then why are you angry with me?'

'Abby, if I were your uncle, I'd put you across my knee and administer the thrashing you so justly deserve!'

'Why?' She couldn't understand his attitude. He had wanted to kiss her, to fondle her—and she had not objected. So where had she gone wrong? What would Ella have done that she had not? Had her inexperience, her lack of sophistication been so obvious after all? 'I—I thought you liked—touching me,' she whispered.

Luke succeeded in bringing the Lamborghini round in a half circle, as much by skidding dangerously on the slippery surface as by any expertise at driving, and then he turned to face her, his expression forbidding.

'Abby, did no one ever tell you, you don't go around letting strange men—take advantage of you?'

'I—yes, of course.'

'So?'

'You're not a—strange man.'

'What in hell am I, then?'

'You're—you're—Luke. And,' she bent her head, 'I knew what I was doing.'

'Like hell you did!'

'I did. I did!' She looked up at him earnestly. 'I wanted you to—kiss me.'

'Oh, God!' He laid his head back against the rest, his eyes closed. 'Abby, you can't possibly know what you're saying.'

'I do. Honestly.'

'Honestly!' His eyes opened again. 'Honestly, Abby? Little girl, you hated me touching you, you resisted me every inch of the way.'

'I didn't!'

She was indignant, and he summoned a weary grimace of amusement. 'No,' he conceded dryly. 'Not physically, perhaps. But when a man kisses a woman, he expects some response. You were dead, Abby. You didn't like me touching you—you *suffered* it!'

'No!' All her new-found confidence fled in a moment. 'That's not true. I—all right, maybe I'm not as—well, experienced as the women you're used to, but I'll learn——'

'Not from me, Abby.'

'Why not?'

His face twisted. 'Would you really like me to tell you?' He shook his head. 'Why not? All right, Abby—it's because I value my self-respect. And God help me, a few minutes ago I was in danger of losing it!'

'You mean...' Abby linked her fingers tightly together. 'You mean—you felt——'

'I mean I nearly lost control, Abby. I nearly took what you so innocently offered!'

Abby turned her head, staring blindly through the streaming panes of glass. What did he mean? That he had wanted to make love to her? Or that any woman would have done equally as well? If only she understood him better!

Luke thrust the car into gear and released the clutch

cautiously. The tyres spun for a moment before gaining traction, but steadily the car began to move along the muddy track. The wipers working full-time cleared the windscreen, but Luke needed all his concentration for his driving, and Abby had plenty of time to contemplate ruefully on what her next move should be.

Daniel McGregor was waiting for them when they got back to the presbytery, declaiming sympathetically on the state of the weather, even while he looked askance at Luke's bare midriff.

'I got wet,' Luke answered flatly in reply to his host's query. 'I had to get out of the car to—attend to the wipers. My sweater was soaked, so I took it off.'

'Of course, of course.' Daniel seemed to accept this explanation, Abby saw with relief, as the old man shifted his attention to her. 'Most sensible. So, Abby, your outing was washed out, after all.'

Abby nodded, praying he would notice nothing amiss in her appearance, half convinced that Luke's lovemaking had left a physical scar. 'It's—it's a horrible afternoon. If you'll excuse me, I'll go and get changed. I—feel sticky.'

Daniel McGregor inclined his head towards Luke. 'I hope you'll go and put some clothes on, too, my boy,' he commented as Abby ran up the stairs. 'Mustn't risk catching a chill. This climate can be treacherous.'

During the night, Abby heard Luke coughing. The sound woke her up, echoing as it did through the stillness of the old building. She sat up in bed, shivering as the cold air attacked her warm flesh. She wondered if she should go to him and ask whether there was anything he wanted. But then the images this evoked made her slide down beneath the covers again, aware that right at this moment she did not have the courage to face the possible outcome of such an invasion. She lay for a while in the darkness, contemplating what it would be like to lie in Luke's arms, and fell asleep to dream violently of Aunt Ella's reaction to such a betrayal.

When Abby came down for breakfast next morning, she was heavy-eyed and uneasy, the overtones of her dream lingering into the morning hours. Only her uncle was at the table, and as she slipped into her seat wondering how she could broach the subject of Luke's whereabouts, his first words saved her the necessity.

'I've rung Doctor McGuire,' he said, looking up gravely from his cereal. 'I'm very much afraid Mr Jordan has caught a chill, after all. He's most unwell this morning.'

Abby busied herself with a piece of toast she didn't really want. 'Is he?' she managed casually. 'You've seen him?'

'Mrs Tully encountered him on the landing, on his way to the bathroom. She came to me at once. He was obviously running a temperature and having difficulty with his breathing. I insisted he went back to bed, and called McGuire immediately.'

'I see.' Abby didn't quite know what else to say. 'It's probably just—a cold.'

'Let us hope so. Mrs Tully has enough to do here without running up and down stairs after an invalid.'

'I could do that,' said Abby quietly. 'I—wouldn't mind.'

'I don't think a man's bedroom is a suitable place for a girl of your age, Abby,' retorted her uncle sharply, 'and I'm sure Mrs Tully would agree with me.'

Abby was sure she would, particularly after what the housekeeper had said to her the previous afternoon.

'If there is any nursing to be done, Mrs Tully will have to cope as best she can,' he went on firmly. 'I'd really rather you kept out of the way, Abby. Do you understand me?'

Abby pushed the toast round her plate. 'Yes, Uncle Daniel.' Then she looked up. 'Can I go and see how he is?'

'For the present, I think it would be as well to leave matters to Mrs Tully and myself. We can keep you informed of any change in his condition. If, as you suggest, it is just a cold, he'll be up and about again in a couple of days.'

But Luke was not up and about again for almost a week. Even though Father McGregor had called the doctor immediately, a more serious pulmonary infection had developed by the time he arrived, and it was several days before Luke's temperature came anywhere near normal. He needed daily injections to combat the inflammation, and in the uncanny hush which seemed to have descended on the house all that could be heard was the harshness of his breathing and the spasmodic bouts of coughing to clear the fluid from his lungs. Abby fretted about the downstairs rooms, blaming herself for his illness, wishing there was something, *anything*, they would let her do. It wasn't so bad when she was at the Dalrymples', although they showed a healthy interest in the goings-on at the presbytery, but back at the house again, she could settle to nothing.

One evening the telephone rang while Abby was moping in Uncle Daniel's study, trying to make sense out of some enormous tome on fly fishing. With a feeling of trepidation, she lifted the receiver, always aware that it could be her aunt at the other end of the line, but relieved again to find it was Scott.

'Hi there, Abby,' he greeted her cheerfully. 'How are you?'

'I'm fine, thank you, Scott. How are you?'

'Better in health than temper, as they say. Now then, have you still got Luke there? I want a word with him.'

His tone was ominous, and Abby wondered if he resented Luke spending so long a way from town. 'As a matter of fact, Luke is here,' she said. 'But you can't speak to him.'

'Why not?' Scott sounded impatient now.

'Because he's ill—sick; he caught a chill.'

'The devil he did!' Scott said an uncomplimentary word. 'How sick?'

'He's recovering—slowly. I think it was almost pneumonia.'

'My God! How did he do that?' Scott's anger had given way to concern.

'He got soaked one afternoon when we were out. You know how unpredictable the weather is here.'

'I know.' Scott sounded resigned. 'So when do you think he'll be well enough to speak to me?'

'I'm not sure.' Abby frowned. 'I could ask him to ring you, if you like. When he's able.'

'Yes, that's probably the best idea.' Scott paused. 'Tell him—tell him I've got Reiter interested in the new series. That should cheer him up, if he needs it. And tell him I

51

want him back in town as soon as possible.'

Abby pressed her lips together, but her next question was irresistible. 'Does—does Aunt Ella know where he is?'

Scott sniffed impatiently. 'Not yet. But she's due back from Italy tomorrow. I'm not looking forward to having to tell her, believe me!'

Abby's fingers curved more closely round the receiver. 'You expected Luke to be back to tell her himself, didn't you?' she suggested shrewdly, and the short laugh he gave was a little bitter.

'You're a fine judge of character, young Abby,' he retorted. 'But don't get too clever for your own good.'

Abby guessed her barb had gone a little too near the bone for Scott's liking, and after a few words of farewell, he rang off. When she had replaced the receiver, she sat staring at it for several more minutes. So Aunt Ella was coming back tomorrow. And after that—what? When she learned of Luke's condition, would she come up here? It was possible. She no longer had any reason to stay away. Or she might telephone. Abby shifted to the other side of the room. She must remember not to answer the telephone after today.

Uncle Daniel did not join her at the table for dinner that evening, and when Mrs Tully appeared with the casserole, Abby looked at her anxiously.

'Lu—that is, Mr Jordan—he's not worse, is he?'

The housekeeper's expression was reproving. 'Of course not, miss. Didn't I tell you myself this morning, Mr Jordan is making a steady recovery? He's still very weak, of course, and he's not stomaching a lot of food, but he's definitely on the mend. Doctor McGuire said so.'

Abby expelled her breath on a sigh. 'Then why isn't Uncle Daniel taking dinner? He's not ill, is he?'

Mrs Tully set the casserole dish before her. 'It's Mrs Lewis,' she explained, with a shake of her head. 'She's not expected to last till morning.'

'Oh, I'm sorry.'

Abby bent her head. She had scarcely known the elderly lady who lived alone in a cottage on the outskirts of the village. Once Mrs Lewis had kept the schoolhouse in the days when every village had its own class of pupils. But she had retired years before Abby was old enough to attend school, and in any case these days the children were taken the fifteen miles to the local county school in a mini-bus. Nevertheless, Ardnalui would miss her passing.

Mrs Tully smoothed the tablecloth, and just when Abby expected her to go, she said: 'Was that a call for Father McGregor earlier on this evening?'

Abby spooned some of the casserole on to her plate. She would not deliver her message to Mrs Tully.

'As—as a matter of fact, it was for me,' she said, lifting her head to meet Mrs Tully's disbelieving eyes, knowing the other woman would not go so far as to ask her who had called.

'I see.' After a brief battle of wills, Mrs Tully flicked a speck of dust from the corner of the mantelshelf. 'Very well, miss.' She paused. 'I hope you enjoy your dinner.'

You really hope it chokes me, thought Abby, as the housekeeper left the room, and attacked the meat and vegetables on her plate with more determination than hunger.

Uncle Daniel had not returned by the time Abby went to bed, and she climbed the stairs to her room wondering whether she really ought to have given Mrs Tully Scott's message. The housekeeper would have delivered it tonight, whereas now it would be morning before Luke knew of it. And then only if her uncle was back. She could hardly invent a second call for Mrs Tully's benefit.

Still, it was too late to worry about it now, and putting on her cotton nightgown she slid between the sheets. In spite of her anxiety, she fell asleep almost immediately, only to be wakened some time later by the distinct sound of somebody moving about on the landing. The illuminated dial of her alarm clock told her it was half past two, and she blinked frowningly into the darkness, wondering who could be about at this time of the night.

With a sigh, she slid out of bed and padded to her door, opening it silently and peering out. The light was on in the bathroom, and as she waited, the door opened and Luke's robed figure appeared, visible before the light by the bathroom door was switched off. But evidently he had seen her too, for a moment later the light was switched on again,

53

and he stood looking at her across the width of the landing. He was paler than she remembered, his tan fading slightly to give him a rather sallow look, and the belt of the bath-robe revealed that he had lost weight. Yet for all that, with his silvery hair rumpled from the pillow, he was disturbingly attractive.

Deciding it was up to her to make the first overtures, she whispered softly: 'Are you all right?'

His mouth turned down at the corners. 'Do you really care?'

'Of course. What do you mean?'

'I mean, you haven't exactly fallen over yourself to enquire about my welfare.'

'Oh!' Abby forgot she was just wearing her nightgown and padded across the landing. 'Uncle Daniel told me not to—well, interfere. I—I wanted to see you, but——' She sighed. 'What are you doing out of bed?'

Luke indicated the glass in his hand. 'Water,' he told her dryly. 'Your uncle usually provides me with a jug of water last thing at night. I haven't seen him since lunchtime today, though.'

'No. He is—he *was*—that is, I don't know whether he's back yet, but he was visiting an old lady who's very sick.'

'I see.'

They were silent for a moment, and suddenly Abby was overwhelmingly conscious of the scant cover given by her nightgown and the tumbled darkness of her hair. Luke's eyes were very intent and she wished she knew what he was thinking.

Then he shivered, and seizing on it, Abby gestured towards his bedroom door. 'It's freezing here,' she exclaimed, and indeed it was, although she had only just noticed it. 'You ought to go back to bed before you catch another chill.'

'I'm not quite such a weakling,' he assured her dryly, 'McGuire insists that the infection was a virus which could have attacked at any time. I don't normally come down with consumption at the first soaking.'

Abby bit her lip. 'Nevertheless, I think you should go back to bed,' she insisted, and with a shrug he moved obediently into his bedroom.

She turned out the bathroom light and followed him to his door. By the light of the bedside lamp, she could see the untidy state of his bed, and ignoring the knowledge of what Uncle Daniel would say if he knew, she brushed past Luke and began straightening the sheets and pillows.

'I can do that,' he protested, but obviously standing for so long had tired him, because he sank down on to the end of the bed, and drank the water rather wearily.

Abby finished her task, and said: 'You can get in now.'

'Can I?' Luke's lips twisted as he got to his feet. 'Are you going to join me?'

His words startled her and the colour flamed into her face as she backed away towards the door.

'Relax!' he said shortly. 'I didn't mean it. But it's obviously slipped your notice that when I shed this robe, I shan't be decent.'

Abby caught her breath on a gulp. His legs were bare, but the significance of this had escaped her until now. She shivered, shaking her head in dismay. 'I—I'm sorry, I'll go. I didn't realise.' Her hand encountered the handle of the door behind her. 'Goodnight—oh!' This as she remembered Scott's telephone call.

'Now what is it?'

Luke sounded irritated and weary and Abby backed up against the door so that it clicked shut behind her. The sound echoed in the silence, and she prayed no one had heard it. But at least with the door closed, there was less chance of anyone hearing their conversation.

'There—there was a call for you this evening,' she said. 'I forgot about it until now. From—from Scott.'

'Indeed?' Luke looked down at his bed. Then with a sigh, he said: 'Look, do you mind if I get into bed? I feel bloody awful!'

'Of course not.' She took a step away from the door again, realised what she was doing, and turned her back.

'Cool it,' he advised impatiently. 'I'll keep my robe on for now. Go on.' He settled comfortably against his pillows. 'What did Scott say? As if I can't guess.'

Abby turned to find him resting tiredly against the pillows, and his unexpected vulnerability did strange things

55

to her. She wished there was something she could do to quicken his recovery.

'Well . . .' She wrapped her arms about her shoulders to stave off the feeling of chill which was rapidly enveloping her. 'He said to tell you that someone called—Reiter? Is that right?' He nodded and she went on: 'Well, he said that this man Reiter is interested in the new series.'

'Did he?' Luke sounded a little more alert now. 'Did he tell you to what degree he was interested?'

'To what degree?' Abby was confused.

'Financially. No?' Luke nodded. 'Obviously, he didn't. You'd have remembered if he had.'

Abby frowned, trying to remembered what else Scott had said. But she was chilled to the bone now, and she was having difficulty in stopping herself from shivering openly.

Luke regarded her broodingly for a moment and then he said quietly: 'Unless you plan to leave the rest of the conversation until morning, I suggest you get into bed, too. Your teeth are chattering.'

'G-get into bed?' Abby was aghast. '*Your* bed?'

'To keep warm, yes. Oh, Abby—Abby!' He sounded driven with exasperation. 'I shan't touch you. If you don't want to do that, go back to bed and come and see me to-morrow. I guess I can wait for the complaints which I'm sure are to come!'

'Uncle Daniel might not let me—that is——' Abby took an uncertain step towards the bed, knowing that the chances of her having another opportunity to speak to him before he was up and about again were very slim. Then, as the familiar panic rose inside her: 'I—I can't get into your bed!'

'Why not?'

'It's not right.'

'Well, it hardly constitutes a sinful act,' he observed impatiently. 'Besides, who's to know?'

'We'll know,' she whispered.

'So what? I won't tell anyone if you don't,' he returned with heavy sarcasm.

Abby hesitated, wondering fatalistically why she did so. This was her opportunity to achieve her objective, handed to her on a plate! Why didn't she take it? This was what she had wanted, what she had planned for. Was she about to let herself down at the last moment?

Gulping back her fears, she came to the bed and he moved aside obligingly to let her climb in. Her cold feet brushed his bare leg, and a curious expression crossed his face as she tucked the covers closely about her.

'Are you comfortable?' he inquired, when she became still and she nodded. 'It's not quite as bad as you expected, is it?'

'It's not bad at all,' she murmured huskily, but she could not read his reactions to this through the narrowed veil of his lashes.

'I suggest you get on,' he advised briefly, and she hurried to do so.

'He said that he wants you back in town as quickly as possible. I don't think he expected you to stay away so long.'

'I don't suppose he did. Nor did I, to be honest.' His mouth was wry. 'Scott likes manipulating people. He doesn't like it when his protégées assume their independence.'

'He also said that—that Aunt Ella is due back in England tomorrow.'

Luke rested his head back against the board at the top of the bed. 'Yes, I know that.' He looked at her out of the corners of his eyes. 'I guess Scott's worried because he's going to have to tell her where I am.'

Abby clasped her hands. 'That bothers you?'

Luke moved his head slowly in a negative gesture. 'No.'

'Why—why should Scott object to telling her? He—he sent you up here, didn't he?'

Luke gave her an old-fashioned look. 'You know Scott, Abby. He doesn't always say what he means.'

Abby frowned, concentrating on the outline of her feet, visible beneath the covers. 'Is he—going to make the television series here?'

Luke shrugged. 'I shouldn't think so.'

Abby quivered. 'So—so why did he send you up here?'

Luke made an abortive gesture. 'Your guess is probably as good as mine.'

Abby tried to speak, swallowed her breath and had to

clear her throat before going on: 'I—I'd like to hear your guess.'

Luke's brows drew together. 'Would you?' He shifted more comfortably against the pillows and the warmth of his body spread across to her. 'Well, what you may or may not know is that Scott does not like—your aunt. He has no time for her. They only tolerate one another because of the mutual benefits of their combined talents.'

Abby's attention was riveted on him. This was something she had not known. Scott had never revealed his feelings towards her mother's sister.

'So,' Luke went on slowly, 'my guess is that Scott saw this opportunity to cause a rift between Ella and me—and took it.'

Abby chose her words carefully: 'You believe that Ella will be angry when she finds out where you are?'

Luke turned to look at her steadily, his eyes taking in the long cuffed sleeves of her nightgown, and the roundly swelling curves it only narrow disguised, the tangled glory of her hair.

'Yes,' he said, and his voice was husky now. 'I don't think Ella would approve of this at all, do you?'

Abby's shallow breathing threatened to choke her. 'But —but when you first came here——'

'—I didn't know you then,' he finished flatly. 'I'm remembering something Scott said when I asked him if he was sure that Ella had had no hand in your upbringing. I think I know the answer now.'

Abby trembled. 'Well, I—I've told you what I came to tell you now, so I'd better go——'

'Why?'

'What do you mean, why?'

'I mean,' said Luke, in that same flat voice, 'that your bed will be cold by this time. Why don't you stay here with me? There's plenty of room and at least you'd be warm. I promise I won't lay a hand on you.'

Abby drew an unsteady breath. 'I couldn't do that!'

'All right, then. Go!'

His voice was without expression, and ignoring her he began to slide under the covers, yawning wearily. Abby watched him. She believed him when he said he wouldn't touch her, but more importantly, would Ella? If she spent the night with him now, he would not be able to deny it, and Ella would never believe that it was innocent. By staying here now, she could achieve her objective without either losing her innocence, or her self-respect. What sweet revenge that would be, when she confronted her aunt with the knowledge . . .

With a small sigh, she wriggled lower down the bed and he turned his head on the pillow to look at her. 'You're staying?' he inquired dryly, and she nodded. 'I'm staying,' she agreed, and he stretched out a lazy hand and switched out the lamp.

Abby, surprisingly enough, went to sleep almost immediately. Luke's own breathing was soothing, and although she had expected to lie awake for hours, she found herself curling into a ball against his back and drifting irresistibly into oblivion.

She awakened to a curious buzzing sound, and for a moment had difficulty in orientating herself to her surroundings. But her hair was imprisoned by Luke's head, close beside hers on the pillow, and his hand was resting heavily on her arm, as if resisting any attempt she might make to get away from him. In sleep, he was relaxed, and vulnerable as before, and Abby found she had no desire to move. But it was light outside, and with this realisation came the further realisation that the sound she could hear was her alarm clock.

She started anxiously, disturbing Luke, but before she could move to stop it, the bell silenced itself. It had obviously run down and she breathed a sigh of relief, even though she had never allowed that to happen before. She had momentarily relaxed back against the pillow, and suddenly she became aware that Luke was awake and watching her.

'What happened?' he enquired drowsily. 'Did someone come in?'

Abby made a sound of exasperation. 'Do you think I'd still be lying here if they had? No, my alarm went off. It startled me.'

'Oh, God, alarms!' Luke rolled on to his back, stretching lazily. 'I used to be governed by them as well.' He rolled back to face her. 'But no longer.'

'You're lucky,' she said, realising that she ought to move at once.

'Am I?' he asked, and the expression in his sleepy green eyes made her catch her breath.

'I have to go,' she said unevenly, but he moved to prop himself up on one elbow, looking down at her, his other hand resting on the mattress at the far side of her, successfully preventing her escape.

'I never saw a woman who looked good in the morning until now,' he murmured huskily, and the warm colour flooded her cheeks.

'I—I suppose you—you've had plenty of experience,' she stammered, and he half smiled.

'Some,' he agreed, taking a strand of her hair between his fingers and raising it to his lips. 'Your hair smells good, too. Fresh and clean—no lingering traces of smoke or alcohol...'

'Luke, please...'

'Scott knew what he was doing when he sent me up here,' he muttered, his voice thickening. 'He knew I'd find you—irresistible...' And with a groan, he lowered himself to her, his mouth caressing the creamy curve of her jawline before seeking the parted softness of hers.

Abby didn't know what was happening to her. His mouth was playing with hers, rubbing and lifting, rubbing and lifting, until she forgot all about Ella and where she was, and even her reasons for being there. With a little sigh, she wound her arms round his neck, and when next he would have drawn away, she put her hand behind the back of his head and held him closer. It wasn't like the last time he had kissed her, when she had been too shaken to respond. This time she felt her whole body melting under the weight of his, and she could tell from the unsteadiness of his breathing and the hardening muscles pressing against hers that Luke was no longer playing games.

'Oh, my God! *Abby!*'

At first Abby scarcely recognised the agonised cry, but when she opened her eyes and saw Uncle Daniel standing horrified beside the bed, she wanted to die. Luke flung himself away from her, raking his hands through his hair, and she struggled into a sitting position, staring up at the old man through wild, tearful eyes.

'Oh, Abby, Abby,' he was saying, over and over again, and she could see there were tears on his cheeks. She scrambled out of bed, wringing her hands helplessly, not knowing how to begin to explain.

'I wish you wouldn't distress yourself, sir.' Luke was getting out of bed, tying the belt of his bathrobe, and although he spoke quietly they could hear every word. 'I realise this must have come as a great shock to you, but it's really not as bad as it appears.'

Abby turned resentful eyes on him, wishing she had the strength of resistance to fall back on. But she had not. She had invited his lovemaking, and however hard it was to bear, she had responded to it. But Luke was speaking again, and she tried to assimilate what he was saying.

'... and as Abby and I intend to get married—with your blessing, I hope—I wish you could accept what we have done as simply giving in to something that got too strong for us. I know it was wrong, but ...'

Married!

Abby heard the word as if from a far distance, hardly understanding in those first terrible moments what it was that Luke was saying. And then she heard the words again, from her uncle this time, and her lips formed its phrasing almost involuntarily. *'Married?'*

Luke looked at her, and there was a steely glint in his eyes which only minutes before had been passionately compelling. 'I know you wanted to wait a while, Abby, before telling your uncle, but in the circumstances ...'

'You hardly know one another!' protested Daniel McGregor weakly.

'On the contrary,' replied Luke, putting his arm about Abby's shoulders and drawing her resisting body to his side, 'Abby and I know one another well enough. It isn't always time that brings about a closer understanding, Father, a deeper recognition of the things one wants. Sometimes, two people just—know.'

'Uncle Daniel ...'

Abby tried to speak, but the pressure about her shoulders and another look into Luke's dark face silenced her, and instead the old man shook his head incredulously.

'I can't say anything just now,' he muttered, taking a handkerchief out of his pocket and blowing his nose. 'I need time—to think.' He looked at Abby. 'I don't know what to say. I'm disappointed in your behaviour, of course, but I'm not unaware that this sort of thing goes on. And as Mr Jordan—*Luke*—wants to marry you, who am I to object?'

'Uncle Daniel——'

'Don't say any more, Abby.' He cleared his throat, looking about the room uncomfortably. 'I suggest you return to your own bedroom now and prepare yourself for the day. Mrs Dalrymple will be expecting you, and Luke naturally needs to remain in bed.'

Abby looked helplessly at Luke, resentment giving way under a tide of anxiety. Why had he said what he had? He had no intention of marrying her! He was her aunt's lover, he had practically admitted it. Didn't he realise that by making her uncle believe he was serious, he was ultimately making it harder for all of them to bear?

CHAPTER FIVE

THREE weeks later, Abby sat beside Luke in the Lamborghini, driving south for the first time in her life. After the roads she was accustomed to, the motorway was a revelation, and Luke appeared to pay scant attention to the frequent signs which indicated a seventy miles an hour speed limit.

But perhaps that was because he was angry with her, she thought uneasily, and indeed since that night they had spent together, he had seemed so. She hardly dared to speculate on what he was thinking, and she wished she knew more about this man who was now her husband.

Her husband!

She gazed down with trepidation at the ring on her finger, the ring which less than eight hours ago had still been in Scott's waistcoat pocket. It was an exquisite piece of craftmanship, broad and faceted; gold, and not the platinum she had been afraid Luke might choose.

Yet she still did not understand why he had done it. Or indeed, how she had come to let him! It had not been part of her plan to marry him—just to take him away from Ella, in the same way her aunt had destroyed her parents' marriage seven years ago.

Of course, Luke did not know that old history. If he had, her ambitions would have come to nothing. As it was, he had, as Uncle Daniel put it, compromised her, and his offer of marriage had been to placate Uncle Daniel's sensitivities.

Even so, he need not have gone through with it. Once the storm of that awful scene had died down, Abby had gone to her adopted uncle and explained what had happened. She had assured him that Luke had not seduced her, as he had suspected, and that there was no earthly reason for him to marry her when he couldn't possibly want to do so.

But there Luke had been unexpectedly adamant. Far from withdrawing from his offer as she had anticipated—indeed, *hoped*, for her own peace of mind—he would do, he had seemed to take an almost malicious delight in thwarting her, reiterating his desire to marry her. Abby had been helpless in his hands, unable to deny publicly the things he said without revealing her own true feelings, and in so doing destroying her uncle's faith in her once and for all.

And that, she found, was something she could not do. It had been easy to plan, to fantasise what she would do in any given set of circumstances. But when she was faced with reality, with the endearing belief her uncle had always shown in her, she had found she could not hurt him as she would surely do if she told the truth. But that didn't prevent her from having private battles with Luke, and bearing the brunt of the anger this evoked. He needed a wife, he had told her, and he had decided that she would do admirably. If she didn't like it, she had only herself to blame, and he would not be responsible for breaking an old man's heart.

Then, when in spite of Abby's silent opposition all the

machinery of the actual wedding had been set in motion, Luke had gone back to London—to see Scott, and Ella, no doubt, although they had heard nothing from her, and to put his own affairs in order. He had returned last evening, accompanied by Scott, who was to be his best man. He had seemed like a stranger to her, tall and distinguished, in his dark brown corded suit, and all her earlier fears had materialised with a vengeance. *Vengeance is mine, saith the Lord*, she had quoted silently to herself, and wondered if this was His way of paying her back for the petty revenge she had planned.

During the evening, Luke had spent some time closeted with Uncle Daniel in his study, and it had been left to Abby to entertain Scott. She had wished she could have avoided this *tête-à-tête*, but it would most certainly have been impolite to walk out and leave him.

So they made small talk until Scott's feelings got the better of him, and he exclaimed forcefully: 'For God's sake, Abby, you can't go through with this!'

Abby was sitting on the couch in the room Mrs Tully always called the parlour, but she was far from relaxed, and having Scott standing over her as he was did not help.

'Have you said that to Luke?' she inquired, in what she hoped was a matter-of-fact tone.

'Of course I have,' he snapped, his hands balled in his trouser pockets.

'And what did he say?'

'He told me to mind my own bloody business!'

Abby's lips twitched, but it was an hysterical kind of amusement that gripped her. 'Then perhaps I ought to do the same,' she said.

Scott snorted. 'If I'd known this would happen . . .'

'I know. You wouldn't have sent him up here.'

'Like hell, I would. My God, it's a relief—an actual relief to get away from the studio, do you know that? And I love my work. You know that. But the atmosphere there . . .' He shook his head vehemently.

Abby licked her lips. 'Do you mean—Aunt Ella?'

'Do I mean Aunt Ella?' he mimicked. 'Of course I mean Ella! Have you any idea what this marriage means to her?'

Abby quivered. 'I—I know how my mother felt when

Daddy went away,' she murmured.

Scott grunted. 'Your mother was a lady, Abby. You know I always thought so. I never forgave myself for bringing Ella with me that Christmas . . .'

Abby sighed, feeling the familiar pang of nostalgia that thinking of her mother always brought. Then she said honestly: 'It need not have been you, Scott. Aunt Ella is —was—Mummy's sister, you know. She and Daddy—they might inevitably have met.'

'I doubt it.' Scott sounded sceptical. 'Ella couldn't wait to shake the dust of Ardnalui off her feet. If she hadn't thought I wanted her to accompany me to Scotland, she would never have come. But she was feeling her way in those days, and I was useful to her.'

'You still are.'

'Oh, yes, I know. We make good movies together. But Ella doesn't *need* me any more. She did then.' He shook his head. 'I'm not proud of the fact that I continued to let her work for me even after—after she and Mario were living together.'

'Oh, Scott!' Abby got to her feet, tucking her thumbs into the low belt of her jeans. 'Don't go on blaming yourself. You had a studio to run. And Aunt Ella is a good actress, isn't she?'

'The best.'

'There you are, then.' Abby tucked her fingers through his arm. 'I think we ought to say no more about it.'

'How can I do that when without what I did then, there'd be no wedding now?'

Abby's hand fell away. 'Please, Scott.'

'You're really going to marry Luke?'

'I have no choice.'

Scott made an angry sound. 'Perhaps you don't at that. Once Luke makes up his mind there's no gainsaying him.'

The wedding was a small affair by village standards, although everyone who could crowded into the church to hear the service. Father McGregor had married them himself, and during the Mass that followed Abby had tried to empty her mind of the eventual outcome of what she was doing. Only Mrs Tully, as well as the principal participants, attended the luncheon which followed; a cold buffet,

65

so that the housekeeper was free to join them.

It had all been slightly unreal to Abby, and the kiss Luke had bestowed on her temple after the service had relieved none of her anxieties. She was married now, and Luke had the right to do with her as he willed.

Allowing herself a fleeting glance at Luke's stern profile as he concentrated on the road ahead, she ran her fingers over the pleated skirt of the cream suit Mrs Tully had made for her to go away in. Not that they were having a honeymoon as such. Luke had too many commitments for that, or so he said. But even London would be strange to Abby, and she couldn't deny a certain excitment at the thought of living there.

Although the nearest town to Ardnalui did not sport a fashionable dress house, it did possess a shop selling dress materials and patterns, and for the wedding itself, the housekeeper had insisted on making her a white dress. Abby had had misgivings. She had never felt like a bride in the true sense of the word. Brides were happy, eager to be alone with their husbands—not wan and apprehensive of what was to happen after the ceremony. But that morning, dressed in the gown of fragile lace over a silk underskirt, her dark hair a perfect foil against its purity, she had had to admit that she looked bridelike.

Now, in this suit, she was once more aware of the enormous step she had taken. Wife to a man like Luke Jordan. A man so many years older than she was. No longer Abby —no, *Abigail* Rodriguez, but Abigail Jordan—*Mrs* Luke Jordan. She drew a trembling breath. What a tangled web she had woven since first she learned of her aunt's infatuation for this man!

'Are you hungry?'

Luke's words interrupted the uneasy tenor of her thoughts and startled her. 'I—what? Oh, no—not very.'

Luke compressed his lips. 'It's almost eight. I thought we might stop at the next service area and have a light meal. It will save having to prepare something when we get home.'

Home! Abby felt a sinking sensation in her stomach. Her home was in Ardnalui, over the Border, already in another country. And was it really eight o'clock. It was still daylight and she had been indifferent to the passing of time. They must have been on the roads for hours. Luke was bound to be tired—and hungry.

'If that's what you want to do...' she ventured, awkwardly, and his lips tightened.

'Isn't it what you want to do? Or would you rather press on?'

Abby straightened her spin. 'What—what time will we get—there?' she asked. She could hardly think of his apartment as *home*. She didn't even know where it was.

'Where?' Luke's response was clipped.

'Why, to your apartment, of course.'

'That depends on whether we stop or not. It's going to be dark anyway before we get there. An hour more or less isn't going to make much difference.'

'All right, let's stop, then.'

'Right.'

Luke was silent again and Abby sighed. 'You still didn't tell me. What time we should—reach London.'

'Around ten-thirty, I should think,' he replied, glancing at his wrist watch. 'Barring accidents.'

Abby nodded. Ten-thirty. Just in time for bed!

The grill room at the service area was tastefully decorated and discreetly lit. The walls were dark red and matched the shades on the lamps which occupied every table. Luke had soup, and steak, and salad, and an enormous plate of french frieds, while Abby had great difficulty in swallowing a prawn cocktail and a plain omelette. They had wine with the meal, a delicacy Abby had previously only tasted very occasionally, but she found its dryness palatable, and it helped to get the food down. The sweet trolley displayed a variety of rich concoctions, sherry trifle, brandy snaps with cream, meringues and gateaux and cream cakes. Luke obviously expected her to choose something, and rather against the somewhat queasy dictates of her stomach she chose the strawberry gateau. A thick slice was placed in front of her, but she avoided looking at it while Luke refused the contents of the trolley and asked for cheese and biscuits. The plainer fare would have suited her admirably and she looked on enviously while the waiter cut him a chunk of smooth Wensleydale.

Luke caught her eyes upon his plate and regarded her tolerantly. 'Would you have preferred this?' he asked.

Abby looked down at the gateau oozing cream. 'I'm sure this will be very nice,' she answered evasively.

'But not for someone not used to eating such rich food at this time of night,' Luke commented. 'Do you want to swap?'

Abby gasped. 'Oh, no, I couldn't take your cheese!'

'Why not?' Luke sounded amused. 'I haven't touched it.'

'I know, but...' Abby looked about her nervously. 'Someone might see. Besides, it was what you wanted...'

Luke gave her an old-fashioned look and reaching across the table he replaced the gateau with his own plate of cheese and crackers. 'There you are. I hope you enjoy it. Although I'd advise you to go easy on the cheese at this time of night. You might have nightmares, and we wouldn't want that, would we?'

His eyes mocked her, and she coloured brilliantly as she applied herself to buttering the crackers. Yet for all that, his understanding was reassuring, and he didn't seem so much like a stranger after all.

Back in the car again, Abby felt drowsy. The food, which had banished the fluttery feeling in the pit of her stomach, and the warming qualities of the wine, had both served to relax her, and snuggled against the soft leather she felt pleasantly sleepy.

She must have slept, because when she opened her eyes again, the darkness outside the car was illuminated by dozens of street lamps, and the neon façades of shops and cinemas. She blinked rapidly and sat up, hoping she had not slept with her mouth open or anything, and looked about her. 'Is this—London?'

'The outskirts,' Luke agreed, sounding slightly weary. 'It won't be long now.'

'I must have slept,' she ventured, and he glanced sideways at her.

'Over an hour,' he agreed. 'I wished I could have joined you.'

Abby made no reply to this. It reminded her too acutely of that night they had slept together, and of all the other

68

nights they might be expected to do so. So she stared wide-eyed at the brightly lighted streets, and tried to forget why she was there. She had visited Glasgow once on her way to Madrid to stay with her grandparents, but that was years ago now, and besides, it had been daylight. London at night was busier than she had imagined it would be at noon.

As they drove nearer to the city itself, Abby became confused with the traffic—the line-up at the traffic lights terrified her, as did the stream of cars overtaking them on the left-hand side, and the one-way system made reaching their destination that much more complicated. Luke seemed unperturbed by the turmoil and confusion, but it was possible to see the lines of strain around his eyes which the arduous hours of driving had traced. Uncle Daniel had suggested they take the journey in easy stages, and she knew he had been thinking of her when he said that, but Luke had speedily disabused him of such a notion. He needed to be back in town for the following day, he had said, and Uncle Daniel had retired gracefully. Scott was coming back by train. He was not overly fond of driving, and the prospect of being cooped up in the back of Luke's car for hour after hour did not appeal to him.

When it became apparent that Luke's apartment must be in the very heart of the city, Abby began to wonder how on earth she would ever sleep again with all this noise. She was used to the peace and tranquillity of Ardnalui. London was loud and noisy, and not at all the romantic way she had pictured it to be.

They turned a corner into a wide thoroughfare with what appeared to be a park running side by side with the road. Then, before she had time to absorb this, Luke turned sharply right and she saw they were in a small square, dominated by a block of skyscraper proportions. Shallow steps led up to swing glass doors, but they drove past and turned down a steep incline into what seemed to be an underpass. But it wasn't. It was an underground garage, already half full of expensive vehicles.

Luke drove the Lamborghini to a space at the end, and after parking it to his liking, switched off the engine. The silence was hollow and unexpected, and Abby turned to look at him nervously.

'Is this it?'

'This is it,' he agreed.

She shrugged her slim shoulders. 'What is it called?'

'The block? Frenchman's Court. The square? Marlborough.'

'Marlborough Square.' Abby said the words as Luke thrust open his door and climbed stiffly out of the car. 'Frenchman's Court, Marlborough Square.' She liked it.

Luke jerked open her door and she swung her legs out as he went to open the boot. All her belongings were stowed in a worn brown suitcase and a canvas holdall. Luke had only an overnight case in which he had carried his pyjamas and shaving equipment, and the fresh tan shirt he had worn that morning. Thinking about his clothes made Abby realise she knew nothing about his domestic arrangements, how the apartment was kept clean, who did the washing, and who provided his food.

Luke locked the car and scooping her holdall under one arm, he took a case in each hand and strode towards the lifts. Abby followed him, shivering a little as they entered the narrow tube which swept them up fourteen floors to the penthouse. It was not like any lift she had used before, and her stomach had hardly had time to adjust itself before the door was sliding back to reveal a pile-carpeted corridor. Only two doors opened off the corridor, and Luke briefly remarked that there were only two apartments on this floor.

He set the cases on the floor while he pulled his keys out of his pocket and inserted them in the lock, and then the door swung open on to a shadowy hallway. Luke touched a switch, and at once a mellow amber light bathed biscuit brown walls and dark green carpeting.

'Go ahead,' he said to Abby, and with nervous tread she stepped into her new home.

The hall was large, with several doors opening from it, as well as a short flight of stairs which Luke explained led to the bedrooms. Then he opened a door to their right, turned on another switch, and Abby walked forward into the huge living room of the apartment.

The illumination in here came from lamps and wall fittings, casting pools of amber and gold over the patina of dark wood and panelling. A fireplace, which surely could not ever be needed, was flanked by tall carved bookcases, while the tapestry-covered chairs and high-backed settee matched the heavy brocade curtains that stood open before long windows. A desk stood by the windows, broad and leather-topped, presently free of any encumbering papers, and there were small antique tables here and there, and a chest supporting a Chinese vase filled with silvery-plumed pampas grass. The carpet was a circular design in green and gold and aubergine, the pattern of which was echoed in the moulding of the high ceiling. It was totally different from the modern room she had envisaged, and she turned to face Luke incredulously.

'I—I never knew you could find a room like this in—in a skyscraper block!' she exclaimed.

Luke smiled at her reaction. He had left the cases in the hall, and now he unbuttoned his jacket and hooked his thumbs into the pockets of the matching waistcoat.

'You can do anything if you can afford it,' he remarked dryly. 'No, seriously, I was brought up in what I suppose you would call modern surroundings. At any rate, we had cheap modern furniture, and I remember my mother saved until she could afford cheap fitted carpets. By ordinary standards, I suppose, we were reasonably well off. Then, when—Alison and I got married ...' Abby felt a curious twinge at the mention of his first wife ... 'when we got married, she wanted one of those square detached houses on a new estate.' He sighed, running his fingers over the base of a bronze carving that stood on a cabinet by the door. 'She got what she wanted, of course, but I hated it. After we split up, I vowed I would never live in those surroundings ever again. I think I'd rather have bought our furniture at a secondhand store and lived in one of those terraced back-to-backs, so long as it had character.'

Abby kicked off her shoes to feel the soft pile beneath her toes, and nodded slowly. 'I know what you mean,' she said, moving over to the windows to gaze out at the hundreds of twinkling lights below them.

'I hoped you would,' he said, behind her, and she felt a

71

moment's anxiety at the possessiveness of his tone.

'Shall I draw the curtains?' she asked jerkily, in an effort to lighten the mood, and he shrugged his shoulders indifferently.

'You can if you like, but there's nothing out there. Just space. The nearest tall building is at least the width of the park away. That's why I chose the apartment on this side of the block.'

Abby digested this and turned to find him going out of the room again. 'Where are you going?'

Luke paused. 'I thought I'd get rid of the cases out of the hall. Do you want to see your bedroom? Then later maybe I can show you the kitchen, and you can make us both a drink. You can do that, can't you?'

'I'm quite a good cook!' she exclaimed indignantly. 'I used to look after Uncle Daniel when Mrs Tully was ill or on holiday.'

Luke looked suitably impressed, but she guessed he found her retaliation amusing. Sighing, she picked up her shoes and carried them after him.

The shallow staircase seemed to be a concession to the artistic design of the apartment rather than serving any useful purpose. At its head, a second hall-cum-landing gave access to four more rooms, one of which was a bathroom for the use of guests. The three bedrooms all had their own private bathroom, Luke explained, opening the door of one of them and carrying her belongings inside.

Abby followed him into the room reluctantly, but again its exquisite appointments made her briefly forget her fears. The carpet here was a creamy gold, reflected in the long silk curtains at the windows, and in the embossed bedspread. The bed was not a fourposter although it did have four posts, and the headboard was carved with scrollwork which was evidently old. The other furniture was made of mahogany, strong, solid items, built on a similar scale to the huge bed. Abby's eyes went directly to the dressing table, but there was nothing there to indicate that Luke used this room.

Now he set her suitcase down on a fringed tapestry-covered ottoman and said: 'Well? Do you like it?'

Abby, whose eyes had been drawn to ceiling carvings

which matched the scrollwork on the headboard, gave a little sigh. 'It's—beautiful!' she said honestly. 'You must be very rich!'

Luke's mouth turned down slightly at the corners. 'And you ought to know better than to say things like that,' he remarked dryly.

Abby coloured. 'Well...' she defended herself uncomfortably, 'you must know I'm right.'

'Does that matter to you?'

Abby hesitated. 'I don't think I know what you mean.'

'Do you mind if I have a lot of money? Does the idea appeal, or doesn't it?'

Abby looked at him thoughtfully, for once able to meet his eyes without evasion. He looked exhausted, and a wave of emotion swept over her, rushing her into speech:

'I've never wanted to be rich, if that's what you mean,' she said. 'It may seem rather naïve to you, but I don't think I need a lot of money. Oh, this apartment is beautiful, of course, but—I think I could live in that back-to-back you talked about.'

Luke expelled his breath on a heavy sigh. 'I believe you,' he said, moving past her to the door. 'Now, would you like to know where I sleep?'

Abby nodded, not trusting herself to speak, and he threw open the door of the adjacent room. All the rooms in the apartment were of generous proportions and this was no exception. If anything, it was slightly larger than Abby's room, with furnishings of dark oak against pale walls. Chocolate brown carpeting was relieved by a circular rug beside the wide bed, and the bedspread was apricot-coloured, like the curtains.

'I would have given you this room,' he said quietly, 'except that I thought you might find the decor rather sombre.'

'Oh, no!' she exclaimed, touching the shade of a bronze lamp beside the bed, her stockinged toes curling into the rich pile of the rug. 'I like it. It's—restful.'

'Would you prefer to change rooms?' Luke offered, gesturing towards his overnight case, but Abby quickly shook her head.

'Of course not. I like my room very much. I just—like this room, too.'

Luke's tired eyes glinted mockingly. 'I suggest you go and make that drink we talked about, before the obvious solution occurs to me,' he remarked.

If the main rooms of the apartment had a period air about them, the kitchen at least was aggressively modern. Satin-smooth working surfaces concealed a refrigerator and washer-cum-tumble drier, and the stainless steel sink unit contained a waste disposal unit. The kitchen was large, too, large enough to eat in, thought Abby, who had surreptitiously peeped into the dining room and found it big enough to seat more than twenty people round the long polished refectory table. Fitted cupboards lined the walls and when she opened the doors, she gasped as the shelves moved as well, making the act of taking things from the cupboards that much easier. There was a narrow breakfast bar, and two tall stools, and Abby wondered if Luke used this when he was here alone, instead of sitting in magnificent isolation in the dining room. But perhaps he seldom ate alone, she thought, not altogether liking its implications, and determinedly took a pint of milk from the fridge and pouring it into a saucepan, set it on the hotplate section of the split-level cooker.

Luke reappeared as she was stirring sugar into beakers of hot chocolate. He had shed his suit for white silk pyjamas, and his hair was damp from the shower he must have taken. Abby averted her eyes from the shadowy outline of his body beneath the fine material, but he seemed indifferent to her embarrassment.

'It—it's hot chocolate,' she said, continuing to stir rapidly, and Luke came across and took the spoon from her unresisting fingers.

'You're not drilling for oil,' he remarked dryly, and picking up one of the beakers raised it to his lips. 'Mmm, it's good. Exactly what you're supposed to drink before going to bed. Even on honeymoon!'

'We're not on honeymoon!' exclaimed Abby crossly, disturbed by her own reaction to him. 'Anyway, what was I supposed to make?'

'Coffee would have been nice.'

'You don't drink coffee before going to bed!'

'Well, not tonight anyway,' he agreed lazily. 'Shall we adjourn to the living room? It's warmer in there.'

To Abby, used to cold rooms and even colder passageways, the apartment was all beautifully warm, but it was true, the kitchen's air-conditioning kept it somewhat cooler.

In the living room, Luke lounged into one of the easy chairs, draping his leg over the arm. Abby, trying not to be aware of him watching her, wandered about the room examining a miniature here, a carving there, anything to avoid the intimacy which might precipitate the inevitable. Just because he had given her a bedroom to herself it did not mean that he did not intend to share it with her, at least for part of the night, and that prospect filled her with alarm. How had it happened? she asked herself futilely, knowing exactly what she had done. It might not have been so bad if she had loved him, but she didn't. He terrified her at times, and there had been no one to discuss her fears with, no one to reassure her that the things he might demand of her were neither terrifying nor frightening. As it was, she saw him as an experienced man of the world, and herself as an ignorant schoolgirl. To imagine him forcing himself upon her, losing control as they put it in books, behaving like an animal... She shuddered. It would never happen. She would never let it.

'Are you tired?'

He was speaking, and she swung round on her heel to face him, plucking at the collar of her suit. 'Yes,' she said, after a moment's indecision. If she said *No*, he might read that as an invitation.

'Finish your chocolate and we'll go to bed,' he said, stifling a yawn. 'I'm tired, too. That was some drive.'

Abby nodded jerkily and finished the liquid in her beaker obediently. Luke swung his leg to the floor and stood up, but although she quivered when he approached her, it was just to take the empty beaker from her hands.

'Go on,' he said, half impatiently. 'You know the way. Goodnight, Abby.'

Her wide-eyed expression must have given her away, because as she turned to leave, he added dryly: 'That's

75

right. I'm not about to demand my rights—not tonight, at any rate. Sleep well.'

The bathroom adjoining Abby's room echoed the cream and gold pattern of the bedroom, but tonight Abby was too weary to pay it a great deal of attention. She admired the chrome fittings of the shower unit, but contented herself with washing in the basin, and after cleaning her teeth she put on her cotton nightgown and tumbled into bed. The sheets were gold-coloured, too, and made of silk, and her toes moved luxuriously against their softness. She didn't think Uncle Daniel would approve of such extravagance, and a momentary pang of homesickness swept over her. It was then she realised how quiet the apartment was. Even at this time of night, and it was almost midnight, the sounds of the city had not abated, but up here it was just a comforting hum. She switched out the light and stretched her arms above her head. Well, she was here, and incredibly she was married. And perhaps tomorrow she would be expected to confront Ella.

She was drifting into sleep when the strident ringing of the telephone brought her sharply awake again. It rang for some time, and anxiety invaded her vaguely confused brain. She didn't know of anyone who would ring at this time of night without there being an emergency, and remembrance of Uncle Daniel's great age and the shock he must have received at her assumed betrayal of everything he had taught her might well have caused him real pain. Perhaps he had been taken ill, perhaps—agonisingly—he had had a heart attack...

She heard the sound of a door opening and abruptly the telephone stopped ringing. Luke had gone to answer it, and remembering how tired he had been, she felt a sense of responsibility.

Throwing aside the bedcovers, she got up, and leaving her room, went barefoot down the stairs to the living room door. Even before she reached the shaft of light thrown from the room beyond, she could hear Luke's voice, and the suppressed anger it contained. She couldn't hear what he was saying, but she guessed whoever was on the other end of the line was getting the sharp edge of his tongue.

Then, just as she reached the door, she heard the sound of the receiver being thrust down savagely on to its rest, and the light was extinguished as Luke came across the room.

Abby had no time to turn and leave, but even so she was shocked when Luke practically walked into her.

'What the hell—*Abby*!' he exclaimed impatiently, grasping her arms in the darkness. 'What are you doing out of bed?'

'I—the telephone,' she said lamely, realising whoever it had been, it had had nothing whatsoever to do with her.

Luke switched on the hall light, releasing her as he did so. Now she saw he slept only in his pyjama trousers, his lean chest bare.

'Do you want to know who it was?' he demanded, and she moved her shoulders awkwardly.

'I—thought it might have been Mrs Tully,' she murmured, realising how weak that sounded, even to her ears, now that she was wide awake and alert again.

Luke sighed. 'Well, it wasn't,' he said shortly. 'It was your dear aunt checking up on us.'

'Aunt Ella?'

'How many aunts do you have?'

Abby bit her lip. 'At this time of night?'

Luke made an exasperated sound. 'My dear infant, it's only half past twelve! To Ella, that's the middle of the evening!'

Abby coloured vividly. 'I'm sorry. I—I should have stayed in bed.'

'Yes, you should,' he agreed harshly.

She shivered. 'Goodnight again, then.'

Luke regarded her steadily for a second and then he said: 'Oh, *Abby*!' in a curiously strained voice, and before she could stop him, he had picked her up and carried her back upstairs. But not to her room. He kicked open his own door and deposited her among the chocolate brown covers of his bed. Abby trembled violently, too shocked to make any protest, even when he climbed in beside her. Then, amazingly, he switched out the light and turned his back on her.

'God knows how long I can keep this up,' he muttered, savagely, and she realised he intended going to sleep . . .

CHAPTER SIX

ABBY lay awake long after Luke's breathing had become deep and faintly stertorous. He was exhausted, she knew, and there was something very satisfying about having him sleeping soundly beside her. She could have got out of bed again and gone back to her own room. She doubted he would have been disturbed by her movements. But, curiously enough, she had no desire to do so, and it was this as much as anything which kept her awake. She couldn't understand what it was about him which could terrify her one minute, and then arouse all her feminine responses the next. The fact remained, she did not understand him, but there were times, like now, when being close to him was the most desirable thing imaginable...

In spite of her comparatively late night, Abby was awake reasonably early the next morning. She was not used to sharing a bed with anybody, and she wondered if Luke's ease of doing so came from long practice. The idea was distasteful to her, and she refused to consider why.

Wakening to find one of his legs imprisoning both of hers and his face buried comfortably in the curve of her neck, she decided she should move before he came awake. She remembered that other occasion when he had awakened to find her beside him, and how his morning reaction to the circumstances had been so much more demanding than it had been the night before.

All the same, she was loath to move away from him, and she lay for several minutes savouring the drowsy warmth of his body. Her hand was resting on his thigh, and she couldn't resist moving her fingers against the soft material, feeling the hardness of muscle beneath. She curled her toes sensuously against the sheets and wondered why she had ever imagined that only white linen looked good on a bed. Chocolate brown silk was infinitely more attractive.

At last, when Luke began to stir a little, snuggling his face deeper into her hair, his hand sliding possessively across her midriff, Abby knew she had to get up. With a lithe movement, she wriggled out of his embrace, and stood for a minute beside the bed, looking down at him. His hair was tousled, and the lines of tiredness had been erased from his face. His limbs, outlined beneath the covers, were relaxed and reclining, and the urgency of a sudden desire to get back into bed surprised her by its strength. Then, determinedly, she turned away, refusing to be seduced by the undoubtedly sexual attraction of his lean body.

She collected her dressing gown from her bedroom, a pink candlewick garment, designed more for warmth than elegance, and went down the stairs to the kitchen. Already, and it was only a little after eight, the central heating had taken the chill from the air, and she fastened the cord of her gown loosely before plugging in the electric kettle. She busied herself waiting for it to boil by seeking out a tray and the teapot, setting teacups on the tray and adding the cream jug and sugar basin. She almost jumped out of her skin when the door behind her opened, and a woman's voice said:

'*Oh*! Good morning. Is it—Mrs Jordan?'

Abby swung round, her heart thumping, to confront a middle-aged woman wearing a poplin overcoat and carrying a shopping bag, her hair half hidden beneath a headscarf.

'I—good morning. Yes, I—I'm Mrs Jordan.' And she was. Only she still couldn't believe it! But who else had this woman expected to find here?

'Pleased to meet you, Mrs Jordan. I'm Mrs Hobbs,' said her visitor, gathering her astonishment and coming forward, holding out her hand. Abby shook it politely, and the woman went on: 'I expect Mr Jordan's told you about me. I do his washing and cleaning—and cook for him when necessary.'

'Oh! Oh, yes.' Abby managed not to sound as surprised as she felt. It was obvious the woman found her appearance surprising, too, but for an entirely different reason, she guessed shrewdly. She looked like no one's idea of the successful author's wife! 'Do you—that is, does my—husband'—*that didn't come out too badly!*—'does he employ you every day, Mrs Hobbs?'

Whether the woman didn't care for this kind of questioning, Abby didn't know, but the kettle was steaming, and Mrs Hobbs turned it off and taking the teapot, warmed it, before putting in the teabags Abby had found. 'I come as often as he asks me,' she said at last, when the tea was made, successfully, Abby felt, reducing her efforts to nil. 'There now. Shall I carry the tray for you?'

'No!' Of that Abby was very certain. 'I—I can manage.' She tightened the cord of her dressing gown and ran combing fingers through her tangled hair. 'You—er—you just go ahead and do what you normally do, Mrs Hobbs.'

'I usually make Mr Jordan's breakfast,' said the woman, taking off the head-scarf to reveal pepper and salt hair, cut short for convenience. 'Would you like breakfast too, Mrs Jordan?'

Abby sighed. She had picked up the tray, but now she hovered uncertainly, not sure what to suggest.

'I think you'd better leave breakfast until Mr Jordan gets up,' she decided at last, taking the easiest way out, and Mrs Hobbs raised her eyebrows as Abby backed out of the kitchen.

Luke was half awake when Abby came back into his bedroom and set the tray down on a small chest by the door. As she closed the door, he opened his eyes, and a strange, satisfied expression crossed his face.

'Well, well,' he remarked drowsily. 'My wife has made tea. How nice!'

Abby regarded him impatiently. 'You might have warned me you had a daily woman,' she protested. 'She nearly scared me out of my skin.'

Luke grinned lazily. 'Who? Mrs Hobbs? Sorry about that.' He yawned, apologised, and added: 'I don't suppose she was overjoyed to see you either.'

Abby frowned. 'Why not?'

Luke rubbed the hair on his chest absent-mindedly, and then his eyes darkened with emotion. 'Come here, Abby. You haven't kissed me good morning yet.'

Abby shifted nervously from one foot to the other, but she remained where she was. 'Why wouldn't Mrs Hobbs want to see me?' she insisted.

Luke groaned and dragged himself into a sitting position. 'What is it they say about two women in one kitchen?'

he remarked. Then: 'So—are we having tea, or aren't we?'

'Of course.' Sighing, Abby returned to the tray, adding two spoonsful of sugar to Luke's cup at his request. But when she held out the cup to him to take, he reached over and caught a handful of her dressing gown, pulling her closer to him.

'You'll spill the tea!' she cried breathlessly, but he just said: 'To hell with the tea!' and dragged her down on to the bed beside him. The hot liquid was spilled all over the bedcovers, and Abby heard the china cup and saucer tumble on to the floor as Luke knelt over her, lowering his mouth to hers with lazy determination.

Their mouths touched and clung, and his hands pushed the offending pink candlewick aside, seeking the rounded curves still concealed beneath the cotton nightgown.

'You wear a hell of a lot of unnecessary gear,' he muttered against her mouth, and Abby found herself agreeing with him, finding unexpected pleasure in smoothing her palms over the taut muscles of his back, wanting the closeness of his flesh against hers. He was lying over her now, and she was conscious of every hard muscle of his body straining against her.

'You know what I want to do, don't you?' he asked softly, his warm breath filling her mouth, and suddenly she was no longer afraid. He was her husband—and it would be almost a relief to shed the burden that innocence had placed upon her. Unknowingly provocative, she arched her back against him, and felt his violent rejection when the telephone started to ring as it had done the night before.

The shrill sound of the bell brought Abby to her senses, and with the return to sanity came an almost unbearable feeling of disgust and shame. What was she doing, letting Luke touch her as he had, seeking the embraces of a man who at best she scarcely liked, let alone loved? They were married, it was true, but that was something else, something which even now she realised could be annulled once Uncle Daniel's sense of propriety had been satisfied.

'For God's sake, Abby,' Luke groaned, as she sought to free herself. 'Don't go! Don't leave me like this! If it's your aunt on the phone, let Mrs Hobbs tell her to go jump in the lake!'

Abby moved her head helplessly from side to side. 'No —please! Let me get up! I want to get up, Luke!'

With a savage oath, he rolled away from her, lying prone on the bed, his head resting on his arm, and Abby struggled to her feet. As she did so, Mrs Hobbs knocked at the door.

'Are you there, Mr Jordan?' she called. 'Miss Mackay is on the phone to speak to you.'

Abby stiffened and looked at Luke's still form. He had made no attempt to answer the daily woman, and in a hushed voice Abby whispered: 'Luke!' But still he didn't move, and with a sigh she went nearer and touched his shoulder. He flinched away from her hand, and when he turned to scowl at her, she almost gasped aloud at the violence of his expression. Then he levered himself into a sitting position, and with his back to Abby called:

'Tell her I can't speak to her now, Mrs Hobbs.'

'Are you sure, sir?' Mrs Hobbs sounded concerned. 'I think she said it was urgent.'

'I'm sorry, Mrs Hobbs,' retorted Luke, getting off the bed, 'but that's my answer.'

'Very good, sir.'

With a rustle of her apron, the daily woman moved away, and then Luke gave a deep sigh and padded barefoot into his bathroom. He didn't look at Abby again. She might have been invisible. And with a feeling of unwarranted, but nevertheless guilty, remorse, she stumbled out of the room.

She took a shower before dressing in her newly laundered jeans and a denim shirt. She was brushing her hair when she remembered the soiled bedclothes. She chewed anxiously at her lower lip, imagining Mrs Hobbs reaction when she found the bedspread stained with tea. The sheets, too, would probably require washing. It was all right for Luke to dismiss the incident, but her upbringing had instilled in her a certain code of conduct that was hard to ignore.

Luke's bedroom door was open, she discovered, and a swift look around assured her that he had probably gone downstairs. The tumbled bed confronted her, and without stopping to consider the advisability of what she intended, she quickly stripped off the sheets and bedspread and hauled them after her into the bathroom.

Luke's bathroom was similar to hers, the bath bronze and deep. Turning on the cold tap, she pushed the stained bedding down into the water, practically filling the bath before feeling satisfied. Then she went back into the bedroom and surveyed the bare bed. If only she knew where the fresh sheets were kept she could remake it without Mrs Hobbs being any the wiser. Then, after the daily woman had gone, she could transfer the sheets and bedspread to the washer in the kitchen and have them laundered before she returned tomorrow.

With a sigh, she looked round the room. Where might sheets be kept? An ottoman seemed the most likely place, but it contained only curtains, and the chest by the door yielded a stack of books and magazines.

She had opened the long wardrobe doors and was searching some fitted shelves when a voice interrupted her.

'What in God's name do you think you're doing?'

It was Luke, of course, tall and immaculate now in a black suede suit, his silvery hair lying thick and smooth against his head. He stood behind her, feet slightly apart, watching her with the cool appraisal of an interrogator.

Abby took a deep breath and closed the doors of the wardrobe, leaning back against them for support. 'I—I was looking for bedding, if you must know.' She indicated the bare mattress behind him. 'I looked in the ottoman and the chest, and then I thought that it might be——'

'—in my wardrobe,' he queried dryly. 'Hardly a possibility, I should have thought.'

'Where does Mrs Hobbs keep it?'

'In the linen cupboard, I would imagine,' he replied evenly. 'In any case,' he glanced round at the bed, 'such matters need not concern you.'

'But they do concern me,' Abby exclaimed. 'I—I couldn't leave the bed in *that* state.'

'Why not?' A faint note of tolerance entered his voice. 'Abby, that's what I pay Mrs Hobbs for.'

Abby sighed. 'It's all right for you,' she mumbled unhappily.

Luke made an impatient gesture. 'Explain to me the essence of that remark.'

Abby looked up at him reluctantly. 'Well, as you said, you're her employer. She knows you. She—she respects you.'

'Why shouldn't she respect you, too? Luke demanded. 'You're my wife.'

'Am I?' Abby was near to tears. The events of the morning combined with the frustration of not being able to hide what had happened to her satisfaction had all left her feeling totally inadequate. 'I—I don't know why I married you.'

'As I recall it, you were not given much choice in the matter,' Luke told her quietly. Then he pushed long fingers through his hair in a curiously uncertain gesture. 'Oh, Abby, I'm sorry. I mean, for—what happened earlier. I didn't intend——' He broke off abruptly, looking down at her in such a way that, ridiculously, she wanted to comfort him.

'I—I'm sorry, too,' she breathed huskily, and he stretched out a hand and wound a strand of her hair round his fingers.

'Come on,' he said, tugging gently at the dark silk, 'Mrs Hobbs is waiting to serve breakfast.'

They ate in the dining room, at one end of the long table, and looking about her admiringly at the maroon damask walls and gleaming candelabrum on the carved sideboard Abby couldn't help thinking how much cosier it would have been for them to eat in the kitchen. But Mrs Hobbs obviously took her duties seriously and looking at Luke across the polished surface of the table, Abby thought how incongruous she must seem in shabby jeans and denim shirt compared to his casual elegance. No wonder the daily had looked at her so disparagingly.

'Now what are you thinking?' Luke asked, with an acute perception that was disturbing. He had finished his plate of kidneys and bacon and was regarding her tolerantly as she sat, elbows resting on the table, her coffee cup cradled between her fingers.

Abby put down her cup and shrugged. 'Nothing much.'

'I know you better than that, Abby,' he reminded her dryly. 'Come on, I want to know.'

Abby hesitated. Then she said slowly: 'If—if I'm to stay here——'

'And you are!'

'—then I think—there should be some changes.'

Luke looked interested. 'Go on.'

Abby frowned. 'Well—Mrs Hobbs, for example.'

'Yes? What about Mrs Hobbs?'

But before Abby could formulate what she wanted to say, that lady reappeared in the doorway, eyebrows raised politely.

'Would you like some more toast, Mr Jordan?' she inquired, almost ingratiatingly, Abby felt, but Luke shook his head.

'I don't think so, thank you, Mrs Hobbs,' he assured her levelly. 'You can get on.'

'Thank you, sir.'

The daily withdrew again, and Abby pursed her lips. 'You see what I mean!' she exclaimed. 'We can't even have a private conversation without being interrupted!'

Luke's lips twitched. 'I gather you don't like Mrs Hobbs.'

Abby sighed frustratedly. 'It's not that I don't like her —oh!' She looked doubtfully towards the door. 'You don't suppose she's listening, do you?'

Luke regarded her steadily for a moment, and then he got to his feet and walked patiently across the room, swinging open the door so she could see the empty hall beyond. 'Satisfied?'

Abby felt duly chastened, but at his request she went on, albeit a little less aggressively: 'It's just that—well, I could prepare our breakfast, and then—and then we wouldn't have to eat in here,' she finished rapidly.

Luke resumed his seat, leaning back so that the chair tipped on to its rear legs. 'Why not? Don't you like this room?'

'Of course I like it.' Abby fidgeted with her cutlery. 'It's a beautiful room. But it's not a breakfast room really, is it?'

'I'm afraid we don't have a breakfast room.'

'But we could eat in the kitchen. Don't you see? If there were just the two of us. It's cosy in there. And you wouldn't have to—well, I shouldn't feel so out of place!'

His chair met the floor squarely again with a thud. 'What do you mean?' he demanded, and there was an edge of impatience creeping back into his voice. 'Why should you feel out of place in here?'

Abby hunched her shoulders. 'Well,' she defended herself awkwardly, 'if—if we ate in the kitchen, you wouldn't have to wear a jacket, and——'

'What the hell does my wearing a jacket have to do with it?'

Abby looked at him anxiously. 'I'm trying to explain. I mean, I'm not dressed up. I'm just wearing denims ...'

'Oh, my God!' He shook his head, half indulgently now. 'I'm not dressed up! If you want I shouldn't wear a jacket —okay, I'll take it off.'

'You don't understand,' she murmured miserably. 'I'd like to do things for myself. I could even wash those sheets if you'd let me.'

Luke got up from his chair and came round the table towards her, taking the chair immediately beside hers. 'Now, listen,' he said, stroking back her hair behind her ear so that he could see her profile, 'I don't want my wife wearing herself out washing sheets and worrying about preparing meals.'

Abby licked her lips. This close, he lost that air of detachment he had had across the table, and she remembered too well their last encounter. 'I—I shouldn't wear myself out. I'm not offering to do everything.'

'Just almost everything,' he remarked wryly.

'A—a wife should take care of—of her husband,' she ventured. 'Shouldn't she?'

'Hmm ... mm.' His eyes lingered disturbingly on her mouth and a pregnant pause descended. Then he dragged his gaze away and got up from the chair. 'All right, Abby,' he agreed a little roughly. 'How would it be if I allowed you to make our breakfast, and lunch, too, when we're at home?'

Abby's eyes sparkled. Then she frowned. 'What about Mrs Hobbs?'

Luke ran a hand round the back of his neck. 'Well, I suppose she would still prepare dinner, when necessary, and continue doing the housework.'

Abby clasped her hands together. 'And could you ask her to come later in the morning. Say—about ten, or half past? Then we wouldn't have to get up so early.'

Luke turned and grinned at her then, shaking his head. 'Oh, Abby,' he exclaimed, 'do you honestly imagine I'm going to get up at seven o'clock to have breakfast before the housekeeper arrives?' He walked towards the door. 'Naturally I'll tell her to come later. But don't be surprised if she gives notice.'

'Why?' Abby rose to her feet now.

Luke shrugged. 'Good housekeepers aren't that easy to come by.'

'Well, if she leaves, she leaves,' said Abby philosophically, half hoping she would, and Luke gave her another wry stare before leaving the room.

Abby was in the living room when Luke reappeared, and she gazed at him expectantly.

'She's staying,' he remarked flatly. 'Now, we have to talk.'

'Wh-what about?'

'You, mostly.'

'What about me?'

'I took the liberty of telephoning the wife of a friend of mine, Frances Dwyer ...'

'Why?' Abby was apprehensive.

'Let me finish and you'll find out,' he said steadily. 'As I was saying, I phoned Frances and suggested that you and she went shopping——'

'Shopping?' Abby stared at him. 'Shopping for what?'

'Abby, don't be so obtuse!' He sighed. 'You need some clothes. A whole wardrobe, if you like.'

'I didn't realise you found my clothes so objectionable,' she retorted, with dignity.

'I don't find your clothes objectionable,' he stated, pulling out a case of cheroots from his pocket. 'Abby, don't make this harder for me than it already is. I just want you to spend some money on yourself.'

'Your money?'

'Of course.'

Abby sniffed. 'And I suppose the next thing you'll want is for me to have my hair cut!'

'No.' He thrust the cheroots back into his pocket and came towards her angrily. 'On no account are you to have your hair cut, do you hear?' He grasped a handful, his mouth twisting almost sensuously. 'You have glorious hair, Abby, and I never want you to have it cut.'

Abby trembled, and he looked down at her exasperatedly. 'Abby, stop provoking me! I want you to be happy here, but you must stop fighting me or I'll——'

'Well, well! Behold the newlyweds!'

Abby started violently, automatically stepping nearer to Luke, and his hand slid from her hair, over her nape and down her spine, to rest in the small of her back. The unexpected interruption had startled him, too, but he recovered more quickly than Abby. Before she could turn her head to see who had spoken, he said flatly: 'Who let you in here, Ella?' and she knew the drawling voice belonged to her aunt.

CHAPTER SEVEN

'Why, darling, what a greeting!'

Ella Mackay was ready for this encounter and was consequently more prepared for it. As Abby turned to survey the woman who had wrecked her parents' marriage, she had to concede that Ella had seldom looked better. As tall as Abby, she had more flesh on her bones, which gave her the voluptuous appearance so admired on the screen. She, too, had dark hair, but hers was shorter, swinging on her shoulders. She was wearing a clinging crêpe gown which drew attention to the generous curves of her body, and Abby thought it looked like an evening dress. The sable scarf hanging from her arm seemed to confirm it.

'Mrs Hobbs let me in,' Ella was saying now, draping the

fur over the back of an armchair. 'Didn't you hear the bell?' She came towards them smilingly. 'Hello, Abby!' A light kiss was bestowed on the girl's cheek. 'Lovely to see you again. And Luke ...' She reached up and kissed his cheek too. 'Well, well! It is good to see you back, darling.'

Abby was tense. Ella was too friendly, too charming; it didn't tally with what Scott had told her, and it was certainly not what she had expected.

'Did you have a good journey?' she was asking now, taking some cigarettes out of the bag hanging from her wrist, and waiting for Luke to supply her with a light. 'You didn't return my calls and I simply couldn't wait to come and offer my congratulations!'

Luke had to release Abby to take his lighter out of his pocket, and she wondered bitterly whether the gambit had been designed to achieve just this. Ella covered his hand with her own as she steadied the flame to the tip of her cigarette, and Luke's mouth was unusually tight when she stepped away.

'Thank you, darling,' she acknowledged warmly, and then turned her attention back to the girl. 'It's been a long time, hasn't it, Abby? But it's wonderful to see you. However, if Luke will forgive me, it seems a shame that you had to get married before seeing London for the first time. It's such an exciting place for—young people. But then McGregor was always years behind the times.'

Abby frowned. 'Uncle Daniel never stopped me from coming to London.'

'Didn't he?' Ella raised narrow arched brows. 'I thought he must have done. I didn't think any girl as obviously—attractive—as you would turn down the invitation.'

'What invitation?'

Abby was confused, casting a bewildered look in Luke's direction, but his features were harshly controlled.

'My invitation,' Ella went on, sounding as confused as Abby herself. 'Do you mean to tell me it was never passed on?' She gasped. 'Abby, you don't imagine I didn't realise how you must have felt when your mother died?'

Abby felt cold. 'I'm afraid I don't know what you're talking about,' she said.

Ella stared at her reproachfully. 'You don't know, do

you?' she exclaimed. 'McGregor didn't tell you!' She turned appealingly to Luke. 'Do you wonder I have no time for that old man?'

'That will do, Ella.'

Luke's voice was curiously flat, and glancing at him Abby was almost shocked by the cold cynicism in his expression. Was it true? Had Ella tried to contact her after her mother's death? And had Uncle Daniel prevented her? It didn't excuse what she had done, but it might mean she was not as unfeeling as Abby had thought.

'Do you mean ...' she was beginning, when Luke cut her short.

'Don't believe a word she says,' he inserted harshly. 'I don't imagine your aunt considered your feelings at all. Not at least, until this moment.'

To Abby's amazement Ella laughed then, gurgling uncontrollable laughter which had a trace of hysteria about it, or would have had if she had not pressed her palm to her lips, stifling the sound.

'Oh, Luke!' she cried, sobering. 'You know me so well, darling. I'm sorry. But I couldn't resist the temptation to play the rôle of the wronged woman for a change.'

Abby felt an instinctive feeling of distaste, and her eyes moved from the amused woman in front of her to the man at her side. Luke gave her a slightly impatient stare and then addressed her aunt.

'Why have you come here, Ella? I know you better than to believe it was to offer your good wishes!'

'But it was!' Ella pouted her lips prettily, a gesture which had earned her scores of fans on the screen. 'Darling, don't be mean. Abby is my niece, after all, and you are my favourite person. Why shouldn't I want to offer my felicitations now that you two have—got together?' Her lips twisted. 'Although I have to say no one would guess at the relationship.'

'Ella!'

Ignoring Luke's warning, she went on: 'Well, it's true, darling. Abby is a little—unsophisticated, isn't she? For your tastes?' She paused. 'I wonder what your precious family will say.'

Abby was chilled by this exchange. There was so much

beneath the surface of what her aunt was saying, so many undercurrents which she could only begin to be aware of. That Ella could say one thing and mean another was becoming very clear to her, and the ability her aunt had of acting a part that was completely at variance with what she had been led to believe was disconcerting. Besides, this was not at all how she had planned it. Or indeed what she had expected. Anger, jealousy, bitterness—she felt she could have dealt with them more easily than this smiling insincerity.

But Ella's mention of Luke's family diverted Abby's thoughts. Even though he had told her about his mother and brothers and sisters, she had forgotten them, and she wondered why none of them had attended the wedding. Surely his mother might have made the journey.

'I'm sure my—family will welcome Abby with open arms,' Luke was saying now. 'The fact is, they don't know about her yet. But I shall tell them, never fear.'

'After the event,' Ella pointed out maliciously. 'Don't you think that's a little late?'

'Why didn't you come to the wedding, Aunt Ella?' asked Abby suddenly, the instinctively chosen words bringing the first sign of anger to Ella's glittering blue eyes.

Luke's lips twitched at this and he cast a look, almost of admiration, in his wife's direction. 'That's quite a point,' he agreed equably. 'Why didn't you come, Ella? I'm sure you would have been most welcome.'

What Ella might have replied was cut off by the ringing of the bell and leaving the two women Luke went to answer the door himself. Abby, alone with her aunt, avoided her avid stare, and was relieved when Luke returned only seconds later accompanied by a blonde girl only a few years older than herself. The girl saw Ella first and her eyebrows ascended interrogatively before she exchanged an offhand greeting with her. Then she saw Abby and Luke made the introductions.

'This is Frances, Abby,' he said, putting out a hand to draw her forward. 'Frances, this is my wife—this is Abby.'

'Hello, Abby.' Frances's smile was open and friendly. 'I've been looking forward to meeting you.'

'How nice!' Ella's drawl was sarcastic, and Abby stiffened, but Frances could handle it.

'That's some morning gown you're wearing, Ella,' she commented dryly. 'You must give me the name of your dress-maker.'

Ella's smile was a trifle forced. 'Still the same old Frances, eh? Tell me, how is Mike these days?'

Frances shrugged. 'Why don't you ask him? He tells me you ring him pretty frequently.'

Ella's face convulsed with angry colour and Abby was amazed how Frances's carelessly spoken words could arouse such fury. However, Luke had evidently decided that things had gone far enough, because he interposed himself between the two women, and said quickly:

'Look, I have to go. I'm meeting Scott in thirty minutes.' He put a possessive hand on Abby's arm, making her look at him in surprise. 'You'll be all right, won't you? Frances knows the score.' He took a plastic disc out of his pocket and handed it to her and she saw it was a credit card. 'I've arranged for you to use this. Please. For me.'

Abby's cheeks were as red as Ella's when he had finished, and she had no stomach to voice the protests she had made earlier.

'Wh-when—when will you be back?' she stammered.

Luke sighed. 'I'm not sure. Probably not until late this afternoon. You'll look after her, won't you, Frances?'

'Of cour——'

'Of course Frances will look after her, darling.' Ella was recovering rapidly. 'And you can give me a lift, can't you? You do pass my apartment on your way, don't you?'

Luke turned from Abby reluctantly. 'I suppose so,' he conceded grimly, nodding impatiently before turning back to his wife again.

All of a sudden there were too many people in the room, and Abby wondered apprehensively whether this was an example of how it would be. She had no conception of Luke's life here in London—the people he knew, the places he visited. And Ella ... What would she do now?

Luke bent his head and for a brief moment his lips brushed hers. Then he had straightened and was crossing the room, Ella collecting the fur and trailing it after him. Abby wanted to say something, anything to prevent him from abandoning her like this, but the words stuck in her throat and with a farewell nod, they departed.

There was a moment's silence after the door had closed and then Frances moved, shedding the jacket of the apricot slacks suit she was wearing and sinking down luxuriously into an armchair.

'This is a gorgeous apartment, isn't it?' she remarked, looking up at Abby's taut face. 'And Luke's a gorgeous man. I've always thought so.'

Abby dragged her thoughts back to the present with difficulty. She had been picturing Luke and Ella in the lift together and the images that evoked brought a stirring nausea to the pit of her stomach.

'I—oh, yes,' she said, moving her slim shoulders carelessly. 'I like it.'

Frances sighed, straightening her spine away from the yielding back of the chair. 'Abby, don't worry!'

'Worry?' Abby tried to be nonchalant. 'I don't know what you mean.'

Frances regarded her steadily for several seconds, and then she conceded defeat. 'All right, we'll leave it. Now, how about some coffee before we go shopping?'

Abby sighed. 'About going shopping ...'

'You're not about to tell me you don't want to go?'

'Well ...'

'Oh, come on, Abby. I don't know a woman who doesn't enjoy buying clothes! And Luke only wants to see you wearing things he's paid for. Give him that pleasure, at least.'

Abby half smiled, determinedly thrusting all thoughts of her husband's association with her aunt to the back of her mind. After all, she had achieved more than her objective. Why should she care what happened now? Let Ella do her worst. Luke was her husband. There was no altering that.

'I'll speak to Mrs Hobbs,' she said, but before the words were out of her mouth, that lady appeared in the open doorway.

'Excuse me, Mrs Jordan,' she said, casting a brief smile of acknowledgement in Frances's direction, 'but can you tell me what these sheets are doing in Mr Jordan's bath?'

Abby's cheeks flamed, and she guessed Mrs Hobbs was

93

enjoying her embarrassment. 'I—well, I stripped them off the bed,' she said uncomfortably. 'I put them in the bath to soak.'

'I see, madam.' The designation was ludicrous and Abby knew it. 'Was there some reason?'

'I hardly think Mrs Jordan would put sheets in to soak without there being a reason, Mrs Hobbs,' remarked Frances dryly, earning herself a resentful glare.

'That's right.' Mentally, Abby gathered herself. 'Mr Jordan upset his tea this morning. If you leave the bedding where it is, I'll deal with it myself.'

'I'm sure there's no need to adopt that attitude, madam.' Mrs Hobbs drew herself up to her full height. 'I've always served to please Mr Jordan, and he's never complained about my ability.'

'And I am not complaining about your ability either, Mrs Hobbs,' Abby assured her, gaining confidence by the minute. 'But naturally now there's a woman in the apartment it won't be necessary for you to do everything yourself.'

Mrs Hobbs folded her hands together. 'I see, madam.'

Abby glanced at Frances and saw her slightly amused but approving smile, and went on: 'And now, could—could——'

'Mrs Dwyer,' supplied Frances quickly.

'—could Mrs Dwyer and I have some coffee? Before we go shopping.'

In spite of her misgivings, Abby enjoyed visiting the shops and boutiques, trying on garments of all kinds, laughing at the way clothes could alter her personality, giving her a sophistication which was barely skin deep. But it made her realise that appearances could be deceiving, and how, in the right clothes, one could assume a surface maturity.

London itself seemed less frightening on foot. Oxford Street was only a ten-minute walk from where Luke had his apartment, and Frances suggested they left her car in the underground garage. It was a warm morning, and although Abby had been doubtful about going out in her jeans, she was soon glad she had allowed Frances to persuade her not to change. London was full of young people all dressed as she was dressed, and her attire seemed the uniform of the day.

As they shopped, they talked, and Abby learned that Frances's husband, Mike, was a professional photographer. Learning his name reminded her of that remark Ella had made, although she was too polite to ask what she had meant. She could guess—but that didn't seem fair somehow.

They decided to have lunch in Harrods, and over the meal, Abby asked Frances whether she had any children.

'I'm afraid not.' The older girl shook her head rather regretfully. 'Mike and I have been married for eight years, but no luck. Why? Do you and Luke intend having children right away?'

That was the kind of question Abby could do well without, but she managed to evade a direct answer by merely smiling and shaking her head. Already she was learning the art of dissembling, she thought uneasily. It was a little disturbing.

'Oh, well ...' Frances rubbed her flat stomach contentedly. 'That was a marvellous meal!' She blinked at Abby. 'What are we going to buy this afternoon?'

'Don't you think we've spent enough?' exclaimed Abby, who had found using the credit card rather disconcerting. She had no accurate idea of how much they had spent, and the pile of boxes Frances had already had despatched direct to the apartment seemed a more than sufficient extravagance.

'Oh, come on,' exclaimed Frances now, bending to pick up her handbag. 'All we've bought so far is day wear. You need at least a dozen evening gowns, a couple of trouser suits—some culottes——'

'Really, I don't think ...'

'What don't you think?' Frances rested her elbow on the table and supported her chin with one hand. 'Abby, far be it from me to interfere, but—well, don't you think you owe it to yourself to—to look your best? I mean, Luke's an important man. People know him, recognise him. He's invited to press gatherings—and parties—and dinners, and you'll be expected to go with him. People will want to meet you, too. You're his wife!' She paused. 'You don't want him to take Ella instead, do you?'

Abby coloured. 'I—I——'

Frances sighed. 'Look, honey, I know she's your aunt and all. Luke told me. But don't underestimate her.' She frowned down at the tablecloth. 'Perhaps you don't know this—but once Ella thought Luke intended to marry her.'

Abby took a deep breath. 'Yes, I know that.'

'You do?' Frances looked relieved. 'Thank goodness for that. Heavens, I hate gossiping, but I was afraid—You might not have known!'

Abby shook her head. 'Ardnalui is not as remote as all that.'

Frances gave an embarrassed little laugh. 'Well, let's go, shall we? I know a super little boutique where they sell exactly the kind of thing you want.'

They arrived back at the apartment in the late afternoon to find the hall littered with dress boxes. Mrs Hobbs let them in, and she looked rather harassed.

'I don't know what to do with all these things, Mrs Jordan,' she exclaimed, indicating the tilting cardboard containers. 'I would have unpacked them and put them away for you, but I didn't know which bedroom you were using.'

Abby's cheeks flamed once more and Frances closed the door behind them and said at once: 'Luke prefers the brown suite and you know it, Mrs Hobbs. We'll have some tea when you've the time.'

In the living room, Abby turned to Frances in embarrassment. 'She doesn't like me, does she?' she exclaimed. 'I wonder why.'

Frances lounged into a chair. 'I shouldn't let it worry you. You'll soon be able to handle her.'

'But I shan't.' Abby paced anxiously up and down. 'I've never dealt with—with anyone like her.'

'Luke told us that you lived with your uncle and his housekeeper. Wasn't she like Mrs Hobbs?'

'Who? Mrs Tully?' Abby stopped pacing to smile. 'Heavens, no! She treated me more like a mother. I wouldn't have dared to give her orders!'

Frances smiled sympathetically. 'You'll learn. Now—did you enjoy yourself?'

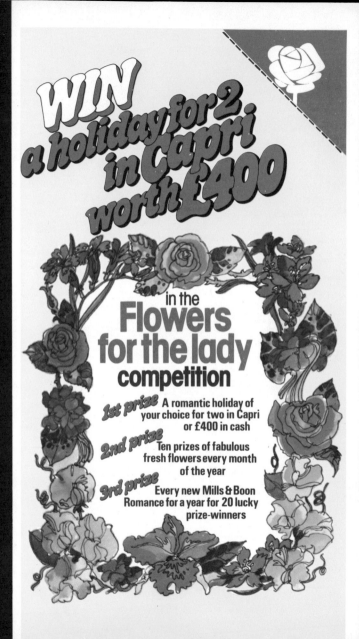

Elaine Westwood
fiftyish, red head, the hard life farming in the Australian outback has lined her pretty plump face. With no children, her home and garden are her only loves.
(Dreamtime at Big Sky)

Abby Rodriguez
half Spanish, half Scots, early twenties, came from a broken home, then orphaned. Tall, slim with black hair and dark eyes; dresses in jeans and sweaters. Works as a nanny in Scotland.
(Alien Wife)

Lady Ross
mistress of the magnificent Swans' Reach. A grandmother, frail with silvery hair and topaz eyes, a sweet temperament, with soft disarming ways. Elegant and cultivated.
(Swans' Reach)

Toni
twenty-one with delicate childlike features, thick tawny brown hair, green eyes and full soft mouth. Interested in art, loves the West Country. Golden tanned skin. A good swimmer.
(The Mark of Tregarron)

Fran Casey
tall blonde with pale blue eyes. Smooth sophisticated and elegant. A jealous woman in her late twenties. Enjoys riding. Self-confident.
(The Mark of Tregarron)

HOW TO ENTER

Above you will find five portraits, lettered A–E, selected from this month's Mills & Boon Romances. Underneath you will find a description of each person's character. Simply study the portraits, read the descriptions and decide which of the five flowers listed on the entry form is most likely to appeal to each person. Write the letters of your choice in the spaces provided under 1st entry on the entry form and complete the sentence "Every month blossoms when I read Mills & Boon because................." (in not more than 10 words). Send your entry together with three Rose Tokens cut from entry forms in all March Mills & Boon Romances to the address on the entry form. If you send six Rose Tokens you may have two attempts, nine Tokens for three attempts and a fourth attempt for just one more Token! It's easy! So good luck and happy reading.
All March Titles have the special Rose Tokens........

1. A Lyon's Share by Janet Dailey.
2. Laird of Doorn by Sue Peters.
3. The Silver Link by Mary Wibberley.
4. Dreamtime at Big Sky by Dorothy Cork.
5. The Intruder by Jane Donnelly.
6. Swans' Reach by Margaret Way.
7. The Mark of Tregarron by Lucy Gillen.
8. Inherit the Sun by Rebecca Stratton.
9. Alien Wife by Anne Mather.
10. The Valley of Palms by Jean S. MacLeod.

RULES

1. The instructions given above form part of the rules.
2. The competition is open to any Mills & Boon reader who is resident in the United Kingdom or Eire, except employees (and their families) of Mills & Boon and any other person directly concerned with the competition.
3. All entries must be on the official entry form, and be written in ink or ball point pen and block capitals. Any which are not clearly legible or with omissions or otherwise not conforming to the rules and instructions of the competition will not be considered.
4. Each entry must be accompanied by three Mills & Boon Rose Tokens (except the fourth entry which requires only one additional Token).
5. No responsibility will be accepted for entries lost, delayed, mislaid or damaged in the post. Proof of posting will not be accepted as proof of receipt.
6. Entries must be received by last post on 30th April 1977.
7. The Judges will examine all entries. The first prize will be awarded to the

entrant who, in the opinion of the Judges, has selected the most suitable flower for each of the characters and who has in not more than ten words completed the sentence 'Every month blossoms when I read Mills & Boon because............' in the most romantic and original way. The second and third prizes will be awarded to the entrants submitting the next most meritorious entries.
8. The Judges' decision will be final and legally binding. No correspondence will be entered into. No competitor may win more than one prize.
9. Prizewinners will be notified by post and announced in the Competitors Journal.
10. Entries become the property of Mills & Boon and will not be returned under any circumstances.
11. All entries must be sent pre-paid post to the competition address. Entrants wishing to obtain a full list of prize-winners should include a large stamped addressed envelope with their entry marked 'Winners'.

Now complete the following sentence in the most romantic and original way: "Every month blossoms when I read Mills & Boon because

	1st entry	2nd entry	3rd entry	4th entry
ROSE				
ORCHID				
VIOLET				
SWEET PEA				
FREESIA				
Tokens required	3	6	9	10

_____ (In not more than 10 words)

Name _____ Address _____

Post your entry to: Mills & Boon, "Flowers for the Lady", PO Box 6, Kettering, Northants. Closing date 30.4.1977

Abby shook her head reminiscently. 'I can't believe all those clothes are really mine.'

'Well, they are. And I can't wait to see Luke's face when he sees you in that white chiffon. It's dreamy!'

Abby remembered the gown well, although her feelings were less enthusiastic. Swathes of filmy gauze that scarcely disguised the curves beneath seemed more in keeping with a nightdress than an evening gown, but the saleswoman had been most insistent. Nevertheless, her unsophisticated senses recoiled from its daring simplicity, even though her first glimpse of herself in the gown had created an illusion of enchantment which only her puritan upbringing had destroyed. She had been persuaded to buy more clothes than she had ever had in her life before, and whether or not Luke could comfortably afford them mattered less than the betrayal of her own convictions. Luke—Ella—Frances —they didn't understand. She had never intended to go this far. And with every day that passed she was getting deeper and deeper into a mesh of deceit.

Mrs Hobbs returned with a tray of afternoon tea as Frances was suggesting they might get together again later in the week.

'Mike's working on a new commission at the moment and I see next to nothing of him, and as Luke is going to be pretty busy, too, at the studios, why don't we have lunch together one day and go to a matinée?'

'The tea, madam.' Mrs Hobbs deposited the tray on a low table near Abby's legs. 'I'll attend to the unpacking now.'

'I——' Abby was about to say that she could manage when she caught Frances's warning eye and stifled the protest. 'Thank you.'

'Mr Jordan telephoned too, madam,' Mrs Hobbs added straightening.

'He did?' Abby looked up at her. 'What did he say?'

'He said to tell you not to wait dinner for him, madam,' replied the woman, not without some satisfaction, Abby felt. 'He doesn't expect to be home much before ten.'

'Ten?' Abby couldn't hide her consternation.

'That's right, madam.'

Mrs Hobbs excused herself then and walked regally

across the room, her head held high. Abby watched her go, biting her lip. The woman had given no reason for Luke's prolonged absence, and she must know that Abby was bound to be feeling rather homesick now, in spite of Frances's companionship. Of course, Luke must know that, too, she realised bitterly, but he was still not coming home.

As the door closed, Frances expelled her breath on an angry exclamation. 'That woman!' she said fiercely. 'You'll have to get Luke to find someone else. Someone who isn't——' She broke off abruptly. 'Anyway, I shouldn't let her see she can upset you so easily.'

Abby bent her head to the teacups. 'Did I do that?'

Frances's expression was resigned. 'Let's say you didn't look pleased about it.' She sighed. 'You'd think Luke——' She broke off again. 'Oh, yes—two lumps, please.'

Abby sipped her tea determinedly, trying not to think about Luke at all. It shouldn't matter to her what he did now. On the contrary, she should be glad he was leaving her to her own devices and not threatening her composure with his undoubted sexual attraction. They were married. She had thwarted Ella publicly, if no other way. So why was she feeling so terribly depressed?

'I expect it's Scott's fault,' said Frances suddenly. 'He works himself like a dog, and he expects everyone who works with him to do the same.'

Abby lifted her head. 'Yes.'

'He's quite a slave-driver. Mike once did some stills for him, and he wanted them the next day!' Frances forced a laugh.

Abby licked her upper lip. 'Frances, it doesn't matter. Really.'

'Doesn't it?' Frances's eyes narrowed. Then she sighed impatiently. 'Well, I think he wants hanging.'

'Scott?'

'No. Luke!'

'Luke?' Abby's eyes were wide and confused. 'What are you talking about?'

'Oh—nothing.' Frances put down her cup and got up to walk about the room. 'Mike and I are going to a dinner party this evening or I'd have suggested you came to us. If it were just one of those casual gigs where one more or less doesn't make a great deal of difference, you could have come along. But this is a formal affair . . .'

'Honestly, Frances, you don't have to worry about me.' Abby set down her cup with rather a clatter in the saucer. 'I don't think I'd have the strength to go anywhere this evening. I'm tired. It's been an exhausting day. I shall probably go to bed before Luke gets home. I mean—well, he may be later than he expects.'

Frances regarded her solemnly. 'Are you sure? Are you sure you'll be okay?'

'Heavens, yes.' Abby got to her feet now. 'I'm not a child, Frances. I have been alone before.'

Frances shook her head. 'You don't look very old to me. What are you? Eighteen? Nineteen?' Abby nodded. 'And I'm twenty-seven. I feel old enough to be your mother.'

Abby giggled then. 'You'd have broken the record if you were!' She paused. 'And thank you. For—everything.'

Frances nodded. 'Yes, I ought to be going. Shall I ring you later in the week?'

'Oh, please,' Abby nodded. 'I'll look forward to it.'

After Frances had gone, the apartment did seem silent, though. Being alone in London was different from being alone in Ardnalui. There she had known she had only to set foot outside the door to find someone to talk to, but here, surrounded by millions of people, she was completely cut off from everyone.

But there was the telephone, she thought suddenly. She could ring Uncle Daniel. It would be marvellous to hear a familiar voice again.

There was a directory beside the telephone, but she discarded this in favour of the code book. However, it was impossible to dial direct to Ardnalui and she eventually had to ask the operator to get the number. She heard the ringing tone and felt almost elated when the receiver was lifted. But it was Mrs Tully who came on the line.

'Why, Abby!' she exclaimed, shouting as she always did over the phone. 'Is something wrong?'

'No. No,' Abby hastened to reassure her. 'No, I just thought I'd ring Uncle Daniel and tell him we've arrived safely and settled down at the apartment.'

'You have? But your uncle's not in the house at the

moment, Abby,' exclaimed Mrs Tully, dousing the girl's excitement without knowing it. 'Have you forgotten so soon? He's always over at the church at this time of day.'

Abby had forgotten. Her day in London had been so full of incident, she had omitted to remember Uncle Daniel's evening call to prayer.

'I'm sorry,' she said, miserably, guessing how disappointed Uncle Daniel would be when he learned she had called. 'I'm afraid I didn't think.'

Perhaps the housekeeper sensed something of the dejection Abby was feeling, because she went on almost gently to say: 'I expect the excitement of it all put ordinary things out of your mind, lass. And I'm sure your uncle will be as glad as I am that everything is going well for you.'

Abby was half wishing she had never made the call, but she said: 'Yes. Everything's fine.'

'Give our regards to your husband,' added Mrs Tully warmly, and after sending Uncle Daniel her love, Abby rang off.

Linking her fingers loosely together, she paced restlessly to the long windows, looking out unseeingly. What now? She glanced at the slim gold watch on her wrist, which had been Uncle Daniel's present to her on her eighteenth birthday. Six o'clock! The evening stretched emptily ahead of her. Oh, why couldn't Luke have come home tonight of all nights?

Leaving the living room, she went up the stairs to the bedrooms, pausing by Luke's door when she saw Mrs Hobbs folding delicate shreds of underwear into the drawers of a chest. Of course, Frances had been responsible for this, but how could she have deterred her without arousing her suspicions? Mrs Hobbs saw her hesitation, and said sharply: 'You do want these things in here, don't you, Mrs Jordan?'

'I—yes.' Abby stepped determinedly into the room. The bed had been remade and nothing remained to reveal what had happened that morning. 'Have you nearly finished?'

Mrs Hobbs nodded. 'Nearly. Are there any more to come?'

Abby ran her fingers over the wooden bedhead. 'One or two,' she conceded reluctantly. 'But don't worry, I'll attend to them.'

Mrs Hobbs contained any protest she might have made and instead asked: 'Will you be wanting dinner this evening, madam?'

Abby quickly shook her head. 'I'm not very hungry.' She paused. 'By the way ...' She forced herself to go on. 'Did—er—did my husband give any reason why he would be so—so late?'

Mrs Hobbs regarded her without liking. 'I thought you'd know why he'd be so late, madam,' she remarked insolently.

Abby felt the hot colour running up her cheeks again. 'Well, I don't,' she retorted, determined not to back down before this frontal attack. 'Do you?'

Mrs Hobbs moved her shoulders indifferently. 'I expect he's having dinner with Miss Mackay, Mrs Jordan. He often does when they've been working together all day.'

Abby turned away, refusing to allow the woman to see the pain she had deliberately inflicted. 'I see,' she said, between taut lips. 'Thank you, Mrs Hobbs. You can go now.'

'But I haven't finished——'

'I said—you can go.' Abby turned again, controlling herself with difficulty. 'And don't bother coming in at all tomorrow. I can manage.'

Mrs Hobbs looked astounded. No doubt her previous experience with Abby had led her to believe that she could get away with anything, but suddenly the rabbit had turned into the fox.

'I'll have to speak to Mr Jordan,' she insisted, her hands locked tightly together. 'He pays my wages——'

'That won't be necessary,' said Abby, realising with a pang of self-disgust that she could enjoy hurting people, too. 'I will speak to Mr Jordan myself. And naturally, as his wife, I'll be paying your wages in future.'

But after the outer door had slammed behind the irate figure of Mrs Hobbs, all the fight went out of her. It was all very well speaking to the daily woman like that, but what if Luke should oppose her? How galling it would be to have to back down now.

With a sigh she sank down on the bed, burying her face in her hands. What was she doing here, in this place? she asked herself desperately. Was any kind of revenge worth the mental torment she had inflicted on herself?

CHAPTER EIGHT

ABBY opened her eyes to a darkened room and lay for several minutes trying to decide where she was. She was in London, of course, she remembered that, but what had awakened her? And why was it dark outside? She sat up, and as she did so she realised she was still dressed in the shirt and jeans she had worn to go shopping.

At once she sighed as complete recall brought the realisation of why she was here. She must have fallen asleep on Luke's bed. The last thing she remembered was stretching out her aching limbs, and she lifted a hand to her eyes and could still feel the puffiness that an hour of weeping had caused.

She almost jumped out of her skin when the door was suddenly opened and the light switch turned to fill the room with blinding, revealing light. Abby gasped, her hands going automatically to her throat before falling weakly into her lap as she recognised Luke standing squarely in the doorway.

'So there you are!' he exclaimed, not without some relief, she thought. 'Didn't you hear me calling you?'

That must have been what had woken her. She shook her head. 'I—I was asleep.'

'So I see.' Luke advanced into the room, unfastening his tie, and she could see the lines of strain around his eyes and mouth. He paused in front of her, his lips tightening into a thin line. 'Why have you been crying?'

Abby drew a deep breath, and got up from the bed, turning to smooth the crumpled bedcover. 'No reason,' she replied perkily. 'I—er—I'll go and make some coffee.'

'You'd better make something more substantial than that,' essayed Luke, taking off his jacket and beginning to unbutton his shirt. 'I see Mrs Hobbs cleared everything away.'

Abby bit her lip. 'I—Mrs Hobbs didn't make any dinner, if that's what you mean.'

Luke's fingers stayed. 'Why not?'

'I—I wasn't hungry.'

'I am.'

'Oh!' Abby was nonplussed for a moment. 'Haven't you had dinner?'

'Had dinner?' he thundered angrily, and she realised he had been holding himself in check ever since he entered the bedroom. 'I've had nothing of any consequence since this morning! I've been working. Didn't you get my message? Why do you think I'm so late?'

Abby sniffed. 'I—I thought you might be—well, having dinner out. Mrs Hobbs said that you had said not to wait dinner for you——'

'That's right. I did.' Luke finished unfastening his shirt and threw it off on to the bed. 'I didn't deny wanting any dinner, did I?'

Abby shifted from one foot to the other. 'Well, I thought ...'

'Yes? What did you think?' Luke was grim.

Abby sighed. 'Mrs Hobbs said you—you sometimes had dinner with—with Aunt Ella ...'

'Oh, did she? Thank you, Mrs Hobbs.' Luke was furious. 'And I suppose that's why you've been moping about in here, feeling sorry for yourself!' He uttered an oath. 'My God!' He kicked off his suede boots carelessly. 'Well, I didn't. So what are you going to do about it? Boil me an egg?'

Abby squared her shoulders. It was all very well for him to feel resentful, but she still hadn't forgiven him for abandoning her on her first evening in London, working or not.

'I don't have to do anything,' she said, with great temerity. 'It doesn't occur to you that I might be feeling— lonely, or homesick, does it?'

'Of course it occurred to me!' he snapped. 'I got away as soon as I could. It may interest you to know that Scott and his assistant are at this moment enjoying steaks at the Mara Club, but I insisted on coming home. To my wife!'

103

Abby's shoulders sagged. 'Oh!'

'Yes. *Oh!*' He started to unfasten his pants and she beat a hasty retreat towards the door.

'I can cook,' she said, averting her eyes. 'What would you like?'

Luke kicked off his pants and walked towards his bathroom door. 'Anything,' he muttered in a resigned tone. 'Just anything.'

In the kitchen, Abby swiftly examined the contents of the refrigerator. There were the usual things—butter, milk, ham, the makings of a salad, some fresh fruit and vegetables. There was also a leg of lamb, which Abby guessed had been intended to supply the main course at dinner. It was too late now to cook so large a piece of meat, but it did give her an idea.

A quick examination of the store cupboards unearthed a jar of curry powder, and fastening a tea towel apronwise around her middle, she gathered the ingredients she needed. Soon onions were frying in the pan, filling the air with their distinctive aroma, as she finely chopped sufficient meat from the joint and seasoned it.

Luke came into the kitchen as she was whipping up a powdered dessert to add to dishes of fresh strawberries. He had showered and changed into close-fitting denim pants and a collarless sweat shirt. His hair clung wetly to his neck, artificially darkened by the water. He frowned at her ministrations, at the hectic colour in her cheeks, and the way she fumbled what she was doing under his intent gaze.

Then he sighed, putting one hand at the back of his neck. 'An omelette would have done,' he exclaimed ruefully. 'There was no need to go to all this trouble. Not at this time of night.'

'I don't mind,' said Abby quickly. She had barely had time to notice it was after eleven, and the sleep she had had earlier had refreshed her. 'Will you have it in here?'

Luke shrugged. 'Wherever you like.' He paused. 'Do you want a starter?'

'A starter?' Abby turned hastily to remove a pan of rice from the hotplate. 'What's that?'

'Sherry. Or a Martini. Tomato juice, even.'

'Oh. Well—no, thanks.' Abby carried the steaming pan to the sink. 'But you go ahead.'

'Thanks.' Luke hesitated a moment longer and then left her to it, not returning until she tentatively called him.

They began with egg mayonnaise and rolls, which she had warmed in the oven. Abby wasn't feeling particularly hungry, but she had prepared enough for herself so that Luke wouldn't feel he was eating alone. The lamb curry was delicious, hot and spicy, a rich accompaniment to the finely flaked rice. Luke drank lager with the meal, but although he suggested that Abby might prefer wine, she insisted she was happy with water. She served the strawberries with a creamy whipped sauce, and the percolator was bubbling when she asked whether he would like cheese and crackers.

Luke expelled his breath on an expressive sigh. 'You must be joking! I couldn't eat another thing.' Then he smiled, and ridiculously her pulses raced. 'But that was delightful. And I apologise for my rudeness earlier.'

Abby turned away, ostensibly to turn off the coffee pot. 'I—I'm glad you enjoyed it,' she said. 'If—if you'd like to go into the living room, I'll bring your coffee through.'

'What? And leave you with all this washing up?' Luke shook his head. 'Come on, let me help you.'

Although Abby insisted that she could manage, Luke ignored her, clearing the breakfast bar where they had eaten and carrying the dishes to the sink. So Abby washed, and Luke dried, and as they worked, he talked to her about his day and asked about hers.

'We bought an awful lot of things,' she confessed, plunging her hands into the soapy water to rescue a single dessert spoon. 'But Frances seemed to think they were necessary.'

'And no doubt Frances also thought that tonight I should have been home to take you out to dinner wearing one of these new outfits,' he comented dryly. Her embarrassed glance gave her away, and he nodded. 'I should—I know. You shouldn't be spending hours in the kitchen preparing a meal for me on your first real night in London.'

'Oh, but I enjoyed it,' she exclaimed, turning wide dark eyes in his direction. 'Honestly, I did.'

Luke looked down at the dish he was drying, his expression suddenly grim. 'All right, all right,' he said abruptly. Then: 'Is that all?'

Abby nodded, and without another word he left her, going into the living room and leaving her to prepare the coffee. When she carried the tray into the room, he was lounging moodily on the couch, his long legs stretched out over the arm. But he swung his feet to the floor as she came in, and getting up, took the tray from her.

Abby perched nervously on the edge of an armchair. Now that the meal was over and there was nothing with which to occupy herself, all her earlier anxieties returned to haunt her. Luke set the tray on the table beside her and then resumed his seat on the couch. Abby busied herself with the coffee cups, and started when he said quietly: 'Do you intend to sleep in my room tonight?'

She dropped the spoon she had been using and stared at him aghast, and his tawny eyes narrowed. 'It's a reasonable question, isn't it?' he inquired. 'After all, your clothes are apparently occupying space in my wardrobe.'

'Oh!' Abby had forgotten that. 'Mrs Hobbs—Mrs Hobbs put them there.' She forced herself to look down at the tray. 'Cream—cream and sugar?'

'Just sugar. Why?'

'Well, some people like cream and sugar——'

'Abby!'

His tone was warning, and she let her hands fall loosely between her knees. 'As—as a matter of fact, Frances asked her to do it,' she admitted with a sigh. 'I—I didn't know how to—how to tell her.'

Luke's mouth twisted. 'Tell her what? That we don't share a room?'

'Well—yes.'

'But we have done,' he pointed out dryly. 'Twice.'

Abby's breathing was becoming a little constricted. 'I'll —I'll move them out again in the morning.'

'No.' Luke spoke flatly. 'Leave them where they are. I, too, prefer not to have to make those kind of explanations to my friends or my family.'

The mention of his family brought Abby to her feet, unable to relax under his scrutiny. 'Wh-what explanations will you give your family, Luke?' she demanded tremulously. 'What reason do you have for marrying me?'

Luke looked up at her steadily. 'I don't have to give them reasons. Besides, when they see you, they'll know.'

'What will they know? That I look like my aunt? That I'm a younger version of her?'

'No.' Luke stifled an expletive as he stood up in one lithe easy movement. 'You are not like your aunt,' he told her harshly. 'Not in any way. You may bear a small resemblance to her, the kind of physical resemblance that often runs in families, but that's all. Basically, you're completely different.'

Abby gulped. 'But there was no need to marry me, was there? I mean, Uncle Daniel would have got over the shock of finding us together. What are your family going to think when they meet me? I'm not at all the kind of wife they'll expect you to have.'

Luke sighed then, looking down at her half impatiently. 'Abby, I married you because *I* chose to do so, not because of what Daniel McGregor saw. Oh, I admit, his appearance precipitated the event, but the idea was already in my mind.'

'It was?'

Abby was aghast, all her earlier apprehensions flooding back to alarm her. A chilling finger ran the whole length of her spine. His words were so final somehow. As though he foresaw no possible grounds for a separation at some future date as she had vaguely imagined.

'Abby.' He was speaking again, and she forced herself to listen. 'I realise I must seem very old to you, but back in Ardnalui you seemed to enjoy my company. I need a wife. And some time in the not too distant future, I'd like children——'

'Children!' Abby almost choked on the word. 'But—but what if we're not compatible?' she stammered. 'What if I want to leave you?'

'Leave me?' A certain hardness entered his eyes. 'Why should you want do that? We've barely been married forty-eight hours.'

Abby flushed. 'I—I don't mean now, exactly. I mean—in the future . . .' she finished lamely.

Luke regarded her so intently that she could not look at him, but concentrated instead on the hair protruding

107

through the unfastened neck of his sweat shirt. The silence seemed to stretch to eternity, and Abby could feel her knees wobbling inside her jeans.

'I gather from that that the only reason you married me was to pacify your uncle,' he said at last.

'I—well, of course.'

'So I don't attract you as a husband?'

Abby felt terrible. 'On—on the contrary, you—you're a very attractive man.'

'Damn you, that's not what I asked.' He lifted his hands and gripped her shoulders. 'Look at me.'

When she still failed to do so, he deliberately tightened his grip and the pain was so intense that she lifted her head almost automatically. She had never seen him look so angry, the tawny eyes glittering with a smouldering fire that had no warmth in it.

'Well?' he said. 'I don't attract you. That is what you're saying, isn't it?'

Abby trembled violently. 'Please! Let me go.'

'Not yet.'

Luke's eyes dropped to her mouth, soft and vulnerable, parted in her distress. The tip of her tongue appeared to tantalise him, and with an exclamation that was half a groan, he dragged her closer and lowered his mouth to hers.

The emotions that claimed Abby in those first moments turned her blood to liquid fire, and sent her senses spinning dizzily. Whether it was that he began by being angry with her and intended showing her how puny would her efforts be to resist him, she never knew. All she did know was that his nearness no longer terrified her—on the contrary, she was experiencing the most wanton desires to tear his shirt from his body and feel his skin against hers. And not just his skin—the muscles and sinews and strength of his body. His hands moved possessively over her, sliding beneath her shirt with a familiarity that weakened her knees and made her cling helplessly to him.

Then, when all coherent thought had ceased and she was eagerly seeking to prolong the feel of his mouth bruising hers, he set her free, releasing her so roughly that she staggered as she tried to regain her balance on legs that no longer wanted to support her.

'Go to bed, Abby!' he comanded harshly, as she stood there looking at him, the back of one hand against her lips.

Abby didn't move. 'Luke, I ...' she began uncertainly, only to be silenced by the anger he unleashed on her.

'Oh, for God's sake, Abby,' he muttered, 'get out of here! Don't you know when you're not wanted? Go and nurture those adolescent dreams you have about knights in shining armour. You won't find many of them around here. But don't imagine that our marriage is a temporary affair—that as soon as the proprieties have been satisfied, I'll release you to go running back to Uncle Daniel. I may not value much in this life, but I do value my self-respect. You're my wife, and so you'll stay. And when I decide I want you, I'll take you! Do you understand? But in future I think you'd better stay out of my bed or I won't be answerable for the consequences!'

'Oh, Luke!' Abby gulped. 'I—I never said——'

'Out!' he snapped, abruptly, striding across the room to select a bottle from the tray occupying a side table. 'And don't bother to come back.'

In her own room, Abby paced the floor uneasily, not knowing how to assimilate this entirely new situation. Until now, they had seemed to be playing the game on her terms, albeit more seriously than she had ever intended. But suddenly that had all changed. Luke hadn't just married her to pacify Uncle Daniel, or because he had thought it was expected of him. She should have known he was not a man to be caught that easily. He had married her because he wanted a wife, a mother for the children he apparently intended to have; and her vain ideas of thwarting Ella were made insignificant by comparison. Did he really mean it? Had he had some notion of her intentions and taken advantage of them? But if he expected this marriage to work, he meant her to be his wife in every meaning of the word ...

She halted by the windows, hands gripping the sill until the knuckles grew white. She had never given marriage a great deal of thought. If she ever had thought about it, it had been in terms of something distant and vaguely unreal, and certainly none of the boys she had dated in the village had lived up to her expectations of a husband.

But Luke Jordan ... She shook her head disbelievingly. He was so much older than she was. Eighteen years at least. He had probably known half a dozen women before she was born! And Uncle Daniel had told her he had been only eighteen when he married his first wife. Alison. Abby licked her dry lips. Their initials were the same, but she doubted they had shared any other similarities. After all, Alison must have wanted to marry Luke, whereas she ...

She turned to rest back against the sill, surveying her room without enjoyment. No wonder he had hoped she would like it here. This was to be her home—but for how long? If, and it was an alarming thought, they had children, would he expect to bring them up here, in this rarefied atmosphere, without a garden where they could play. *They!* A slightly hysterical sob rose in her throat. Was she really seriously contemplating bearing Luke's children, suffering the indignities—not to mention the agonies—of childbirth, for a man she had thought she could simply use? But what alternative did she have?

A shudder ran through her as she recalled those moments in his arms tonight. He had been intent on humiliating her, of course, in proving to himself, as well as to her, that she was not as indifferent to him as she would like to think. Had he succeeded? He was an experienced man, after all, while she felt completely at his mercy. Nevertheless, it had not been fear which had weakened her knees and caused that dark tide of feeling to run like fluid fire through her veins.

She heard Luke come to his room, but not until the apartment was silent did Abby shed her clothes and slip between the sheets of her bed. Even then she lay awake for hours before sleep came to claim her, hours which weighed heavily on her when she confronted her reflection in the pale light of morning.

It was after eight when she got out of bed, but with consciousness had come the remembrance of her orders to Mrs Hobbs not to put in an appearance today, and she knew she had to make the effort to prepare Luke's breakfast.

She showered quickly, but disdained the clothes Luke's money had provided in favour of her old denims. With her hair secured in two elastic bands, she made her way to the

110

kitchen, and the coffee pot was percolating when Luke made his appearance. Even so, she had not expected him to be up yet, and his presence in the kitchen brought the usual flush of colour to her pale cheeks.

'What are you doing?' he demanded in a cold voice, going to the fridge and extracting a pint of milk. He removed the cap and drank thirstily from the bottle, and distracted, Abby watched the strong muscles of his throat moving rythmically.

'I—well, I'm preparing breakfast,' she replied unevenly.

'I can see that.' Luke lowered the bottle. It was already half empty. 'Where is Mrs Hobbs? Hasn't she arrived yet?'

'No, I—I asked her not to come in today.'

The words tumbled out before she could think of any suitable excuse for the woman's non-appearance, and Luke stared at her narrowly. 'What did you say?'

'I—I asked her not to come in today.'

'Why not?'

'Because—because—she was insolent to me,' said Abby defensively.

'Insolent?' Luke frowned. 'In what way insolent?'

Abby sighed. 'Does it matter?'

'Yes, I rather think it does.'

She bent her head. 'Oh, well, it was nothing really. I—your telephone message last evening—she implied I ought to know why you were going to be late.'

'Did she?'

'Yes. Then she said about—about you—and Aunt Ella ...'

'What about me and Ella?'

'I—I told you. Last night ...'

'I see. You mean that business of us having dinner together.'

'Yes.'

'And that was all?'

'Oh, yes—*yes*!' Abby moved her hands frustratedly. 'It wasn't just *what* she said. It—it was the way she said it.'

Luke finished the pint of milk with an ease that staggered her, then he wiped his mouth with the back of his hand. 'So Mrs Hobbs has been dismissed?'

'No.' Abby lowered the heat on the grill. 'I just asked

her not to come in today.' She paused, eyeing him anxiously. 'Are—are you very angry?'

Luke gave her an old-fashioned look. 'Good lord, why should I be angry? You're my wife, Abby, not my housekeeper. If you choose to relieve Mrs Hobbs of some of her duties, that's your affair.'

Abby breathed a sigh of relief. 'Well, it's ready, if you are. The breakfast, I mean.' She bit her lip, regarding his fine grey mohair suit with uncertainty. 'Shall I lay the table in the dining room?'

Luke took one of the stools at the breakfast bar. 'No, no. This will do.' He flicked back his cuff and considered the watch on his wrist. 'I don't have time to stand on ceremony.'

Abby wondered at the feeling of dismay his words engendered. She ought to have been glad he was leaving her yet again. It was easier for her when he was not around, wasn't it? But the prospect of a long day spent in her own company was not appealing.

'Are—are you working again today?' she inquired casually, and he looked at her darkly.

'Do you really care?' he countered, and she bent her head to the fresh grapefruit in her dish.

'I—I just wondered,' she murmured, trying not to sound as anxious as she felt, and heard his swiftly indrawn breath.

'Look, Abby,' he said harshly, leaning across the bar towards her, 'this situation isn't entirely of my making. I didn't know what you had in mind when you married me, but until you begin to accept the way it is, I think it's better for both of us if we see as little of one another as possible.'

Abby gasped. 'But—but what am I to do?'

'That's up to you.' Luke resumed eating his grapefruit. 'Ring Frances. You got along all right with her, didn't you? Although I have to admit the clothes you're wearing don't look much different from the ones you brought from Scotland.'

Abby flushed. 'These are the clothes I brought from Scotland.' She pressed her lips tightly together. 'I—I don't like the idea of being a—a bought woman!'

'A bought woman!' Luke sounded sickened by her attitude. 'For God's sake, Abby, grow up! You're living in some kind of dream world! A *husband* is entitled to buy clothes for his *wife*! How can you call yourself a bought woman, when you have my ring on your finger?'

Abby put down her spoon, and as her hands dropped to her lap, they sought the broad gold band on her finger. 'I—I don't feel married,' she said, and then shivered at the look in his eyes.

'I shall be at the studios all day,' was all he said, however. 'But on Friday evening, your aunt is giving a party for us. I shall expect you to come with me.'

Abby gulped. 'It's not me she wants to see, is it?'

Luke thrust back his stool and got to his feet. 'Goodbye, Abby,' he said harshly, and strode towards the door.

'But——' Abby scrambled up. 'Your eggs——'

'I'm not hungry,' he retorted grimly, and she heard the outer door slam at his departure.

The kitchen seemed painfully empty without his powerful presence. His half-eaten grapefruit still lay in the dish, and under the grill a plate of bacon, eggs and mushrooms shrivelled heedlessly.

The telephone rang as she was making the beds. It was Scott, and Abby almost dropped the phone in her eagerness to speak to a friendly human being. But when he asked for Luke, her brief excitement faded.

'He's not here,' she said reluctantly.

'No?' Scott sounded surprised. 'But—oh, well, never mind.'

'But what, Scott?' Abby had heard his hesitation. 'What were you going to say?'

'It doesn't matter——'

'Scott, please!'

The urgency in her voice must have got through to him, because finally he said: 'Well, he did say he was going to spend the day with you, Abby. He felt pretty lousy about leaving you yesterday, but that was unavoidable.'

'Oh!'

Abby's throat felt tight, and she was quiet for so long that Scott had to say: 'Abby? Abby, are you still there?'

'Yes.' She spoke the words with difficulty. 'I'm here.'

'Well, it doesn't mean anything, you know,' Scott blustered. 'I mean, I shouldn't worry about it. Luke must have remembered something I've forgotten——'

'Don't feel bad, Scott,' Abby interrupted him, with a heavy sigh. 'I know why Luke has gone out. But I'll tell him you rang.'

CHAPTER NINE

ABBY spent the day familiarising herself with the apartment and its environs. In the late afternoon, she went out and bought some bread and some meat to make a casserole for dinner. But although the meal was ready at seven-thirty, Luke had not returned home, and she eventually went to bed soon after ten, swallowing several aspirins in an effort to make her sleep. But it was not a good idea, and her nerves being what they were, she vomited them up again half an hour later. She must have fallen asleep towards midnight, and exhaustion kept her in its grip until the pale light of morning stole into her room.

She got up urgently, reluctantly aware that she was eager to find out whether Luke had returned during the night. If he hadn't she didn't like to contemplate what she would do, but a stealthy glimpse of his bare torso emerging from the dark sheets of his bed where he sprawled in sleep brought an uneasy feeling of relief to her tense metabolism.

In the kitchen, another acknowledgement of his return greeted her. He had re-heated the casserole she had made under the grill, and his dirty dishes, plus an empty ice-cream carton, bore witness to the fact that wherever he had been, he had not eaten. She was amazed at the feeling of satisfaction this gave her, and put it down to her desire to frustrate Ella's plans. Surely, if he had been with her aunt, she would have provided him with a meal! But where he had been, she didn't care to speculate.

He had not appeared by the time she had prepared breakfast, and she hesitated a while before setting a silver tray she found beneath the cutlery drawer. But the food would spoil if she left it much longer, and it was already almost nine and Mrs Hobbs could be expected to appear by ten, there was nothing else for it but to take it to him.

She tapped tentatively at his door before going in, but he was already awake, stretched lazily against his pillows, the sheets enfolding his lower limbs like a second skin. Observing the tray in her hands, he hauled himself up into a sitting position, his eyes narrowing as he noticed the nervousness with which she set the tray before him.

'Why did you knock?' he challenged, as she straightened away from the bed. 'You didn't before.'

Abby coloured. 'Were you awake? I—I thought you were probably tired, after—after your late night.'

Luke's mouth drew down at the corners. 'Are you censuring me?'

'No.' She moved her shoulders jerkily. 'Is that all right for you?'

'Where's yours?'

'Oh ...' Abby had omitted to make herself anything to eat. She simply didn't think she could swallow anything. 'I —I'm not hungry.'

Luke regarded the contents of the tray without enthusiasm. 'What did you do with yourself yesterday?'

Abby shifted her weight from one foot to the other. 'Nothing much.'

'Did you go out?'

'No. That is'—she paused—'only to the shops in the afternoon.'

'I see.' Luke was regarding her with a steady disruptive gaze that was disconcerting. 'I telephoned yesterday afternoon. It must have been while you were out. I thought you were deliberately not answering the phone.'

'But I wouldn't do that!' Abby was horrified. 'It might have been something important.'

'As it happens, it was. I met Heinrich Reiter for lunch. Do you remember the name? Afterwards, he suggested we flew down to Cornwall and viewed the village he plans to use for the series. I didn't know what time I'd be back, and I thought I ought to let you know.'

'You—you didn't have dinner ...'

'You saw the dishes? No, we didn't have dinner. It was somewhat of a disaster really. We flew down in Heinrich's own plane, but the damn thing refused to start later on, and we had to charter a flight back. Consequently, it was almost

115

midnight by the time we got back to town.'

'I see.'

'Do you believe me?' His eyes were dark and interrogative.

'Is there any reason why I shouldn't?' she countered quickly.

He shrugged, the muscles of his shoulders moving beneath the smooth skin. 'No. I wouldn't lie to you.'

'Wouldn't you?'

The words were out before she could retract them, and his brows drew together ominously. 'What does that mean?'

Abby would have left him, but his eyes were holding hers and she could not look away. 'I—well, Scott rang yesterday ...'

'Oh, yes? And what did he say?'

'He—he said that—that you had told him you intended to—to spend the day with me,' she floundered.

'That's right,' Luke nodded. 'I did.'

'But—but you didn't.'

'We both know why, don't we?'

Abby bent her head then, pushing her trembling fingers into the pockets of her jeans. She had guessed what he would say. She shouldn't have brought it up. But she was still foolish enough not to want to have any more secrets from him.

'What else did Scott say?'

She moved her shoulders indifferently. 'Nothing much.'

'I suppose, like Frances, he felt sorry for you.'

Abby lifted her head. 'I didn't ask for his sympathy.'

'No.' Luke put the tray aside, and to her astonishment put his legs out of bed. 'Well, I'm sorry about the breakfast, Abby, but I'm not hungry either.'

'You're not?' Her exclamation was unknowingly revealing, and he stood before her, lean and disturbing, in lemon silk pyjama trousers, expressions of self-derision and impatience warring in his dark features.

'I think you'd better go now, Abby,' he said flatly, moving towards his bathroom door. 'I'm sorry about the food, but ...'

Leaving her, he went into his bathroom, and presently she heard the sound of running water. She sighed, a feeling of restlessness and impotence sweeping over her. What was wrong with her? she asked herself impatiently. Why was it when he behaved as she had hoped he would do, she felt cheated somehow? Did she want to fight with him all the time? Did she need the constant stimulation of an uncertain relationship? The fact remained that he did disturb her, and while in the past she had never felt any curiosity about men, Luke Jordan had changed all that.

And how could he not have done? she silently exclaimed. He had kissed her, caressed her—slept with her. It was natural that she felt some sort of inquisitiveness towards him. She would not be human if she did not. Nevertheless, she had been kissed before, and caressed, without feeling any sense of arousal of the kind she was unwillingly feeling now.

With a sigh, she went to pick up the tray. Then she hesitated. What did he intend doing today? Had he made arrangements to see this man Reiter again, or was he going to the studio? Would he be home for lunch?

Licking her lips, she called: 'Luke! Luke, will you be going out this morning?'

There was no reply. The sound of the water had made her voice inaudible to him. She approached the bathroom door and called once more. Again there was no reply, and summoning all her courage, she put her head round the door to speak to him.

Luke was taking a shower, but the cubicle door was open and she gulped as he turned and saw her. Immediately, an expression of exasperation spread over his face, and without showing any of the embarrassment she was feeling, he beckoned her closer.

Reluctantly, Abby walked across the floor, her rubber-soled feet making no sound on the marble tiles. Avoiding looking at him, she said in a loud voice: 'Will you be— will you be home for lunch?'

She thought he hadn't answered and was forced to look up, to find him frowning. 'What?' he mouthed.

'Lunch!' She spoke clearly. 'Will you be in for lunch?'

'Oh.' Luke considered this, continuing to rinse the soap from his body. Now that Abby was watching him, she found she didn't want to look away, and when he looked up and

117

found her eyes upon him, his own eyes darkened impatiently. Then, before she could draw back, he had stretched out a hand and pulled her into the shower beside him, and the cool water was soaking her hair and her face and her clothes.

'Luke!' she protested with a gasp, but he wasn't listening to her. His mouth descended to cover hers, and with his lips parting hers she found it incredibly difficult to co-ordinate any kind of resistance.

He kissed her many times, long searching kisses that assuaged the aching need which was growing inside her. Urgent fingers stripped the sodden garments from her, and their bodies were fused together, oblivious of the water. He bent his head, his mouth seeking the hardening nipples of her breasts, and her hands came up of their own volition to guide his mouth back to hers.

'Dear God, Abby,' he groaned, swinging her up into his arms and carrying her out of the shower and into his room again, 'I told you not to come to my bedroom again unless you were prepared to face the consequences ...'

Someone was knocking at the door, the sound harsh and imperative, dragging Abby back from the edge of oblivion, arousing her to an awareness of the world around her.

She blinked her eyes reluctantly, opening them with a feeling of uncertainty, unable for a few moments to understand why her aching body was draped in silk. And then she remembered what had happened, and a wave of hot colour seemed to envelop her wholly. But although she rolled over urgently in the luxuriant softness of the bed, she found she was alone.

The knocking came again, and with it, the impatient voice of Mrs Hobbs from beyond the bedroom door: 'Mrs Jordan? Are you there? Can I come in?'

Gulping, Abby pulled herself upright in the bed, holding the chocolate brown sheets closely about her. 'What is it, Mrs Hobbs?' she managed, rather apprehensively.

Mrs Hobbs seemed to take her response as permission to enter the room for the door opened and that lady stood on the threshold surveying the tumbled covers of the bed, and the unknowingly sensuous beauty of the embarrassed girl

118

sitting among them, with scarcely concealed distaste. For a moment she stood there in silence, evidently drawing her own conclusions as to what had occurred, and then recovering herself, she said shortly:

'Shall I prepare lunch today, madam? As it's almost twelve?'

'Twelve?' Abby was horrified. 'It can't be!'

'I'm afraid it is, madam.' Mrs Hobbs' expression was vaguely insolent. 'Mr Jordan asked me not to wake you, but as Miss Mackay rang to say that she plans to have lunch with you, I thought you ought to be told.'

Abby caught her breath. 'Aunt Ella ...' she breathed.

Mrs Hobbs lifted her chin. 'Miss Mackay looks too young to be anybody's aunt,' she averred.

Abby accepted this without comment, trying to think. Ella ... planning to join her for lunch? And without an invitation? Did Luke know? Did he intend to join them, too? *Luke* ...

She put her hands to her cheeks to hide the telltale colour that burned there once more. Where was Luke? Where had he gone after he had stifled her fears with his mouth and taken possession of her body with such agonising strength? Dear heaven, she had had no conception of what was involved. No well-meaning biologist, nor any finely-drawn textbook, could have prepared her for the enormity of what had happened. A shiver of aversion ran through her when she allowed these recollections back into her mind, and she had to force herself to concentrate on what Mrs Hobbs was saying before panic sent her rushing for the first train back to Ardnalui.

'I—well, perhaps——' She broke off awkwardly, wishing she was wearing some garment so that she could get out of bed instead of being imprisoned by the older woman's disparaging stare. 'When is—Miss Mackay coming, Mrs Hobbs?'

'I expect she'll be here in about half an hour, madam. What were you planning to serve for lunch today?'

Abby's fists clenched over the sheet. The daily woman must know that so far she had made no plans about today's menus. And there was still the question as to whether Luke intended joining them for the meal. Why couldn't he have made his plans clear instead of leaving her groping again? And the idea of eating lunch with Ella in Luke's presence did not bear thinking about right at this moment.

With a sigh she looked at the older woman, aware that Mrs Hobbs must be able to see the defeated look in her eyes. 'I'll leave it to you, Mrs Hobbs,' she said quietly. 'I'm sure you know what my aunt likes to eat much better than I do.'

Mrs Hobbs gave a rather smug smile. 'Indeed I do, madam. If I had a pound note for every meal Miss Mackay has eaten here, I'd be a wealthy woman by now.'

Abby looked down at her clenched hands. 'Thank you, Mrs Hobbs. You can go now. I—er—I want to get dressed.'

'Yes, madam.' Mrs Hobbs reached for the door handle. 'Oh—and by the way, Mr Jordan said to tell you he'll be back around six,' and the door slammed triumphantly behind her.

Abby stared at the blank panels for several minutes after she had gone. That woman! she thought angrily. She must have known how uncertain Abby was as to Luke's movements, and yet she had deliberately withheld the information until the very last minute. With a smothered ejaculation, she slid out of bed and then stopped aghast as she glimpsed her reflection in the long wardrobe mirrors.

Fortunately, Mrs Hobbs could not have seen all the bruises that marred her creamy flesh, but those that marked the slender bones of her shoulders must have been clearly visible. Bluish-purple, they etched the pressure of Luke's fingers, that demanding pressure that she remembered so well. He was a brute—*an animal*—she thought bitterly, lightly tracing those sensitive areas of her skin with her fingertips. And to think she had been curious about the man-woman relationship, inquisitive of that desire to know all the secrets of her body—and Luke's. She shivered once more. What a rude awakening to the harsh realities of the world she had had! He had been right when he had told her there were no knights on white chargers any more. She doubted there ever had been, and she felt a sense of outraged amazement that she had actually believed that a woman might enjoy sex as much as a man. It was repulsive —and painful. And a woman would have to love a man very much to permit him those privileges very often.

Luke's bathroom brought a further wave of revulsion. Her clothes still lay in the well of the shower cubicle, soaked and impossible to wear. With a grimace of distaste, she wrung them out and after a moment's hesitation, donned Luke's navy towelling bathrobe to carry them into her own bedroom. She draped the crumpled jeans and shirt over the side of her bath, wishing there was some way she could conceal them from Mrs Hobbs' avid stare.

All her clothes were in Luke's bedroom, she now realised, but the unwearability of her favourite garments made the decision to choose something new easier to take. She surveyed the contents of the long wardrobe in his room with a certain amount of reluctant interest, however. After all, she needed all the assurance she could muster, and there was nothing like the right clothes to stimulate a feeling of self-confidence.

Eventually she pulled out a dress of silk jersey, with a cuffed neckline and a swinging skirt which accentuated the slender length of her legs. It was a simple style relying entirely on material and cut for its elegance, and the shades of orange and yellow were a fitting complement to Abby's dark colouring. In high wedged heels, her legs encased in the sheerest nylon, she looked much more the successful writer's wife than she had ever done before, and fleetingly she wondered what Luke would think of the transformation. Then she was angry with herself for even wondering such a thing. After what had happened this morning, seeing Luke again was something to be avoided, not looked for.

Even so, she couldn't help feeling pleased with her appearance, although she doubted it would last once Ella arrived.

Mrs Hobbs was laying the table in the dining room when Abby went in search of her, and her eyes flickered with reluctant surprise when she first saw her young mistress. Then she straightened from setting out the silver cutlery and asked abruptly: 'Was there something you wanted, madam?'

Abby sighed. 'No, not exactly. I—just wondered what you had decided to serve for lunch, Mrs Hobbs.'

A look of resignation crossed the older woman's face. 'Miss Mackay likes smoked salmon, madam. I thought my

121

own paté, followed by smoked salmon and salad with fresh fruit to finish, would be a suitable combination.'

'Oh, yes. Yes. That sounds very nice.' Abby shrugged her shoulders. 'Thank you.'

'What wine would you like me to serve, madam?'

Abby coloured. Wine was something she knew absolutely nothing about, and she was almost sure Mrs Hobbs knew this, too.

'Oh—I'll leave that to you, too, Mrs Hobbs,' she said at last. 'As with everything else, I'm sure you have impeccable taste.'

Mrs Hobbs made no comment, but returned to her task, and with another sigh, Abby left the room. The woman was impossible! She wasn't actually impolite, but her attitude left a lot to be desired, and no matter what Abby said she would go her own way.

The ringing of the doorbell was a respite from her thoughts, and without thinking she went to answer it, finding Mrs Hobbs on her heels as she swung open the door. Ella was standing outside, and like the daily woman she appraised Abby very thoroughly before stepping into the entrance hall.

'Quite a welcoming committee,' she commented maliciously. 'I didn't realise you'd be quite so pleased to see me, Abby.' Her eyes shifted to the other woman. 'And how are you today, Hobby darling? Still smoothing life's way with your efficient presence, I suppose.'

Hobby! Abby drew her lower lip between her teeth. Was this what Frances had wanted to tell her? That Mrs Hobbs and her aunt were old allies?

'Good morning, Miss Mackay,' the daily woman was answering now, her face wreathed in smiles as she took charge of Ella's carelessly discarded cape. 'You've chosen a chilly morning for your visit.'

'Yes, it is rather miserable, isn't it?' agreed Ella, casting a glance at the overcast skies visible beyond the long windows of the living room. 'But I'm sure you've prepared a delightful lunch for us, and that will be well worth waiting for.'

Mrs Hobbs beamed as she went away, and reluctantly, Abby followed her aunt into the comfortably furnished apartment. Obviously, Ella was very much at home here and had every intention of making that situation plain. Closing the heavy doors, she leaned back against them for a moment, unaware as she did so that she was framed against the dark wood in vivid relief. But her aunt was aware of it, and her voice was harsh as she said:

'I thought it was time you and I had a little chat, Abby.'

Abby straightened. 'Oh? Did you?'

'Yes.' Ella flicked a speck of dust from the jacket of the superbly cut cream slacks suit she was wearing. 'And first of all, I suggest we dispense with the conventions. You and I both know why you tricked Luke into this marriage, and I don't mean all that claptrap about Daniel McGregor finding you in bed together.'

Abby could feel the hot colour sweeping up her throat and wished she had more control over her feelings. Ella looked as cool and collected as if they were discussing nothing more personal than the weather.

'Uncle Daniel did find us in bed together,' she managed tightly.

'Did he?' Ella seemed unconcerned. 'Clever!'

'What do you mean?'

'Oh, come on, Abby! You're your mother's daughter—I can see that. And while I hate you for what you're trying to do to me, I can understand why you did it.'

'I'd really rather not discuss my marriage with you.'

'I bet you wouldn't!' Ella gave her an impatient stare. 'But unfortunately, I'm not about to let you get away with that.'

Abby clenched her fists. 'I don't know how you have the nerve to come here and say these things to me!'

Ella's lips twisted. 'No? Why not? It's my future I'm fighting for.'

'Your future!'

'Yes. Why not?' Ella tilted her head. 'Everyone's entitled to fight for what they want.'

'As you fought for my father, I suppose!'

'No.' Ella's expression hardened. 'I didn't fight for your father, Abby. He was a gift!'

Abby gasped. 'How can you say such things!'

'Because they're true!' Ella strode angrily across the

123

carpet. 'My God, you don't actually believe I wanted your father? Except for the purely flattering concept of knowing myself a desirable woman!'

'That's a vile thing to say!'

'Is it? But true, I assure you.'

'Do you think I'd believe you?'

Ella gave a short laugh. 'No, I suppose not.'

'You're an actress! You can play whatever role it suits you.'

'True. But has it ever occurred to you that there are always two sides to every argument?'

'You tantalised my father! You tormented him——'

'No.' Ella was adamant. 'I was young—and beautiful. That's no conceit. I still am—everyone knows it. Your father was tantalised—but by his own emotions, not by me.'

'I don't believe you.'

'That's your prerogative, of course.'

'And he can't defend himself.'

'Nor, it seems, can I.'

Abby twisted her hands together. 'I won't listen to you!'

'Why not? Does the truth frighten you, too?'

'What do you mean—too?'

'Your mother would never believe me. She saw your father as some kind of—of innocent, tempted by corruption.'

'And wasn't he?'

'No.' Ella was angry now. 'My God, Abby, have some sense! Your mother just sat back and let it happen. She let the husband she professed to love make a fool of himself over her sister and she did nothing. Nothing! What would you have done? Would you have let me get away without a fight? Wouldn't you have thrown your father's responsibilities at him? Made him feel the heel he was? But what did your mother do? As I said—*nothing*!'

'My mother was a lady——'

'Cold comfort.'

'I hate you!'

'Yes, you do, don't you? And you know what? I'd rather have your hatred than your mother's martyrdom any day!'

Abby sniffed. 'My father died ...'

'Yes.'

'My mother didn't want to go on living ...'

'Not even for you.'

'I'd expect you to say that!'

Ella shrugged. 'Then you weren't disappointed.' She sighed. 'But don't imagine you're all innocent, Abby. You must be more like me than you even imagine. I can't ever imagine your mother would have done what you've done.'

'Done what?'

'Tricked Luke into marrying you.'

'You don't know that.'

'I think I do.' Ella's lips tightened. 'But I warn you—I'm not your mother.'

'Thank God for that!'

'On the contrary, if I'd had a daughter, I would have hoped she'd be someone like you. Someone with determination, if nothing else.'

'Why have you come here?' demanded Abby.

'To talk to you.'

'Like this?'

Ella shook her head. 'Not exactly. Strange as it may seem, I'm prepared to overlook your—er—unfortunate loyalties, providing we can come to some kind of an agreement.'

'An agreement?' Abby was confused.

'Yes, an agreement. About this—marriage.'

'You can do nothing about that.'

'Can't I? Let's say I haven't even tried.'

'Perhaps you ought to speak to Luke——'

'No.' Ella drew a deep breath. 'For some reason, Luke has got it into his head that you need him more than I do. That's ridiculous, of course, but Luke is an intensely—honest man. Between you, you and Daniel have put him on the spot. And while I can—see—what he finds attractive about you—your similarity to me cannot have gone unnoticed, even if you are a little underweight—I can't help thinking how immature you must seem to a man of his sophistication and intelligence.'

That these thoughts had occurred to Abby must have shown in her face, because Ella's small smile was knowing as she went on: 'I'd give it three months at the outside, before your—er—simple charms begin to pall.'

Abby held up her head. 'And—and what if I told you that—that Luke and I don't—don't sleep together?'

For a moment a shadow darkened the older woman's blue eyes. Then it cleared as she said: 'But you do, don't you? Hobby told me so.'

'Then *Mrs* Hobbs was wrong,' retorted Abby harshly. 'Because we don't.'

Ella took a step towards her. 'You're lying to me.'

'No, I'm not.' Abby stood her ground. 'Oh, I admit, I—I have been in Luke's bed, but not—not for the reasons you think.'

Now it was Ella's turn to stare. 'I don't believe it.'

Abby shrugged. 'As you said earlier, that's your prerogative.'

Ella's teeth ground together. 'Then why did he marry you?'

'You know why. I expect Scott gave you the details.'

'Oh, yes, Scott told me what happened.' Ella was obviously trying to think, trying to assimilate what this new situation might mean. Her eyes narrowed. 'You're telling me that Luke married you without laying a hand on you?'

'Sexually speaking—yes.'

Ella breathed deeply. 'Then why . . .'

Abby turned away. If this was victory, she didn't like the feeling. Somehow none of this was turning out as she had expected. She ought to have known. People were human, not cyphers. Nobody was all bad, just as nobody was quite a saint. The things Ella had told her lingered in her mind, and she couldn't altogether rid herself of the conviction that there just might be some truth in her explanations. Maybe her mother had let her father go too easily—maybe he had been weak . . . She doubted she would ever really know. And Ella had not denied her part in the affair, only justified her actions—or tried to.

The door opened just then, and Mrs Hobbs reappeared. 'Lunch is served, Miss Mackay,' she announced ingratiatingly. 'If you and—Mrs Jordan—will come through?'

'Thank you.'

Ella glanced at her niece, and then preceded her into the dining room. Their places had been set at the end of the long table, and Mrs Hobbs seemed to take it for granted that Ella would occupy the space at the end where Luke had been seated two days ago. Abby was indifferent to the slight, and applied herself to spreading paté on the melba toast the daily woman had provided.

Actually, Abby made quite a good meal, but she noticed that Ella ate next to nothing, much to Mrs Hobbs' concern. She was forced to reassure the woman that the smoked salmon had nothing to do with her lack of appetite, and accepted the second bottle of wine she proffered with more enthusiasm.

Conversation was non-existent throughout the meal, much to Abby's relief, but when Mrs Hobbs had departed after serving their coffee in the living room, Ella seemed to recover her self-assurance.

'The marriage will have to be annulled,' she stated unequivocally, and Abby almost choked before setting her cup back in its saucer.

'Annulled?' she echoed faintly.

'That's right.' Ella's eyes were hard and bright now. 'I want Luke, Abby, and I intend to have him. One way or the other. It's up to you.'

'I don't understand . . .'

'It's quite simple really. You've had your little game, and I admit, you gave me a nasty shock. But that's over now. You achieved your objective, and I can find it in my heart to admire you for it. But I am not like your mother, and I have no intention of allowing you to ruin my life.'

Abby licked lips gone suddenly dry. It was strange hearing Luke spoken about in this way, as though he had no say in the matter. Perhaps Ella did not know him as well as she thought she did if she imagined he would allow himself to be manipulated. Did her aunt really believe that she had manoeuvred him into this marriage? Didn't she know he was far too devious for that?

'Wh-what do you expect me to do?' she ventured unevenly.

Ella made an impatient gesture. 'If—and I still find it hard to believe—Luke really married you to satisfy some quixotic desire to pacify Daniel McGregor, it shouldn't be too difficult for you to ask for a separation as soon as the proprieties have been satisfied.'

127

Abby felt a shiver of remembered passion slide chillingly down her spine. 'And—and what if Luke won't agree to that?' she asked quietly. 'Always assuming that I would.'

'It will be up to you to make sure he does agree to it,' retorted Ella forcefully.

'Why should I do that?'

Ella sighed. 'Abby—please! I'm trying to keep this civil. Don't force me to fight you.'

'How could you do that?'

Ella's cup clattered into its saucer, spilling coffee over the traycloth. 'Abby! I don't want to hurt you.'

'You don't want to hurt me!' Abby found a sense of injustice growing inside her. For a few moments she forgot that only hours before she had been panicking over ways to escape from this situation in which she found herself. Suddenly, she was defending her right to be Luke's wife with a determination that would have shocked her had she stopped to think about it. 'You don't want to hurt me? You come here and tell me you mean to take my husband, and then have the nerve to say you don't want to hurt me!'

'Abby, you took Luke from me. Not the other way about.'

'He's a man, isn't he? He has free will. I didn't force him to the altar at gunpoint. He could have refused ...'

Ella's lips curled. 'I hope you realise what you've just said.'

'I—I——'

'You've just proved my point about your own father.'

Abby's chest heaved. 'Luke was not a married man,' she protested, as emotion brought a lump to her throat.

'Do you really think that matters in the final analysis?' Ella shook her head. 'Abby, you have to face facts. You could never satisfy a man like Luke. If he did decide to make love to you, you'd be terrified! He's used to a woman —not a frightened girl!'

'But——'

Abby opened her mouth to protest and then broke off. To admit that Luke had made love to her—if you could call the assault he had made on her senses love—would give Ella the lever she needed. But how could she even begin to understand Luke's motives for anything, when at every turn he reversed their positions?

'I blame Scott,' Ella was saying now, getting to her feet to pace restlessly across the floor. 'If he hadn't conceived that crazy idea of sending Luke to Ardnalui——'

'You're talking as if Luke had no will of his own!' exclaimed Abby fretfully, and Ella turned to face her.

'Am I? But you're not about to tell me that your involvement with him came about by accident, are you?' she demanded grimly.

Abby looked down at her hands folded in her lap. 'If you really know Luke that well, you should know he has a mind of his own——'

'I know that you and McGregor cooked this up between you——'

'That's not true! Uncle Daniel had nothing to do with it.'

Ella uttered a scornful sound. 'You did it alone? Forgive me if I find that hard to believe.'

'Believe what you like!' cried Abby distractedly.

'Oh, Abby!' Ella pressed her balled fist to her temple. 'You're forcing me to fight you. But remember, I didn't start this.'

'On the contrary,' remarked Abby quietly, 'I think you started it years ago.'

'Well, that at least is honest,' Ella conceded with a sigh. 'All right, Abby, I'll give it to you straight. Luke, your—husband—owes no small slice of his success to me, and he knows it. Without me, he'd be nothing.'

Abby felt a cold hand squeezing her stomach. 'How can you justify that remark?'

'Quite easily. Your husband was an engineer until he met me. It was I who read his first manuscript, who persuaded the publishers to take it. Howard Jennings is a friend of mine. You've heard of Howard Jennings, I suppose.'

Abby was all at sea. 'What has that to do with anything?'

'Simply this: I made him—I can break him.'

'I—I don't believe you.'

'Don't you? You don't sound very sure about it to me.'

'But—but——'

'How?' Ella laughed. 'Corruption is as rife in the theatre as anywhere else. Has Luke mentioned Heinrich Reiter to you? Ah, I see he has. Well, dear Heinrich is a personal admirer of mine. His interest in the new series stems from his desire to have me starring in a production of his. Do I make myself clear, or shall I go the whole way?'

'Luke writes. His books——'

'His books!' Ella snapped her fingers contemptuously. 'His books don't enable him to live in this style. It's the money he's made from films and television which have given him the standing he enjoys today. Take that away and—well ...' She shrugged eloquently.

Abby couldn't take it all in. She understood what Ella was saying easily enough, but she didn't understand why, if this was so, Luke had married *her*. Why hadn't he married Ella? He had had plenty of time to do so. But then marriage was not considered so important among film people these days. Perhaps living together was enough. Had Ella lived here with him? It seemed imperative that she had to know, but it was a question she would never ask Ella herself. It was too degrading, too humiliating ...

'You do understand me, don't you, Abby?'

Ella was speaking again, and Abby raised pained eyes to her aunt's. 'I understand what you're saying,' she said quietly. 'But surely you should be saying these things to Luke.'

'Which proves how little you know of him,' drawled Ella in a resigned tone. 'He's an arrogant devil. If I attempt to threaten him, he's foolhardy enough to tell me to go and get —well, I'm sure you can finish that sentence for yourself.'

'Then perhaps I ought to do the same.'

'What? And jeopardise his whole career without even a by-your-leave?'

'What do you expect me to do?'

'I expect you to be sensible, Abby. You don't really want to be married to a man almost twenty years older than you are! My God, when you're forty, he'll be nearly sixty! You want someone younger, less experienced, less—demanding, shall we say?'

'And if he won't let me go?'

'This is the twentieth century, Abby. There are courts of law. And I'd help you in any way I could.'

'I bet you would.'

130

'Oh, Abby! Be honest! Didn't you really only marry Luke to spite me?'

'All right—all right, yes. *Yes*.' Abby's lips trembled. 'But I wish to God I hadn't.'

'I'll second that,' added Ella, with feeling.

CHAPTER TEN

ELLA'S apartment was thronged with people. Abby had never attended so large a gathering, and the noise was quite deafening. The long sliding doors which divided the huge lounge from the dining area had been rolled back to facilitate the free movement of her visitors from one room to the other, but the press of humanity was such that most guests congregated in small groups and made little effort to circulate. White-coated waiters, hired for the occasion, moved among the guests holding high trays of drinks and canapés, while long tables in the dining room displayed an appetizing cold buffet. But the food was barely touched. Everyone seemed intent on exchanging gossip, and from the fleeting snatches of conversation that came Abby's way, she learned that to be successful was not always to be popular. Music, issuing from quadrophonic speakers, overlaid the buzz of talk and laughter, adding to the general cacophony of sound.

Abby was standing with Scott Anderson, and a couple of his technicians and their wives. Since the moment of their arrival, she had seen next to nothing of Luke, Ella having borne him away to meet someone who was 'absolutely dying' to meet him, and while she told herself she didn't care what he did, somehow it didn't quite convince her. Abby had been left in the able and willing hands of Bruce Conway, Ella's co-star in the movie they had been making in Italy, but while many women found his heavy-eyed attraction and broad muscular figure attractive, Abby did not appreciate his roving eyes and fulsome compliments. She was firmly convinced after Luke's indifferent appraisal of her appearance that she looked no more than averagely attractive, and Bruce's avowals that she was the most beautiful woman in the room left her cold. She had tried not to feel disappointed earlier when Luke had made no comment on her appearance, but another man's admiration was no reassurance. Perhaps she should have worn something more glamorous, she thought. Perhaps Luke had expected more for the money she had spent. Yet in her bedroom, parading before the long mirror, the turquoise blue gown, with its caped neckline that successfully disguised the bruises Luke himself had made, had looked exactly right, without hinting at a sophistication she was so ill-equipped to maintain. She had plaited two narrow strands of her hair and drawn them back to an ivory clasp at the back of her head, and her dark colouring had added to her vaguely alien appearance. She had liked the effect and had half hoped that Luke would too.

But instead he had disappeared with Ella with scarcely a backward glance, and Abby, ignoring Bruce's suggestion that they should find somewhere where they could talk, had looked round desperately for a friendly face. When she saw Scott, relief flooded over her, and she made her way towards him like a drowning man reaching for the shore. Bruce had hung about for a while, but eventually he had got the message, and now Abby was standing beside Scott, feeling the beginnings of a headache probing achingly at her temples.

She ought to have known the evening would be a disaster, she thought dully. After the row they had had the night before, how could it be anything else? And yet the previous evening had not started so badly; at least from a practical point of view. But after Ella's visit, she had been tense and edgy, and perhaps more than willing to release that tension in anger.

Her jeans and shirt had been dried by the late afternoon, and childishly, she had donned them again before Luke came home. Mrs Hobbs had departed before his return, but not before she had outlined serving instructions for the friccassée of beef she had left in the oven for dinner. Abby had been surprised at the daily woman leaving so early, but perhaps Ella had given her instructions, too.

Abby had been watching television in the living room when Luke had appeared, and with her heart beating faster with its memories of the morning returning with renewed intensity, it had been all she could do to remain in her seat when he entered the room.

In a suit of navy blue suede, which fitted his broad shoulders and narrow thighs like a second skin, his curiously light hair mussed slightly as if he had been running his long fingers through its length, he had looked distractingly attractive; and a certain resentment had filled her that he still had the power to stir her senses in spite of those painful recollections she was trying to subdue. There had been a certain tenseness in the air between them, and impatience too on his part when she avoided directly looking at him.

Eventually, after a few polite exchanges, he had left to take a shower, and when his eyes had flickered over her as he left the room, she had felt an increasing feeling of indignation at what she guessed to be the tenor of his thoughts. She despised him for being able to behave as if nothing untoward had happened when he must know that she felt shattered by what had occurred.

But it had not been until after dinner that matters really came to a head. The food had been admirably prepared by Mrs Hobbs, and all Abby had had to do was serve it. As the daily woman had already laid the table in the dining room, it seemed pointless serving the meal in the kitchen, although Abby was supremely conscious of the inadequacy of her jeans when compared to Luke's black corded pants and matching silk shirt. He looked like some brooding angel, watching her pick at her food, with an increasingly devilish look in his eyes.

'What have you been doing with yourself today?' he asked at last, and Abby's fork poked more determinedly at a piece of meat as she answered indifferently: 'Nothing much.'

Luke let her indifference pass unchallenged, and went on: 'Have you been out? I think you should. You're beginning to look quite pale and heavy-eyed.'

'Thank you.'

Abby's brief spurt of sarcasm was doused by the drumming of his fingers against the table. 'Stop this, Abby!' he commanded harshly. 'I've been very patient with you since your arrival here, but I refuse to suffer insolence.'

'*You* refuse?' Abby's resentment spilled over. 'How do you think I feel?'

'Oh, for God's sake——' Luke thrust his chair away from the table and rose to his feet grimly, staring down at her with real dislike in his eyes. 'We may as well have this out here and now. I presume you're referring to this morning.'

'You presume correctly.' Abby refused to go on looking up at him. The situation was too one-sided. He always had the better of her, and towering over her like this, he gave her a curiously panicky feeling deep in her stomach.

'I warned you,' he said now, pushing his half empty plate aside. 'Besides, it was bound to happen sooner or later. You knew that.'

'I—I didn't know you would behave like a—a brute!' she protested unevenly. 'You ... hurt me ...'

'Damn you, what did you expect? Didn't they teach you anything at school?'

'Not—not sexual assault, at any rate,' she managed chokily, and he glared frustratedly at her.

'God, it wasn't assault!' he swore, faint colour coming up under his tan. 'You don't know what the hell you're talking about!'

'You took advantage of me ...'

'You didn't fight me all the way,' he reminded her roughly.

Abby gasped. 'That's a rotten thing to say!'

'But true.' He sighed, raking a hand through his hair. 'Abby, you've got to understand, there are limits——' He broke off, shaking his head. 'I frightened you, I know that, but next time——'

'*Next time!*' His casual assumption that there would be a 'next time' brought Abby to her feet then. 'There won't be a next time!'

'Won't there?' Luke's eyes narrowed then, heavy lids and thick lashes concealing their expression from her. But for all that, Abby was chilled by his stillness, by the threat it represented.

'You—you can't expect—it's too soon—we don't even know if we're suited to one another——'

Words tumbled from her lips, anything to distract him

from the implications of her remark. She sensed she should not challenge him in this way. She needed time. She had to play it cool.

Licking her lips, she said the first thing that came into her head. 'Luke, Ella came here today. She—I—we had lunch together.'

She saw to her relief that she had at last distracted him, if only briefly. 'Ella?' He frowned. 'What did she want?' He paused. 'Did you invite her?'

'No. That is—well, she is my aunt, after all.'

'So *you* keep telling me.'

Abby sighed, bending her head. 'I expect blood is thicker than water.'

'Is it? Is that what she said?'

'No. I—oh, stop trying to tie me up in knots!'

'Am I doing that?'

'You know you are.' She pushed back her hair with a weary hand. 'I have a headache.'

'How convenient!'

'Don't be sarcastic. It's true—I do have a headache. I've had it since this afternoon.'

'Since Ella left, no doubt.' Luke's expression was derisive. 'Well? And did you have a girlish heart-to-heart? Did you confide in her your—er—objections to my attentions?'

'No!' Abby gasped indignantly. 'I—I wouldn't discuss—such things.'

'She would,' averred Luke flatly. 'Look, Abby, I don't know why Ella came here or what she said to you, but I suppose I can guess. Whatever it was, remember this: you're my wife. We're married, for better or for worse, and no matter what motive you had for marrying me, it's done now and we're going to stay that way. Do I make myself understood?'

Abby stared at him tremulously. 'I'm not your property! You—you can't keep me here against my will.'

'Ella's words, one presumes.' His lips twisted. 'For God's sake, Abby, be your age! Ella has her own reasons for splitting us up, you know that. But we're two adult people, so stop behaving like some frightened child!'

'I never wanted to marry you. And you don't really want me——'

'Don't I?' Luke uttered an oath, coming round the table to grasp her shoulders savagely. 'Do you want me to prove you wrong?'

'No. *No!*' Guessing what he meant, Abby struggled to free herself. 'Don't touch me! I—I hate you!'

To her humiliation and dismay, she felt tears of anger and frustration overspill her eyes and flood heedlessly down her cheeks, seeming in their way to confirm his scathing definition of her as a frightened child.

Her tears had a sobering effect on Luke however. As she gazed up at him, looking little older than the daughter he might have had, his face changed, his anger giving way to a curiously vulnerable expression of self contempt. Watching him, Abby felt the painful grip on her shoulders ease and his hands fell to his sides.

And then, ridiculously enough, she had wanted to reach out to him, to reassure him, to restore the man who hitherto she had been trying to escape. But as her hand lifted half appealingly, he swung away from her, striding across the room and down the hall, and seconds later she had heard the outer door of the apartment slam. He had not returned before she went to bed, and in the morning he had been up and dressed before she had dragged herself out of bed. He had left without waiting for breakfast and she had not seen him again until he returned home to change for this party of Ella's.

Realising that Scott was speaking to her now, Abby dragged her thoughts back to the present, trying to ignore the heavy throbbing as her headache increased. 'I'm sorry. What did you say?'

'I said you're looking tired, Abby. What is it? Lack of sleep?'

It was said casually enough, but it could be taken two ways, and Abby glanced round in embarrassment to reassure herself that no one else had overheard. 'No. I—I expect it's living in London after a place like Ardnalui. I used to spend a lot of time in the open air, but here . . .' She shrugged. 'You know what I mean.'

'Of course,' Scott nodded. 'Do you miss it?'

136

Abby bent her head. 'What do you think?'

'Then for God's sake, why did you marry Luke?' demanded Scott, raising his voice slightly, and then lowering it again before they attracted attention. 'You don't love him, do you?'

Abby hesitated for a moment, and then she moved her head vigorously from side to side. Of course she didn't love him. She hated and despised him. He was using her to satisfy some nefarious plan of his own, and he enjoyed humiliating her. But she had hesitated, and that knowledge made her say something she might otherwise never have said: 'Aunt Ella wants the marriage to be annulled.'

Scott glanced at her sideways, and then looking straight ahead, he said: 'But we both know that can't happen, don't we?'

Abby's head jerked up. 'What do you mean?'

'A marriage can only be annulled if it hasn't been consummated,' he remarked quietly.

Abby's cheeks flamed. 'But you don't know——'

'Don't I?' Scott shook his head. 'Abby, Luke came to my house last night, did you know that?' Abby showed her unawareness of that fact, and he went on: 'He was rather morose. You had had a row, I assumed. I'm afraid we got rather drunk.'

'And—and Luke told—you——' Abby broke off with a gulp.

'No, no. Even stoned out of his mind, Luke wouldn't discuss something like that. But I'm not a fool, Abby. I've been around. I know when a man and a woman ...' He sighed. 'Sufficient to say that an annulment is out of the question, isn't it?'

Abby nodded, and he made a resigned gesture. 'So? What are you going to do?'

'To do? Me?' Abby lifted her shoulders helplessly. 'What can I do?'

'What do you want to do?'

What did she want to do? With a pang, Abby realised that she didn't really know. The future seemed totally blank. The only reality was her marriage to Luke—to a man she scarcely knew, a stranger to whom she had committed herself without ever considering the possible consequences. What a fool she had been to imagine she had any control over the destiny of a man like Luke—or her aunt either, for that matter. Luke was right—she had not grown up. She was still a frightened child ...

'Abby!' The friendly voice of Frances Dwyer brought her out of her reverie, and she turned to find the blonde girl confronting her, accompanied by a dark-haired man who she quickly introduced as her husband, Mike. 'Abby, how lovely you look. That gown really suits you.'

Abby gathered herself quickly, unwilling for anyone else to guess that all was not well with her. 'Thank you, Frances. You look pretty good yourself. I didn't know I'd see you here.'

'Oh, Ella invited Mike and me,' replied Frances, grimacing. 'She always likes a photographer on hand in case something important comes up. Isn't that right, darling?'

She turned to the man beside her, and his lean good-looking face broke into a grin. 'That's right. How are you enjoying London, Abby? Have you got around to visiting any of our tourist attractions yet?'

'I'm afraid not.' Abby warmed to the admiration in Mike Dwyer's brown eyes, the tenseness of her headache receding slightly. 'I've hardly been out of the apartment. Luke's been working——'

'When is he not!' declared Frances, turning her attention to Scott. 'Don't you know Abby hasn't even had a honeymoon? Don't you feel a cad for monopolising her bridegroom?'

It was all said jokingly, and Scott took it in good part, much to Abby's relief. After their conversation, he might have been excused for defending himself more strongly, but he merely assured Frances that once the new series was off the ground, Luke could have all the time he wanted.

'Frances tells me that your mother and Ella were sisters,' Mike remarked to Abby, and she nodded quickly. 'You are alike,' he went on thoughtfully, 'but not as alike as I'd have expected. You're much darker than she is, for one thing, your skin is paler, and your bones are more delicately drawn.' He smiled. 'Forgive me, but I see everyone as a possible subject.'

138

Abby hesitated a moment and then she said quietly: 'My father was a Spaniard.'

'Ah!' Mike nodded triumphantly. 'That explains a lot. You have a certain—alien quality that I couldn't quite place. Now I understand.' He paused, continuing to scrutinize her with almost embarrassing intensity. 'Tell me, have you ever thought about taking up modelling?'

'Modelling?' Abby was surprised. 'You mean clothes and things?'

'Not necessarily. I meant photographic modelling——'

'No, she hasn't. And nor will she, so long as I have anything to do with it!'

Luke's hard tone startled all of them, and catching Scott's eye, Abby exchanged a nervous glance with him before turning to her husband. Luke was standing right behind them, tall and disturbing in his dark red velvet dinner suit, his expression far from encouraging as he confronted Mike Dwyer.

'Aw, come on, Luke,' Mike was saying persuasively, 'you've got a beautiful wife. Why shouldn't anyone else have the chance to admire her?'

Luke's hand descended possessively on Abby's shoulder. 'Because she is *my* wife,' he retorted dryly. 'I can do all the admiring necessary, thank you.'

Abby quivered, and feeling it through his fingers, Luke propelled her closer to him so that she came up against the hardness of his chest. Both Scott and Frances were watching them with a certain amount of astonishment, and it was all Abby could do to prevent herself from demanding exactly what Luke thought he was doing. He had virtually abandoned her an hour ago, and now, when she had begun to relax a little, he came back expecting her to fall into his arms like a ripe plum.

With a determined effort, she managed to draw away from him again, speaking deliberately to Mike: 'You're a photographer, aren't you, Mr Dwyer? I suppose you take photographs of lots of beautiful women.'

'The name's Mike, and yes, I guess you could say that.'

'Do you have exhibitions, that sort of thing?'

'Not usually——' Mike was beginning, when Luke interrupted them again.

'Abby! I want to take you to meet Heinrich Reiter——'

'Oh, do you?' Abby turned her head, her dark hair swinging silkily about her shoulders. 'Well, can you wait a little while, Luke? Er—Mike and I—were just getting to know one another.'

It was difficult to know who looked the more astounded. Obviously Luke had never expected Abby to thwart him, but Scott and Mike and Frances all looked taken aback. There was a short pregnant silence of perhaps thirty seconds, and then Mike said uncomfortably: 'You'd better go with Luke, Abby. I—er—we can talk later.'

Abby drew a deep breath. Curiously, she felt in control of the situation for the first time that evening, and she didn't stop to think that perhaps it was the presence of other people that gave her this new-found confidence.

'Oh, very well,' she said, tossing her head. 'Is it important that I meet this man, Luke?'

Luke didn't trust himself to speak to her until they were out of earshot of the others. Then he said, in a voice as cold and hard as steel: 'Don't you ever do that to me again!'

'Do what?'

Abby was being deliberately provocative. While she had been standing with Scott she had managed to swallow two champagne cocktails and the unaccustomed amount of alcohol had combined with the things Mike had said to give her a heady, if fleeting, sense of self-assurance. For the moment, she didn't quite care what she said, and Luke's darkly angry features were almost amusing.

'Abby,' he said grimly, 'don't play games with me. I warn you——'

'Oh, don't be so stuffy, Luke!' she exclaimed, wrinkling her nose at him. 'You can't expect to desert me for more than an hour and then expect me to jump to your bidding the minute you appear.'

'I did not desert you, Abby.'

'What would you call it, then? You knew I would know practically no one here.'

'Ella asked Bruce to keep an eye on you.'

'I didn't want Bruce to keep an eye on me. I prefer to choose my own companions, thank you. And just when somebody interesting started talking to me, you turn up.'

'You think Mike Dwyer is interesting?'

If Abby had been more alert to the danger signals, she might have recognised the trace of quiet menace in Luke's voice. As it was, she went ahead carelessly, nodding her head and saying: 'Yes. Yes, I do. And I think he enjoyed talking to me, if you can believe that. At least he noticed my appearance.'

'What is the essence of that remark?'

Abby sniffed. 'Well, you didn't even notice I wasn't still wearing jeans!' she accused him resentfully.

'I noticed,' he retorted. 'However, I was under the apparently mistaken impression that you would not welcome my admiration.'

Abby gulped, suddenly realising what she was saying. 'I—I don't,' she stammered uneasily.

Luke's eyes bored into hers. 'I wonder,' he said, and a feeling of faintness assailed her. The crowd of people around them suddenly seemed too much for her, and she swayed unsteadily, reaching automatically for Luke's arm as the room swam around her.

Immediately the hardness in his eyes disappeared, and had she not known him better, she would have said genuine concern for her brought his arm around her and accounted for the unusually gentle tone of his voice.

'Are you all right?'

'I—I—it's so hot in here,' she breathed jerkily.

Luke uttered an expletive as someone brushed past, jostling them, then glancing round briefly, he steered her determinedly towards the doors. Of course, they had to encounter Ella as they reached the perimeter of the throng, and her eyes narrowed speculatively before she exclaimed: 'What's the matter? Luke darling, I've been looking everywhere for you. I wanted to tell you—Laurence has agreed to put up the money——'

'Not now, Ella.'

'What do you mean? Not now? Walking off like that and leaving me with him! It was you he wanted to talk to, I told you——'

'Well, I'll have to talk to him some other time. Can't you see? Abby's not well.'

141

Ella's eyes shifted angrily to her niece. 'Why? What's wrong with her?'

'I'm all right, really ...'

The last thing Abby wanted was to cause a fuss. She wished she could get away from all of them. Luke's arm around her waist was altogether too possessive, and the lean muscular hardness of his body behind hers was arousing sensations which she was finding to her dismay were not as undesirable as they had been earlier. It would have been unutterably pleasant to relax against him, to allow him to take charge of things as he was doing, and give herself up to the enjoyment of being cosseted. But instead she made a vain effort to drag herself away from him, and succeeded in arousing his anger as well as his concern.

'I'm taking you home,' he stated categorically, and Ella looked positively venomous.

'You can't do this, Luke! I arranged this party especially for you——'

'Oh, please!' Abby broke away from him at last. 'Leave me alone, both of you! I can go home alone. I can get a cab. It's not far. Perhaps Scott—or the Dwyers—would come with me if you don't want me to go alone——'

As if on cue, Frances appeared behind Luke just then, her face showing her concern. 'Is something wrong, Luke?' she asked, anxiously, glancing at Abby. 'Abby, aren't you feeling well?'

'I'm fine——'

'No, she's not,' stated Luke assertively. 'I'm taking her home.'

'Oh, can't you persuade him to stay, Frances?' exclaimed Ella impatiently. 'I've got Matthew Laurence sitting over there just waiting to put money into the new series, and Luke insists on walking out——'

'I am not walking out, Ella. I am taking my wife home.'

'Your wife!'

'Yes, my wife.'

'I—we could take Abby home if you want to stay,' Frances offered awkwardly, aware of Abby's agonised expression, but Luke was adamant.

'I'm perfectly capable of taking my own wife home, thank you,' he retorted grimly.

'Luke, you can't do this to me!' Ella wailed. 'What am I going to tell Laurence?'

'The truth might be a good idea,' replied Luke, hustling Abby's protesting figure towards the door. 'He's a married man. He just might understand.'

Going down in the lift to the basement area where Luke had left his car, Abby refused to look at him. She was feeling sick and confused, not least by the knowledge that Luke had not been lying to her when he had said he had not deserted her. Meeting this man Laurence was obviously important to him, and if she had not jumped to conclusions they might never have had the argument which had resulted in her feeling so giddily light-headed.

They drove home in silence, and Luke's apartment seemed uncannily silent after the noisy ebullience of Ella's. Abby walked directly into the living room and turned to confront her husband rather unsteadily. Her stomach was feeling rather queasy now, and she wished she had never drunk that second glass of champagne.

'You can go back,' she said jerkily, trying to maintain a composure she was far from feeling. 'I'll be all right, and I really think you should speak to that man Aunt Ella was talking about. I'm sorry if I—well, if I was rude. Put—put it down to the champag—*oh!*'

A sudden wave of uncontrollable nausea swept over her, and pressing a hand to her mouth, she brushed past Luke and stumbled up the few stairs to the guest bathroom. She reached the primrose yellow basin just in time and leant there for some time, retching miserably. She had thought she was alone and when finally the spasms left her she almost jumped out of her skin when he pressed a cool handkerchief into her hand.

She moved her head ignominiously. 'I—I'm sorry,' she murmured in a small voice, but he merely gave her a wry look.

'Come on,' he said. 'Bed!'

'I—I can manage. The—the party ...'

Luke had already unfastened his tie, and now he took off the expensive jacket of his dinner suit before turning down the covers of her bed. 'What party?' he inquired, with lazy complacence, and long after she was lying alone between the cool sheets, Abby remembered the faint smile which had touched his lips. Remembered it—and suffered for it. For in those moments of stress, she had learned that the line between love and hatred was a very narrow line indeed ...

CHAPTER ELEVEN

DURING the following week, Abby saw even less of her husband than she had done before. If she had hoped that the night of the party might represent a turning point in their relationship, she was sadly mistaken, and if anything, Luke was less approachable than ever. She knew he was working, of course. He kept the light on in his bedroom hours after he had gone to bed, and Abby could faintly hear the sound of turning pages. He was not aware that she could hear him, of course, or that she lay awake for hours waiting for him to turn out his light, but her nightly vigils were beginning to tell, and there were unfamiliar dark rings around her eyes.

Her days were less difficult to fill. Since the night of Ella's party, she had been invited to several others by people she had met there, and although she thanked them politely and turned them down, at least she did not feel so lonely in the city.

Frances and Mike were the most welcome callers. She had lunch with Frances two days after the party, and went with her to a matinée in the afternoon. It was one of those sophisticated comedies abounding in the West End at that time, and certainly provided a talking point when she went to dinner with the Dwyers later in the week. They lived in a narrow town house in Kensington, and Abby felt immediately at home there. Her attachment to the place might have had something to do with their shaggy Irish wolfhound, an enormous beast of quite ridiculously amiable temperament, who took an instant liking to Abby, and persisted in propping himself against her legs whenever she was around. That he shed hairs in all the wrong places seemed to worry him not a jot, and his unfailing warmth and good humour did much to restore Abby's sense of perspective.

Luke showed little interest in her movements, driving himself ruthlessly, and consequently she was shocked when he announced on Thursday evening that they were going away for the weekend the following afternoon.

'A—away?' she echoed nervously, getting up from the dinner table where they had been drinking a final cup of coffee. 'Away where?'

'To a place called Rosemeath. It's in Cheshire. Not far from Chester, actually. Right on the borders of Wales.'

'But—but why?'

Abby could think of no reason why he should suggest taking her away, and having waited apprehensively all week for Ella to contact her and complain about her behaviour on the night of the party, she could only assume this was some other business affair.

'My mother lives there,' Luke astounded her by replying. 'And I think it's time you two got to know one another.'

'Your—mother?' Abby's mouth was dry. 'But does she know about me?'

'She knows I'm married again, yes. Apart from that, she knows very little.'

'Has—has she asked to meet me?'

'Is that relevant? I want you to meet her.' He was arrogant suddenly. 'Can you be ready by about two o'clock? I have to attend a script conference in the morning, but I should be able to get away by then.'

'But—but——' Abby sought about desperately for something to say. 'I—I promised to dine with the Dwyers tomorrow evening. They're giving a small dinner party——'

'To hell with the Dwyers! Is that who you've been spending your time with? I hope you haven't been foolish enough to get involved with Mike.'

'I don't know what you mean!' Abby hid her anxiety in resentment. 'I enjoy both their companies—Frances and Mike, and Beau, of course.'

Luke's expression relaxed somewhat. 'Beau Brummell! That disreputable beast! Do you like him?'

'I love him,' exclaimed Abby dramatically, and Luke's mouth twitched.

'Then you should feel quite at home with my mother. She has an assortment of animals, including a pair of spaniels that chew anything in sight.'

Abby paused a moment, looking doubtfully at him. 'Luke, do you—I mean, is there any point in my—meeting your family——'

His lips thinned immediately. 'Naturally there's every point. My mother is your mother-in-law, after all. You're her daughter-in-law. I can think of no better reason than that.'

But lying awake that night, listening to Luke moving about in his bedroom, Abby was not so sure. What would Mrs Jordan say to her? What questions might she ask about their relationship, about the suddenness of their marriage? If only she had had more warning, more time to prepare herself. She was almost sure Luke had sprung it on her deliberately. Was it his way of ensuring she had no escape? *Luke* ...

She turned her face into the pillow, burrowing deep into its silky coolness. For over a week now she had been unable to think of him without experiencing a curious aching in her stomach, and every time he was near her, every nerve in her body seemed taut and vulnerable. Whatever he had done to her, he still had the power to disturb her physically, and she had to continually summon those unpleasant memories to mind when that devastating weakness flooded her lower limbs.

The following afternoon, sitting beside him in the Lamborghini, she tried desperately to compose herself for the ordeal ahead. Meeting one's in-laws for the first time was hard enough in normal circumstances, but for Abby these circumstances were far from normal. She dreaded to think how Luke's mother would react if she ever learned Abby's real reasons for marrying her son, and the fact that Luke himself had wanted to marry her meant little in the face of her deception. Would Mrs Jordan recognise her? Had Luke told her she was Ella Mackay's niece? For it was common knowledge, after all, that until her appearance on the scene, Luke and Ella had been constantly seen in one another's company.

'Relax!' Luke spoke to her now, glancing sideways at

146

her, as they left the rat-race of the M.1 and M.6 behind them, and turned on to the comparative peace of the Whitchurch road. 'She's going to like you.'

'Who? Your mother?' Abby played for time. 'How can you say that?'

'Because you're a very likeable person,' he responded dryly. 'Didn't you know?'

Abby sighed. 'You're teasing me.'

'No, I'm not.' He accelerated past another vehicle. Then, changing the subject, he went on: 'What do you think of this area? Some of the most beautiful countryside in Britain, I always think.'

'It is—pretty,' she conceded slowly, and he suppressed an urge to be impatient with her.

'Whitchurch is not far from where my mother has her smallholding,' he added. 'It's a small town, with one of the most attractive churches in the whole area. Anglican, of course.'

'Do you know the area well?' she asked reluctantly.

'Reasonably. My mother moved out here two years ago when my youngest sister got married. Until then she'd lived in the suburbs of Liverpool, a vastly more urban area.'

'Does—does she live alone?'

'Not completely. My sister Jennifer lives with her.' He ignored Abby's dismayed expression and went on: 'Jenny's never married. She's a couple of years younger than I am, but until they moved out here, hospitals were her whole life. She was a nursing sister, you see, but since they've moved to Rosemeath, she's joined a group of local doctors as their nursing receptionist, which means she has much more free time, and can live at home.'

'I see.' Abby swallowed convulsively. Not only his mother, but also his sister, a spinster lady, who had had a nursing sister. Abby's knowledge of nursing sisters was limited to what she had seen on television or read in books, none of it encouraging.

'You'll like Jenny,' asserted Luke now, apparently sensing her anxieties. 'She and I were always close as children.'

Abby stared unseeingly through the car windows. If she had been asked how she would prefer to face her first meeting with Luke's mother, she would have said from the vantage point of being hostess at the apartment. Coming out here to some isolated smallholding did not seem in keeping with what she had learned of Luke's life in London. But then she knew so little about him really. Why had she begun to associate him with sophisticated parties and expensive apartments when he had seemed equally at home at the presbytery?

They reached the village of Rosemeath soon after six. It was situated in a fold of the hills right on the borders with Wales, a thickly wooded area that at this time of year was burgeoning with new life and colour. They drove along a village street where every garden was bright with lupins and marigolds, fuchsias and pansies, hedges of rhododendrons with their distinctive pink and purple flowers, and roses everywhere. Abby saw cottage doors overgrown with honeysuckle and clematis, growing with more profusion than she had ever seen before.

'Does your mother live here?' she exclaimed, enchanted by her surroundings, and Luke nodded.

'Just beyond the village,' he agreed tolerantly. 'She has a couple of acres of land where she grows fruit and vegetables, and earlier on this year she acquired a greenhouse so that she could try her hand at tomatoes.'

Abby involuntarily straightened her spine. She sounded a formidable lady, and who could doubt it after learning she had succeeded in bringing up her eight children single-handed? Abby's life to date seemed useless by comparison.

The cottages became fewer and further between, and then, just ahead of them, Abby saw a sprawling bungalow-type dwelling, with a dormer window set squarely below the eaves. It was fronted by a garden equally as colourful as those they had passed, but behind the building she could see more land and the tall canes where peas and beans stretched their stems.

Luke glanced her way once more, and nodded. 'Yes, that's it. Penny Lane. Recognise the designation?'

Abby shook her head, and he grimaced. 'Don't tell me you don't remember the Beatles! Anyway, they came from Liverpool, too, and *Penny Lane* was one of their records. It's also a real part of the city, and my mother wanted to perpetuate the connection, I guess.'

148

But Abby was too tense now to pay a great deal of attention to what Luke was saying. They had turned between white gates which stood wide, and as they approached the house a pair of dogs came dashing round from the back of the building. They stood at the head of the drive, barking noisily, and had Abby been nervous of animals she might well have hesitated before opening the car door and getting out. But instead, she went towards the dogs eagerly, and soon they were leaping excitedly about her, licking her hands and wagging their tails, and generally making her feel welcome.

'You like dogs? Oh, thank goodness! I was afraid you might be another of those girls who hate getting hairs on their clothes!'

Abby looked up in surprise to find herself confronted by a small, grey-haired woman, dressed casually in linen slacks and a shirt blouse. Laughter lines fanned out from eyes as tawny-yellow as Luke's, and her mouth displayed a smiling mobility of temperament. She was smiling at Abby now, and Abby herself could scarcely believe that this tiny woman could be the mother of a man as tall and powerful as Luke.

'Er—Mrs Jordan?' she ventured uncertainly, and the woman nodded.

'I'm Luke's mother,' she agreed, coming forward to kiss Abby firmly on both cheeks. 'And you're Abby, of course. I'm very pleased to meet you, my dear.'

Abby was suddenly conscious that Luke had got out of the car, too, and come to join them, tolerantly pushing the excitable animals aside, bending to give his mother a warm embrace.

'You're looking well,' he told his mother as he straightened again. 'Did you see Cheadle about your shoulder?'

Mrs Jordan clicked her tongue with goodnatured impatience. 'Isn't that just like a man?' she complained to Abby, shaking her head. 'He tells you you're looking well, and then reminds you about what was wrong with you the last time he saw you!'

Abby had to smile. 'This is a lovely place,' she exclaimed simply. 'I think anyone could be happy here.'

Mrs Jordan looked pleased. 'Well, come along into the

house. You must be tired after the journey. Will you get the cases, Luke? The kettle is simmering.'

Abby, stumbling over the two spaniels, followed Luke's mother across the stone forecourt, and in through the open front door of the bungalow. A russet-carpeted hall gave access to several rooms, while a narrow passage ran through to the back of the house.

'I'll go and make the tea,' said Mrs Jordan, halting in the hallway. 'That's the living room. If you'd like to go in there, Abby, I shan't be a minute.'

Abby hesitated a moment, and then she said quickly: 'Couldn't I come with you and help? We don't have to stand on ceremony, do we?'

Mrs Jordan's eyes twinkled. 'Of course not, if you feel like that. Come along, then. The kitchen's just along here. Jenny and I usually eat in there when we're on our own. It's cosier, and in the winter it's the only room with an open fire.'

Abby was amazed how easy it was to talk to Luke's mother. But then as yet they had touched on no personal topics, and Abby's genuine pleasure in the house made an ideal point of contact. By the time Luke strolled into the kitchen, Abby and his mother were seated at the formica-topped table discussing the problems of keeping fresh fruit for any length of time in hot weather.

'Where's Jenny?' he inquired, walking casually over to the table and helping himself to a cup of the tea they were sharing.

'She'll be home in about half an hour,' replied his mother, pushing the biscuit barrel towards him. 'I thought we'd eat at about seven-thirty, if that's all right with you. It's just a cold meal. I thought you might prefer that, and it won't take long to prepare.'

'I can help you,' offered Abby, at once, but Mrs Jordan shook her head.

'That won't be necessary, my dear. Jenny will help me.'

'Oh, but Abby likes doing things for herself, don't you, Abby?' remarked Luke dryly. 'She'd dismiss Mrs Hobbs altogether if I let her.'

His mother snorted. 'Well, I can't say I'm surprised. I

150

don't like that woman, Luke. I never have. She was always far too friendly with that Mac——'

'Mother!'

Luke's voice was warning, and she broke off abruptly. But Abby guessed what she had been about to say, and looked down awkwardly into her tea cup.

'Of course, Ella Mackay is your aunt, isn't she, Abby?' Mrs Jordan said, after a moment's respite. 'You're not very much like her, are you?'

'I—some people think I am,' Abby admitted briefly, but Mrs Jordan shook her head.

'They wouldn't if they knew you,' she asserted. 'Your aunt ...' She cast a defensive glance in her son's direction. 'Your aunt—well, she's a different kettle of fish altogether, isn't she? I mean, you wouldn't catch her sitting in my kitchen, or offering to help me prepare the dinner.'

Luke's mouth had turned down at the corners and Abby judged it was time to change the subject. 'Don't you miss the city, Mrs Jordan?' she asked, looking round the quiet kitchen with its Aga range, and shelves of gleaming pots and pans. 'Luke told me you used to live in Liverpool and this must be very different.'

'Oh, it is.' Mrs Jordan relaxed, smiling. 'But I love it. I always wanted to live out in the country, to have a bit of land of my own. And thanks to Luke, I've got it.' She smiled up at her son, who was still gravely staring at some point above both their heads. 'It's good to see you, son.'

Luke's expression softened as he looked down at his mother again. 'And it's good to see you, too,' he conceded wryly. 'When you're not jumping in with both feet where angels fear to tread!'

His mother gurgled with laughter. 'Oh, Luke! I don't learn, do I?' Then she looked thoughtfully at Abby. 'But I'll say this for you—you haven't made a mistake this time. She's a grand lass, that I can tell.'

Abby coloured, but Luke merely looked amused. 'I'm glad you approve. She was terrified of meeting you.'

Abby met his mocking eyes indignantly, and his mother gave a cluck of dismay. 'Why? What tales have you been spreading about me? Just because your mother doesn't suffer fools gladly ...'

151

'He hasn't been spreading tales!' exclaimed Abby, and Luke nodded.

'That's right. I didn't have to. Your reputation must have spread before you,' he teased, and his mother gave him an impatient look.

'You're a devil!' she reproved, turning to Abby. 'My dear, whatever you've heard, all I've ever wanted was for Luke to be happy, and he knows it. Alison was never right for him, and Ella Mackay—well, least said, soonest mended, that's what I say.'

'But I haven't heard anything,' protested Abby, red-faced. 'He's teasing you. I was nervous of coming to meet you, I admit that, but it had nothing to do with anything I'd heard. On the contrary,' she looked defiantly up at her husband, 'he hardly mentioned you to me.'

Mrs Jordan didn't appear at all put out by this news. 'I expect he thought it would be best to leave you to form your own opinions,' she said comfortably. 'And you're here now, that's what's important. Heavens, when Luke rang me last week to tell me he was bringing you to meet me, I could hardly contain my impatience.'

Abby pressed her lips together. 'You're very kind.'

'Not at all. I'm a very determined woman, as you'll find out. But never mind about that now—Luke! Will you carry the cases up to your room, and then show Abby where the bathroom is and so on. There's plenty of hot water if you'd both like a bath before dinner, or the shower works if you can stand the fact that the cold pressure is greater than the hot ...'

Luke's mother chattered on about the problems she had had with the installation of the shower, but Abby was scarcely listening to her. Something Mrs Jordan had said, right at the beginning of her speech, stuck in Abby's mind like a bone in her throat. His mother had asked Luke to take their cases up to his room. *His room!* Not *rooms!* Of course, she should have thought of it before now, but somehow meeting his mother had overshadowed all the smaller details. But now the meeting was over and the other details proved not to be so small after all.

She looked at Luke and found his eyes upon her, and although he didn't speak, she knew he had guessed what

152

was troubling her. But ignoring the alarm signals she was sending his way, he responded to his mother and then said: 'Come on, Abby. I'll show you where you're going to sleep.'

They went back along the hall to where Luke had left their cases, and because Mrs Jordan was still within hearing distance, Abby accompanied him through another door and up a narrow flight of stairs to the room under the eaves. Without the evidence of the windows outside, Abby would never have known the room was there, its access hidden as it was behind the concealing door.

It was a large room, tall in the centre and sloping down towards the eaves, with the staircase coming up to one side, but its size was tempered by the amount of furniture it contained. There was a desk and a couple of easy chairs, two wardrobes and a dressing table, and an old-fashioned tallboy. Bookshelves filled the lower half of the window wall, packed with children's books of all kinds, as well as more contemporary novels, and a stack of games in one corner bore witness to its use as a storeroom as well. But for all that, with green curtains speckled with gold sun-flowers, a fluffy yellow tumble twist on the floor, and a broad double bed with a flowered spread, it was a comfortable room, and certainly matched the homely attributes of its surroundings.

Following Luke up the narrow stairway, Abby emerged into the room as Luke was flinging their suitcases carelessly on the bed, and he turned to face her with a curiously appealing look in his eyes.

'Well?' he said. 'Let's have it, shall we? You don't want to stay here?'

'It's not that.' Abby looked about her quickly, liking the room, unwilling suddenly to spoil what might be a pleasant weekend. She looked at him nervously at last and said: 'I didn't know we would have to share a bed.'

'I realise that. But we've done it before,' he pointed out quietly.

'Even so . . .'

'Unfortunately the bungalow has only two bedrooms apart from this room, and neither of them are big enough to swing a cat. My mother keeps this room aired for me.

153

That old desk over there used to be mine, and most of those books, too, believe it or not. It would never occur to her that we might want separate rooms.'

'But it must have occurred to you,' protested Abby, and after a moment, he nodded. 'So?' she persisted.

His eyes held hers. 'I wanted to sleep with you,' he stated steadily, and the thickening blood seemed to pound more heavily through her veins.

'I—you——'

She couldn't go on, and he looked away from her, going over to the window, having to bend his shoulders to cope with the sloping ceiling. 'You don't need to worry, you know,' he said, staring out across the fields beyond his mother's property, 'I shan't touch you. Not unless you want me to. Surely we can share a bed without creating embarrassment for everyone, including my mother.'

Abby sat down unsteadily on the side of the bed. It was soft and springy, but she scarcely noticed it. 'I—I—all right. So—so long as you mean—what you say.'

He turned then and came back to the bed, straightening his back with evident relief. 'I mean it,' he assured her, his voice quite cool. 'Now, would you like to see the bathroom?'

Abby spent three-quarters of an hour in the bath, and when she returned to the bedroom, wrapped closely in a towelling bathrobe, it was to find that Luke had evidently gone downstairs again. Voices in the garden drifted up to her, and going to the window she looked down to see Luke and his mother, and another, taller woman, walking between the rows of vegetables, admiring the crop. Luke, in his shirtsleeves, looked quite at home as he bent to examine the roots of some radishes, brushing the soil aside and putting one in his mouth with a laughing disregard for his mother's obvious disapproval. Watching him, Abby felt her senses stirring, and was immediately furious with herself. Oh, God, she thought disgustedly, was she really the kind of woman who could be aroused by a purely physical attraction?

The tall woman with Luke and his mother had to be Jennifer Jordan. She had Luke's curiously light hair, although in her case it was worn shoulder-length, in a smooth elegant style. She was attractive, too, and Abby wondered

154

why she had never married. Certainly, all the Jordans she had met to date seemed to have more than their share of charm and good looks.

She was dressed and applying eyeshadow before the dressing table mirror when Luke came back upstairs. He eyed her printed silk skirt and sleeveless blouse in a toning shade of creamy orange silently for a few moments, and then he said: 'Am I allowed to comment?' with wry humour.

Trying to match his mood, Abby put down the brush she had been using and rose to her feet to pirouette before him. 'If you like.'

'I like it. Is it new?'

'If you mean, did you pay for it, then yes,' conceded Abby briefly, and then regretted her curtness when Luke turned away and after collecting a fresh shirt and shorts, disappeared down the stairs again on his way to the bathroom.

Deciding it would be easier if she was not there when he came back, she ran a final comb through her long hair, stepped into cork-heeled sandals, and descended the stairs.

She could hear voices in the kitchen, and squaring her shoulders, she walked quickly along the hall before her courage should fail her. At the door she halted, determination wilting, but she had to go on, and with a deep breath she walked with assumed confidence into the room.

Mrs Jordan had changed from her skirt and slacks into a softly fitting caftan, its embroidered folds flattering her thin figure. She was standing by the table, adding dressing to a huge bowl of salad, but her smile was welcoming for Abby, and she turned at once to her daughter and introduced them.

Jennifer looked tall and elegant in a dark blue slacks suit, its fine material threaded with lurex. Both women had obviously dressed for dinner and Abby, in her knee-length skirt, wondered if she looked as out of place as she suddenly felt.

Jennifer shook hands politely enough, but there was not the easy friendliness there that Abby had felt at once with Mrs Jordan. Jennifer was reserving judgment, she felt, and regarded her brother's young wife with a certain amount of hostility.

155

'What a pretty outfit!' Luke's mother relieved the silence which had followed the introductions with her compliment. 'But you're too pale, Abby. You must get Luke to take you somewhere nice and hot, where you can sunbathe every day. He didn't get his tan in this country, you know.'

'I shouldn't think Luke would want to go away at this time, Mother,' remarked Jennifer shortly, returning to her task of dismembering a pair of cold chickens. 'What with the new series and everything.'

'Oh, Jennifer!' Mrs Jordan looked impatiently at her daughter. 'Have you no imagination? Do you realise this child hasn't even had a honeymoon?'

'Honestly, I don't mind ...' Abby shifted her shoulders uncomfortably. 'I—is there anything I can do? Does this ham want slicing? I'm quite good at slicing meat.'

'Well, I was going to ask Luke to do that,' murmured Mrs Jordan doubtfully. 'Are you sure you can do it?' Then she laughed. 'That's hardly polite, is it, but Max Cheadle does so hate thick meat!'

'Max Cheadle?' Abby repeated the name in surprise, and Mrs Jordan patted her arm with a casual hand.

'Yes. He's Doctor Cheadle, actually. One of Jenny's group of doctors. But he's a family friend, and I've invited him and his nephew, who is also part of the practice, to join us for dinner.'

'Oh.' Abby looked anxiously down at her skirt. 'Then perhaps I should have worn something else——'

'Nonsense.' Mrs Jordan looked quite angry for a moment. 'You look lovely, doesn't she, Jennifer?'

Jennifer contented her mother with a faint smile, but Abby knew that under that mild exterior, the older girl was much less enthusiastic. She wondered why. Jennifer didn't know her. She knew nothing about her. Why should she be so suspicious?

Luke appeared as Abby was removing the apron his mother had lent her to wear while she expertly sliced the ham. He had changed into a dark brown suede suit, his shirt bronze coloured above the closely fitting lines of the waistcoat. His eyes took in the domestic scene with lazy amusement, and then he said unconcernedly: 'There's a car coming up the drive. Are you expecting company?'

Max Cheadle was a man in his late fifties, stocky and distinguished, with a definite glint in his eye when he looked at Luke's mother. He was a widower with no children of his own to indulge, and he seemed to enjoy the family atmosphere he found at Penny Lane. His nephew, Grant Hollings, was a much younger man, younger than Luke, Abby guessed, and while he greeted Jennifer with evident pleasure, his attentions were soon riveted by her sister-in-law. Abby was half embarrassed by his intentness; she was seated between him and his uncle at dinner, with Luke across the table from her, and afterwards Grant arranged it so that she found herself ensconced with him on the low velvet couch in the living room. He wanted to know all about her, he said, and without being rude Abby had no choice but to humour him. If Jennifer was annoyed by this state of affairs, she hid it well, talking almost exclusively to her brother, successfully preventing him from interrupting them, Abby thought anxiously.

Nevertheless, when Grant turned sideways towards her, his arm resting casually along the back of the couch behind her, Luke left his sister with scarcely a backward glance. He crossed the living room in a couple of strides, bending to his wife and taking her hands, pulling her up into the enclosing circle of his arm.

'Sorry, old man,' he smiled down at Grant, but Abby knew the pleasantry did not reach his eyes. 'You don't mind if I steal my wife away, do you? I've something I want to show her.'

Grant got politely to his feet, his own irritation showing. 'You kept her a closely guarded secret, didn't you, Luke?' he inquired maliciously. 'Why? Were you afraid someone might persuade Abby she was too young for you?'

'Of course.' Luke was not to be disconcerted by remarks like that. 'Wouldn't you have done the same?' The pressure of his hand penetrated the thin material of Abby's blouse, making the skin covering her spine tingle. He looked down at her, and her heart palpitated alarmingly. 'Come along, my darling. The moon's risen, and I have a notion to kiss you without observation.'

Abby's cheeks were scarlet as she followed him across the room, albeit without having much choice in the matter. His

157

fingers round her wrist were firm and compelling, and besides, Mrs Jordan was looking on with approving eyes.

But outside she pulled herself away from him, breathing in the scents from the garden through heaving lungs. She realised she was trembling, and that knowledge did not please her one bit.

Taking a deep breath, she said: 'That wasn't necessary, you know. Grant Hollings means nothing to me.'

Luke had moved ahead of her through a trellis leading into a rose garden, that stretched for some distance at the side of the bungalow. But now he turned, and she could see the glow of the small cheroot he had lighted in the fading light. He inhaled deeply, his expression dark and brooding, and then he said flatly: 'Others could be excused for mistaking that impression,' and walked on.

'Oh, heavens!' Abby followed him, throwing up her arms in an impatient gesture. 'I suppose you mean Jennifer. Well, I didn't encourage him, I can assure you, and if Jennifer thinks I did——'

Luke stopped again and looked back at her. 'Did I mention Jennifer?' he countered dryly.

'No, but——' Abby hunched her shoulders. 'I don't think she likes me.'

'And that gives you grounds for accusing her of trying to cause trouble between us, is that it?'

'I didn't do that.'

'Didn't you? Not in so many words, perhaps. But it's eloquent in your meaning. Anyway, I can assure you, Jennifer made no comment on your behaviour. *I* chose to break up your *tête-à-tête*.'

'It wasn't a *tête-à-tête*! Oh, honestly, Luke, this is ridiculous! Grant and I were only talking ...'

Luke turned his back on her and walked on again, and she was obliged to keep up with him although the dampening ground was soaking through the open sandals. She didn't know how far he intended to go, and to return to the house without him would indicate that they had quarrelled.

Overhead, the sickle-shaped arc of the moon sailed coolly between the branches of the beech trees nearby, silver shreds of cloud heralding another fine day. Stars were beginning to appear in the darkening backcloth of the night sky, and with the perfume of the roses all about her, Abby felt seduced by their onslaught on her senses. Luke had stopped to stare down into a small ornamental pond which hitherto Abby had not known existed, and now she came to stand beside him, glimpsing the streak of scales as plump goldfish darted about its depths, feeling a desire to make her peace with him.

'Luke ...' she began appealingly. 'Luke—I'm sorry. Don't let's argue, please. Not tonight.'

Luke turned his head to look at her, and even in the gloom she could see the brilliant glitter of his eyes. 'What would you have us do, then?' he inquired harshly. 'Abby, I'm trying to be patient with you, but you make it bloody difficult.'

Abby gulped. 'I'm sorry.'

'No, you're not,' he contradicted her grimly. 'Oh, go back to the house before my physical needs get the better of good sense,' and without another word he stalked off, leaving her to find her way back to the bungalow alone.

As it happened, Doctor Cheadle and his nephew were on the point of leaving, and consequently Abby's reappearance alone did not arouse as much curiosity as it might have done. Luke appeared as the car disappeared down the drive, and accompanying the three women indoors he successfully disposed of any uncomfortable queries they might have made.

'I'll help you with the washing up, Mrs Jordan,' Abby offered, as they walked into the hall, but Mrs Jordan shook her head vigorously.

'I have a dish-washing machine, thank you, Abby, and Jennifer will help me tidy up,' she assured her firmly. 'You and Luke go to bed.' Her eyes twinkled. 'I'm sure you're longing to be alone.'

Alone! Abby cast a helpless glance in her husband's direction, but he merely smiled at his mother before kissing her cheek and wishing her and Jennifer goodnight.

In their bedroom, Abby confronted him nervously, unbuttoning and buttoning her blouse with unsteady fingers. 'I'll get undressed in the bathroom,' she said, picking up the chiffon nightgown she had laid out on the bed. It was a

159

new nightgown, one of the ones Frances had chosen, but she had never expected Luke to see her in it.

'All right.' Luke sat down on the side of the bed to take his shoes off. 'Which side of the bed do you prefer to sleep?'

Abby flushed. 'Oh, it doesn't matter.'

'All right.' Luke rose to his feet again and began to unbutton his waistcoat, and with a little shrug Abby left the room.

When she returned, only a bedside lamp was burning, and Luke was already in bed, stretched on his stomach at the far side, his face turned away from her. Swallowing her trepidation, Abby climbed delicately between the sheets, trying not to disturb him, and turned out the lamp with trembling fingers.

But she need not have been concerned. Within five minutes of her turning out the light, Luke was breathing deeply and heavily. She moved tentatively without arousing any reaction, and a low sigh escaped her. He was asleep. So why did she feel so suddenly desolated?

CHAPTER TWELVE

WHEN Abby awakened next morning, she was alone in the bed and only the imprint of Luke's head on the pillow beside hers bore witness to his silent occupation. To her dismay, she found it was already after ten o'clock, and remembering how early people rose in the country, she got hastily out of bed and stumbled across to the curtained windows.

There was no sign of life, not even the dogs disturbed the stillness, bees moving busily among the flowers, enjoying the warm sunlight. There were not any sounds from the floor below either, and deciding that a wash would have to do this morning, Abby quickly dressed in the scarlet pants and navy tricel sweater she had worn to travel in the previous day. She brushed her hair, tied it back with a scarlet ribbon at her nape, and without bothering with any make-up went downstairs.

The living room was deserted, but the cushions had all been straightened and fresh flowers stood in a porcelain vase on the screened hearth. Deciding that Luke's mother was probably in the kitchen, she went noiselessly along the hall and opened the kitchen door. Jennifer stood at the sink, scraping potatoes, but she glanced round at Abby's entrance, and a polite if slightly strained smile brought a little colour to her cheeks.

'Good morning,' she greeted the younger girl, wiping her hands on her apron. 'Our country air has obviously been too much for you.'

'I overslept. I'm sorry.' Abby bit her lip. 'Where is everybody?'

'Luke's driven his mother into Wrexham,' explained Jennifer. 'She wanted to wake you and take you with them, but Luke said to let you sleep. The rest appears to have agreed with you.'

'Thank you.' Abby didn't quite know how to accept the wry compliment. 'I—it's a lovely morning, isn't it?'

'Beautiful.'

The outer door stood wide and on impulse, Abby moved towards it, looking out on the vegetable gardens. 'You're very lucky living here,' she said, leaning against the door jamb. 'London's so—noisy.'

Jennifer sounded surprised. 'I'd have thought you'd love it after living in a backwater all your life,' she remarked. 'Your aunt does.'

'Yes.' Abby bit back the denunciation that she and her aunt were two entirely different people. Instead, she said: 'Do you know my aunt very well?'

Jennifer busied herself filling the coffee percolator. 'She's been here a couple of times,' she conceded.

Abby felt a sickly tightening of her stomach muscles. 'To—stay?' she inquired faintly.

Jennifer shook her head. 'Of course not. We don't have the room, for one thing. Besides, she and my mother don't exactly—get on.'

'I see.' Abby was amazed at the relief she felt.

'Mother likes you, though,' added Jennifer, almost as an

161

afterthought, plugging in the percolator. 'She doesn't think you're at all like Ella.'

Abby licked her lips, turning to stare at her sister-in-law. 'But *you* do?'

Jennifer coloured then, turning to take down a pair of china beakers, avoiding the younger girl's eyes. 'I don't know,' she said at last. 'I haven't made up my mind yet. Ella's a consummate actress. You might be, too.'

Abby pressed her lips together. 'Is that why you were so unfriendly last night?'

Jennifer sighed. 'I'm sorry if you thought I was un-friendly. It wasn't intentional. But then—watching you with Grant ...'

'Grant Hollings attached himself to me!' protested Abby hotly, and Jennifer nodded.

'You're probably right. He has a weakness for beautiful girls.'

Abby sighed, not quite knowing why she had to defend herself so vehemently. If Ella had her way, this would be her one and only visit to Penny Lane. What did it matter what Jennifer thought? But it did. Another disturbing facet of her deepening involvement with Luke.

'So you'd prefer to live in the country?' Jennifer had returned to their initial exchange, and Abby nodded. 'Then perhaps you should talk to Luke,' his sister went on. 'I'm pretty sure he gets tired of the city sometimes. But naturally it's Ella's environment, and Alison wasn't much different.'

'Alison?' Abby came to perch on a chair beside the table, refusing Jennifer's offer of something to eat with the aro-matically fragrant coffee. 'Tell me about her.'

Jennifer looked surprised. 'I don't think I should be talk-ing to you about Luke's first wife. Why don't you ask him?'

Abby shrugged, sipping from her beaker. 'I don't think he'd tell me,' she answered honestly. 'But I'd like to know.'

'What?'

'What was she like? Did—did Luke love her?'

Jennifer gave her an old-fashioned look. 'I suppose he thought he did at the time.'

'Did you like her?'

'No.'

'Why not?'

'She was vain, and shallow. She wanted a meal ticket, and Luke provided it.'

Abby half smiled. 'Are you sure you weren't simply jealous?' she ventured daringly. 'Luke told me you and he were very close.'

Jennifer smiled then, the first real smile Abby had shared with her. 'You don't pull your punches, do you? All right, maybe I was jealous. But I was right, too. They were never happy together.'

Abby looked down into her beaker. 'And Ella? You didn't like her either, did you?'

'I *don't* like Ella,' Jennifer amended dryly. 'I never have and I never will. I don't trust her. Oh, I'm sure she thinks as much of Luke as it's possible for a woman like her to think of anybody, but she just wants to own him—to possess him!' She paused. 'You know she expected to marry Luke, don't you? We were all prepared for it. We hardly believed him when he rang and told us he had married you.'

Abby's pulses raced. 'It was a shock to me, too,' she murmured almost inaudibly.

'Not half as much of a shock as it must have been to Ella Mackay,' remarked Jennifer dryly. 'Her own niece! What irony!'

Abby got up from the chair to walk to the window. 'But my aunt did help your brother, didn't she? In the beginning, I mean.'

'Oh, yes.' Jennifer spoke levelly. 'Luke's always been interested in writing, of course, but he went into civil engineering after he'd got his degree, and none of us, including Alison, paid much attention to the scribbling he did. Then there was the divorce, of course, and I suppose with more time on his hands, he began to take it more seriously. Even so, the manuscript of *Pedlar's Pirate* might never have reached the publishers if it hadn't been for Ella.'

'But—but why? How?' Abby had to know.

'Luke had finished the book, but I don't think he thought much of it. Literarily speaking, it had no merit in his eyes, and I think he was afraid his friends would jeer at him if it ever got into print. He was a civil engineer, like I say, and it was pure chance that he met Ella and she discovered he could write. Oh, she wanted him anyway, writer or not. But that was an added bonus as it happened, because *Pedlar's Pirate* was filmed, as you probably know, and Ella took the starring role.'

'But how did they meet?'

'Guess! On a building site.' Jennifer gave a short laugh. 'Ella was filming for a television series and the producer decided they needed an authentic backdrop involving bridge-building. It happened that Luke was supervising the construction of the Limewater viaduct in the Thames valley at that time. It was suitable—and it wasn't far away. The film unit spent two days there, but that was long enough for Ella to get her claws into my brother.'

Abby's enthusiasm was waning. She had half disbelieved the things her aunt had told her, but now it seemed she had been telling the truth after all. And no matter whether she, Abby, was beginning to care about this marriage or not, Ella held the power of his success over them.

She finished her coffee quickly, setting down the beaker more heavily than she should have done, starting at the clatter.

'Of course, I shouldn't be so bitter,' Jennifer was continuing wryly. 'Without Luke's success, Mother would never have been able to buy this place, and having a small-holding has always been her dream. Luke's been generous to all of us. I—well, I was engaged once, but the man I loved was killed in a motor accident. Luke knew how I was burying myself in my work at the hospital. He made sure that when Mother moved out here, I did, too. And it's worked. I feel a different person already.'

'Yes.' Abby drew an unsteady breath. 'He's a kind man. I know that.'

Jennifer hesitated a moment, then she said quietly: 'You love him, don't you, Abby? You really love him, and not his success.'

Abby swung round, prepared to deny her words, but then she found she couldn't do it. The words trembled on her lips, but she could not speak them. And not because she wanted to ingratiate herself with Jennifer either. Dear God, she thought disbelievingly, I think she's right. I do love him! *I do!* But oh, lord, Ella would never let them be

164

happy together, and she held all the cards ...

When Luke and his mother returned from Wrexham, it was to find both Jennifer and Abby sitting sunning themselves in the garden, and Mrs Jordan's relief at their apparent amicability was plainly evident.

To Abby, Luke's return presented both a delight and a threat, and uncaring of what interpretation he might put on her actions, she kept firmly out of his way, helping Jennifer prepare lunch, and afterwards, assisting her to wash up.

In the afternoon, Luke suggested they all take the dogs for a walk, and to Abby's relief, both Mrs Jordan and Jennifer accompanied herself and Luke. It was a beautiful afternoon, the meadows thick with dandelions and buttercups, the grass thick and lush beneath their feet.

Once Abby caught Luke watching her with a brooding impatience overlaying his lean features, but she pretended to ignore it, running on ahead with the spaniels until her whole body seemed bathed with perspiration.

There were just the four of them for dinner that evening, and after a cool bath and a change of clothes, Abby felt pleasantly relaxed when Mrs Jordan suggested that Jennifer should play the piano for them. Abby had noticed the baby grand tucked away in one corner of the living room the night before, but she had assumed as in many households, no one ever used the instrument. She was proved wrong by Jennifer running through a whole series of popular classical pieces, filling the bungalow with a warm, golden sound. It could have been the perfect end to a perfect day, and the knowledge that she had been so wholeheartedly accepted by these people filled Abby with both delight and regret. When she and Luke separated, would they regard her as they had regarded Alison—as someone who had never cared for him? It was an unbearable thought.

Going to bed, Luke repeated the performance of the night before, taking a shower before Abby came upstairs, and being in bed with the lamp burning when she came back from the bathroom. The night was warm, and he had pushed the sheet back to his waist, exposing the brown muscular flesh of his shoulders. It occurred to her that perhaps he slept without any clothes, but the night before

165

she had been too concerned with keeping apart from him to notice.

Sighing, she climbed between the sheets, but instead of turning out the light, she sat for a few moments looking down at him, wondering with a pang whether he would ever share her bed again. Her pulses raced. What was he thinking about, she wondered, his face deliberately turned away from her? Did he ever think about that morning he had forced himself upon her? And why had he said he wanted to sleep with her, and then behaved in such a way that she knew he was hardly conscious of her beside him?

'Luke . . .'

The word was dragged from her, and his response was not encouraging: 'What?' he asked, without moving.

'Luke, I—I like your family.'

'Good.'

He was unresponsive, and on impulse she stretched out her hand and stroked the smooth skin of his shoulder. He flinched away from her hand however, rolling on to his back and taking the sheet with him, his face dark with anger.

'What the hell do you think you're doing?'

Abby sighed once more, unconsciously provocative in the sheer chiffon gown. 'I—just wanted to talk to you,' she protested.

'Not now,' he stated flatly, and rolling on to his stomach again, he buried his face in the pillow.

'Why not?' she persisted. 'Luke, are you angry with me?'

'Angry with you?' He lifted his head, propping himself up on his elbows. 'God, Abby, don't do this to me!'

'Do what?' But she knew. And yet still she went on, compelled by an urge that was older than time. 'Luke, don't turn away . . .'

'What do you want me to do?' he groaned, reaching out a hand and allowing his fingers to close around her bare forearm, smoothing the flesh beneath his fingers. 'Oh, Abby —Abby! Come here . . .'

His mouth blazed a trail of fire from the curve of her throat to the scented hollow between her breasts, his weight pressing her back against the pillows. Common sense told her that she ought to move away, that to submit to him now

166

would only make it more painful for her in the future, but time was running out. Ella, Scott, Jennifer—their images were draining away and in their place was the aching desire to know again the thrusting demand of his hard body.

Her arms slid round his neck, her hands invading the virile thickness of his hair, and when his mouth found hers, her whole being seemed to arch towards his.

He kicked the sheet aside, and her eyes opened and stared half apprehensively into his. Then they shifted questioningly towards the lamp, and a lazy sensuality filled his gaze.

'What's wrong?' he demanded, against her lips, playing with her mouth tantalisingly. 'It was daylight before . . .'

'I know, but——'

His kiss silenced her, and after a few moments she forgot her protest . . .

Hours later, Abby awakened to find herself alone in the bed once more. She was pleasantly lethargic, and for a few moments she bathed in the luxury of physical sensation. But as the ordinary things of the world came back into focus, she sensed a chill which had not been there before. She knew at once what it was. As the waves of indolence receded, she was left with the shattering awareness that until now she had been only half alive. Whatever had gone before, nothing could ever erase the fulfilment she had felt a few hours ago in Luke's arms. Now she knew the real meaning of making love, and Luke's possession of her body had been a satiation of a shared and passionate need. She had never dreamed that deep inside her she possessed such ardent emotions, matching his hunger with her own, instinctively and uninhibitedly letting him see her true nature.

But as she stretched her arms and encountered the empty space beside her, the chill she had sensed earlier deepened into a coldness that wrapped itself around her heart. Ella, she thought, distractedly. Ella wanted Luke—and now she, Abby, understood why.

Blinking, she propped herself up on her elbows, and as she did so she saw Luke standing motionless by the windows, the curtains drawn aside so that he could look out. He was unaware of her watching him, and her heart

167

plunged at the brooding expression the moonlight illuminated on his dark face. What was he thinking? she wondered
anxiously. That she was a poor substitute for her aunt?

Getting out of bed, she padded across to him, touching
his arm so that he started violently.

'Luke ...' she began, but his angry expression silenced
her.

'Go back to bed, Abby!' he told her harshly. 'You'll get
cold.'

It was a mild night, but nevertheless, it was cooler near
the windows, and Luke had put on his bathrobe.

Still Abby hesitated. 'Are—are you coming back to bed?'
she persisted, but he shook his head.

'Not right now.'

Abby bit her lower lip. 'Why not?'

Luke looked down at her, her slender body pale in the
moonlight, and his lips tightened. 'Go to bed, Abby!' he
told her angrily. 'Have you no sense?'

'Sense ...?' She faltered. 'I—don't understand ...'

'Oh, Abby,' he groaned, his voice thickening with
emotion, 'I've got to think, and you make it impossible for
me to do it.'

Abby's spirits rose a little. 'Why think at this time of
night?' she protested, tentatively touching his hand, and
was made weak by the look in his eyes. 'Oh, Luke ...' she
breathed, moving closer to him, and with an exclamation
that was half groan, his arms closed around her, hauling her
close to the stirring maleness of his body.

'Abby, Abby,' he spoke against her mouth, and then
swinging her up into his arms he carried her back to the
bed, allowing the bathrobe to fall unheeded to the floor ...

They returned to London after lunch on Sunday. Mrs
Jordan was disappointed when Luke insisted they could not
stay over until Monday, and even Jennifer added her
appeals to the invitation. But Luke was adamant, and Abby,
disconcerted by Luke's coldness to her since they got up
that morning, decided it might be easier for all of them if
they went back to town.

As on the previous morning, Luke had been up and
dressed before she awakened, and after she had dressed and

gone downstairs, she discovered he was out somewhere with the dogs. Even so, she had not concerned herself until he had returned to the house and responded to her half shy greeting with a cool dispassionate stare. She had hardly been able to believe this was the same man who only hours before had been trembling with passion in her arms. They might have been strangers.

And so it continued all the way back to the apartment. The roads were busy with Sunday traffic, and Luke concentrated exclusively on his driving, pushing the Lamborghini up to speeds which left the majority of the other road users standing. Yet for all that, his driving was not dangerous. Abby sensed that he was completely in control, and gaining some sort of satisfaction from the release of speed.

It was early evening when they let themselves into the penthouse. Abby went into the living room, but Luke went straight up the stairs, taking the cases with him. She didn't know what he intended to do, and she waited nervously for him to come back.

When he returned he was fastening his tie over a clean shirt, and her eyes widened as he secured it in place and buttoned the jacket of his suit.

'Wh-what are you doing?' she exclaimed, and he flexed his shoulder muscles wearily.

'I'm going out,' he told her quietly. 'You'll be all right, won't you?'

'Going out?' Abby's legs gave out on her and she sat down abruptly on a low chair. 'But it's after seven—and you haven't eaten!'

'I'm not hungry,' he replied briefly, walking towards the door again. 'I don't know what time I'll be back.'

Abby got to her feet again. 'But where are you going?'

Luke's lips tightened. 'Does it matter?'

'Of course it matters.' Abby felt angry suddenly. 'I'm your—your wife, Luke. Don't I have a right to know?'

Luke hesitated for a moment, then he said quietly: 'Don't start something you can't finish, Abby.'

'I don't know what you mean. I thought——'

'Abby! You've made it plain right from the start that you

169

only married me for one reason. And I don't mean Uncle Daniel's palpitations either!'

'What?'

Luke raked a hand through his hair, looking disturbingly handsome at that moment. 'Abby, I know about Ella and your father! I've known all along, without you boasting about it to Ella.'

'But I didn't!'

'Oh, don't give me that! You admitted as much to her last week, didn't you?'

Abby's face gave her away. 'You don't understand——'

'Of course I understand. Abby, it was always accepted that we married to assuage Daniel's anxieties. One reason or the other—I didn't care. And you've said all along that I didn't attract you. If I've succeeded in proving you wrong, put it down to male ego. Sex is a great leveller. However, I'm beginning to realise that you may have been right all along.'

'H-how do you mean?'

'Abby, this weekend has made me realise my own limitations. I don't want the kind of association we've had up until now—that *you've got me but it's against my will* type of relationship. Everyone tells me you're too young for me. Well, they're probably right. I am old enough to be your father, after all. Or your *uncle*!'

'*Luke!*'

'Don't you think I'm being sensible, Abby? I mean, just because I've shown you—well, what it can be like between a man and a woman it doesn't mean that you couldn't have an equally satisfying relationship with a much younger man, a man of your own age——'

'Stop it, Luke!'

Her cheeks flamed, but he shook his head. 'Believe it, Abby. It happens all the time.'

'Not to me!'

'You're not so different, my dear,' he retorted cruelly.

'That's a horrible thing to say!'

'Oh, *God*!' He uttered an ugly expletive Abby had never even heard before but which she recognised for what it was. 'I made a mistake, Abby. Shall we leave it at that?'

Abby twisted her hands together, torn about by her

emotions. 'Do you—do you expect me to leave?' she cried.

'Perhaps that might be a good idea,' he agreed flatly. 'As I don't seem able to keep my hands off you . . .'

'Oh, Luke . . .'

But he ignored her, going on: 'Naturally, you don't have to go back to Ardnalui, not if you don't want to. I shall make you a generous allowance——'

'I don't want your money!'

'Don't be quixotic, my dear. You have to live.'

'I'll manage,' she retorted, agonised by the pain he was so deliberately inflicting.

'So . . .' He moved determinedly nearer to the door. 'I'll bid you goodnight.'

'Luke, please . . .'

Still she appealed to him, but he shook his head firmly. 'It's no good, Abby. It never was. I should have known better, but it seems I never learn. I'm sorry.'

For several minutes after he had gone, she remained where she was, standing motionless in the middle of the floor, unable to believe that the scene that had just taken place had actually happened. But gradually the whole degrading horror of it took possession of her and she sank down into the chair again and allowed the pent-up tears to flood unheeded down her pale cheeks.

She cried for over an hour, aching, racking sobs that left her with swollen eyes and a dizzying headache. What had Luke done to her? What awful retribution was this for the paltry revenge she had planned to take on her aunt? He had known all along, that was something she had to adjust to. But who had told him? Ella? Scott? Uncle Daniel? Which of them would risk her happiness in that way? Only Ella, she had to concede. She would do anything to keep Luke, she had proved that. And yet he had still gone through with the marriage. That must have been a great shock to Ella. But why had he done it? To punish Abby? To punish her aunt? Or because, as he had said, he needed a wife, and she had seemed suitable at the time? And he had cared what Uncle Daniel thought, of course.

Yet now he was telling her it was all over. The situation was in no way different, and yet he was telling her to get out. It didn't make sense. Unless . . .

171

She pressed a hand to her throat, suddenly remembering the things Ella had said to her. Was it only last week that her aunt had warned her what she would do if Abby tried to make this marriage work? All last week when Abby had been apprehensively waiting to hear from her, had she been poisoning Luke's mind against her? Using her influence in a subtle way to make him despise his wife? But if Luke had been influenced, it could only be in a financial way, and that made the affair that much more ugly.

This weekend away had been so unexpected. Had this been Luke's way of taking his own kind of revenge before setting her free? He had said he couldn't keep his hands from her, that he had had to prove that he could make her want him to satisfy his ego. Yet even he could have no notion of how deeply he had hurt her. She thanked God she had never told him she loved him in words. She might have proved it by her actions, but no actual words of love had passed her lips.

With a logical assessment of the situation came a certain detachment, a certain hardness that might have had something to do with the fact that her prolonged spell of weeping seemed to have drained her of all emotion. Between them, Luke and her aunt thought they had achieved their objective, but she was not the submissive individual they obviously thought her. Her will was stronger than that. It would be incredibly easy to give in, of course, to crawl back to Ardnalui, to lick her wounds in seclusion, but that was exactly what Ella, at least, expected. Her aunt had been right about one thing. She was not like her mother. She would not give up without a fight, and if Luke thought he could cast her aside in favour of his lucrative career, he was very much mistaken.

With this decision taken, Abby swallowed a couple of aspirin and slept soundlessly for the rest of the night. She didn't hear Luke come home, but she was up before him in the morning, and had his breakfast prepared as if nothing at all was wrong between them.

Luke merely picked at his food, however. He looked pale and drawn, as if he had slept badly, and eventually abandoned his bacon and eggs in favour of several cups of strong coffee.

172

'When—er—have you thought when you might be leaving?' he asked. 'I know a good estate agent who could find you an apart——'

'I'm not leaving,' stated Abby steadily, carrying his dirty dishes to the sink. 'More coffee?'

If she had expected an argument, she was mistaken. Luke regarded her coldly for several seconds before getting to his feet, wiping his face on the table napkin and leaving the kitchen.

He left for the studios without speaking to her again, and Abby found she needed a cup of strong coffee herself before she could continue washing up.

For the next few days, life was not easy. Luke came home in the evenings, long after she had retired for the night, and was up and out in the mornings, sometimes before she herself was up. Mrs Hobbs obviously found the whole situation most unusual, but for some reason best known to herself, she refrained from commenting upon it.

Then one morning Abby came down the stairs into the hall to find several suitcases and a trunk confronting her, and a note from Luke stating he had packed his belongings, and that a carrier would collect them later in the day. It was a terrible shock, and for some time Abby's legs refused to support her. But somehow she managed to get into the kitchen and make herself a cup of coffee, and by the time Mrs Hobbs appeared she could present an expressionless mask.

'Mr Jordan going away, is he?' the daily asked, unable to hide her satisfaction at this turn of events, and Abby clenched her hands to prevent herself from smacking the other woman's smug face.

'Yes,' she said. 'As a matter of fact, he is. And in the circumstances, I shan't require your services any more, Mrs Hobbs.'

That took the smugness from the older woman's face, and her lips curled spitefully. 'You having to manage alone then, *madam*?' she jeered, implying a meanness on Luke's part which was entirely unjustified considering the allowance he had briefly notified her he was paying into a bank account for her. But Abby saw no reason to explain the situation to her, and after much bitter remonstration, Mrs Hobbs departed at lunchtime with a month's wages in her pocket.

The carrier came in the afternoon and carted Luke's belongings away, fending off Abby's casual inquiries as to where he was instructed to deliver them. With his departure, weakness overwhelmed her again, and despising herself for her foolishness, she spent the afternoon in tears.

Frances phoned the following day. 'What's going on?' she asked at once, tautening Abby's nerve-ends. 'Why haven't we heard from you?'

Abby expelled her pent-up breath on a sigh. 'I—well, I've been busy,' she temporised awkwardly.

'Busy?' Frances sounded surprised. 'Abby, has Luke asked you not to call?'

'Heavens, no.' At least she could be honest about that. 'Frances—well, things aren't too easy right now.'

'Oh?' Frances sounded intrigued. 'You surprise me, Abby. I mean, you and Luke seemed so happy together. That night of Ella's party, he was so concerned about you, wasn't he? Everybody noticed—including Ella, I might add.'

'It's a long story,' said Abby now. 'Do you mind if I don't want to talk about it?'

Frances sounded regretful. 'All right, honey. If that's the way you feel.' She broke off and then added: 'Come to dinner this evening.'

'I can't.' Abby was apologetic. 'I'll ring you later in the week, Frances, hmm?'

'I know. Don't ring us, we'll ring you. Okay, Abby, I get the message. See you!' And she rang off.

Contrarily, after she had rung off, Abby half wished she had accepted her invitation. It would have been nice to see Mike again, and the Irish wolfhound! But seeing Mike meant more explanations, and she didn't think she could face them right now.

For two weeks she lived in limbo, never moving far from the apartment, always expecting the phone to ring and Luke to tell her where he was living. It was the least he could do, she thought, but no call came, and gradually her confidence corroded. Perhaps she ought to go back to Ardnalui, after all, although she dreaded seeing Uncle Daniel again and having to tell him what had gone wrong. But it wasn't right for her to be living here, in Luke's apartment, among Luke's possessions, while he was possibly making do with something much less comfortable. Unless he was living with Ella ...

That idea made her feel slightly sick, and she determinedly refused to consider his whereabouts again.

Then, late one evening, the telephone did ring.

Abby had gone to bed. She had got into the habit of retiring early with one of Luke's books and reading until her eyes closed through exhaustion. It worked very well, especially when accompanied by a small glass of whisky, although she was careful never to find any enjoyment in drinking for drinking's sake.

Scrambling out of her bed, she sped down the stairs to the living room, lifting the receiver and saying breathlessly: 'Luke? Luke, is that you?' before Ella's cool voice interrupted her.

'No, damn you, it's not Luke, Abby! It's me! But if Luke's not there, there are a few things I'd like to say to you!'

'If Luke's not——' Abby's words were inaudible, a frown creasing her brow. What did Ella mean? If Luke wasn't here? she wondered. Had Luke told Ella he was coming here this evening? Had she expected to find him at the apartment?

'I've been away for a few days,' Ella was going on coldly, 'but I'm back now, and you and I have some unfinished business!'

Ella had been away?

Abby shook her head confusedly. Was it possible that her aunt didn't know what had happened yet? Hadn't Luke told her? Wherever she had gone, she would be sure to keep him informed of her movements. And if Luke had not yet had the chance, had no one else? Scott, for instance?

'*Abby!*'

Realising Ella was waiting for her to say something, Abby gathered herself with difficulty. 'Yes?'

'Abby, what the hell is going on? I told you I wanted Luke, but if he thinks he can walk out on me, he's mistaken!'

There was a desperate note in Ella's voice which Abby

had never heard before, and she couldn't understand it. Surely Luke intended returning to Ella. Surely that had been his intention all along.

Deciding not to let Ella know exactly how uncertain she felt, Abby ventured: 'I—I don't think I know what you mean,' pulling the phone away from her ear aghast when Ella's language lapsed into the crudest kind of abuse.

'Don't give me that, you little bitch!' Ella exploded, furiously, panting for breath. 'What lies have you been telling him about me? Sucking up to his mother and that ghastly prig, Jennifer—pretending that the money meant nothing to you!' She paused. 'Three scripts he's delivered for the new series! Three scripts—and he says he's doing no more! Proposing to live out in that Godforsaken place —knowing I could never stand that kind of life!'

Abby swallowed the lump in her throat. 'Is—is it a Godforsaken place?' she probed, without committing herself, one way or the other.

'You know it is! Of course, it will be no novelty to you, will it? It's all you're used to—all you've got the sense to need! I'll give you credit, Abby—you play dirtier than I expected.'

'Aunt Ella, I——'

'Don't call me that! Oh, well, what does it matter? Without those scripts, the series is defunct anyway. My God, when Scott told me——'

'Scott?' murmured Abby faintly.

'Of course. Good old Scott!' Ella sounded bitter. 'He's to blame for everything. Do you know, he had the nerve to tell me that he sent Luke up to Ardnalui deliberately——' She broke off abruptly. 'What the hell! It's over now. And as the loser, I think you owe me something, Abby.'

'The loser? I—owe—you——'

'Yes. I want the rest of those scripts, Abby. Okay, I know I let you think that I made Luke, but truth to tell, he made me. Or at least, his scripts did. This series—it was to be the high spot of my career so far, and now ...'

'Do—do you mean Luke's—refused to write—for you——?'

'Don't pretend you don't know, Abby! Don't add insult to injury! Oh, God, I'm even beginning to talk in clichés!'

Ella broke off again, obviously trying to compose herself before going on. 'Listen to me, Abby, speak to Luke for me. Explain about my career, if you can, show him that without him I'm sunk! I need this series. There's nothing else I want to do!'

'He—he won't listen to me——'

'Don't be damn silly! Of course he'll listen to you, if you'll do it. My God, I've never known a man so besotted about a woman—no, not a woman, a girl—a slip of a girl young enough to be his daughter!'

'Wh-what did you say?'

Abby had to ask, but obviously Ella saw nothing unusual in the question. 'You *know*!' she exclaimed. 'Hell, I thought *I* knew Luke, but I didn't. I thought we were alike, but we're not. I'd never have believed, if I hadn't seen it with my own eyes, if I hadn't heard it from his own lips——'

A wild excitement was coursing through Abby's veins. She could hardly believe it, of course, and yet it might explain so much. Was Ella really telling her that Luke cared about her? That he was *besotted* with her? Oh God, if only it were true, she thought agonisingly, devastated by the fear that this might be some new ploy on her aunt's part to humiliate her. But if it was not ...

'Well, anyway,' Ella finished heavily, 'I don't think it's so much to ask, Abby. You've succeeded in taking Luke from me, haven't you, and you have so much. Say you'll speak to him for me! Promise you will!'

Abby licked her dry lips. 'Aunt Ella, I—I'll have to think about it.'

'Think about it?' Ella sounded hysterical. 'Abby, I warn you—I'll do something desperate. I—I'll kill myself!' she added dramatically.

'I don't think so.' It was amazing how calm Abby felt. 'And I can't make any promises. But—but I will try—to speak to Luke.'

'Thank you.' Ella could say no more. 'You'll—let me know?'

'Of course.'

Abby replaced the receiver with almost slow-motion movements. Then she cupped her chin on her hand and sat

177

staring at it for fully fifteen minutes, before lifting it again and dialling Scott's number. He seemed surprised to hear from her, particularly when she began by asking where she could find Luke.

'Oh, Abby love, I can't tell you!' he exclaimed.

'Can't? Or won't?'

'Abby, I promised Luke I'd give his address to no one.'

'Me included?'

'Particularly you, Abby.'

Abby swallowed her disappointment. This was hardly encouraging, but she had to go on. For her own sake. 'Scott, I have to see him. It—it's a matter of—of life and death.'

'Come off it, Abby!'

'No, honestly, Scott, I mean it.'

'What do you mean?'

Abby sought about desperately for something to say. 'I—well, I'm pregnant,' she announced urgently.

Her words produced the desired effect, because when Scott spoke again, his voice was definitely shaken. 'Pregnant? Abby, are you sure?'

'As sure as I can be. I—I want an abortion, Scott.'

'An abortion?' Scott seemed unable to prevent himself from repeating everything she said. 'Abby, you can't do that.'

'Why not? If I can't even speak to Luke . . .'

'Abby, wait!' Scott made an anxious sound. 'Abby, leave this with me. Let me speak to Luke first——'

'No.' Abby was adamant. 'If you don't let me see Luke, I—I'll do something desperate. I—I can, you know. I know how.' She didn't, but Scott was not to know that.

'Abby!' His tone was agonised. 'Abby, you crazy little fool, you can't mean that!' He sighed. 'Oh, God, what am I going to do?'

'Give me Luke's address—or answer for the consequences.'

'Abby! Luke wants to see no one. He won't even answer his telephone.'

'Just give me his address, Scott, please!'

'He'll kill me if I do.'

'He may well do something drastic, if you don't,' she pointed out quietly.

'Abby, leave him alone. I don't think he can take much more.'

Abby's stomach plunged. 'Scott, I have to see him. I—I love him ...'

There was silence for a full minute and then Scott said rather unevenly: 'You love him? Does he know?'

Abby sighed. 'Probably not. Scott!'

'Oh, all right, all right.' She heard him fumbling among some papers. 'I have it here somewhere. Yes, here it is— St Godwin's Head, Trelamphey.'

'Where's that?' exclaimed Abby, writing furiously. 'Cornwall?'

'Pembrokeshire, actually. A few miles beyond Pembroke. On the estuary.'

'South Wales.' Abby frowned. 'Do you know why?'

'Don't you?'

'I thought I didn't.'

'I gather you've spoken to Ella.'

'She didn't know that—that Luke and I had ...'

'No. Luke asked me not to tell anyone.'

'Won't she find out?'

'Not unless you tell her. You haven't, have you?'

'No.' Abby bit her lower lip. 'Scott, do you think he'll see me?'

Scott hesitated a moment, and then he said honestly: 'I don't know. He's in a strange mood. I wouldn't dare to speculate. But you have the best reason in the world for seeing him, don't you? Or do you?'

Abby almost felt he could see her blushing. 'Scott ...'

'All right, I know. I shouldn't hold my breath. But I expect a godson some day, Abby. You owe me that, at least.'

After he had rung off, Abby got quickly up from the chair and then gasped as the room swam dizzily around her, as it had on the night of Ella's party, only this was much worse. Grasping the back of the chair, she remained where she was, willing the dizziness to subside, and presently it did just that.

She sighed, wiping the beads of moisture from her forehead. Obviously she wasn't getting enough to eat, she thought impatiently. Feeling faint was not going to do her any good at all, but the thought of food right then was strangely abhorrent to her.

With a sigh, she made her way back to her bed, already planning what she would do in the morning. She would ring the railway station and find out when she could get a train to Pembroke. If Luke's cottage was in a remote area, perhaps she could hire a car once she got there and drive herself to her destination. Excitement feathered along her spine. She was sure she wouldn't sleep tonight, but she had so much to think about that didn't really worry her.

As it happened, she fell asleep almost as soon as her head touched the pillow. Her conversation with Ella and the battle she had had with Scott must have been more exhausting than she thought, because she knew nothing more until sunlight was filtering determinedly through the break in the curtains.

Immediately the remembrance of what had happened the night before came back to her, and she got eagerly out of bed, impatient with herself for sleeping so long. It was already after nine o'clock, and she might well have missed some important connection.

But as she swung her legs to the floor and rose to her feet, the room swam giddily once more and a wave of nausea sent her rushing into her bathroom. She gripped the basin distractedly, fretful at the notion that being ill at this time was something she could well do without. But even as she bent there, waiting for the sickly feeling to disperse, a startling thought came to her. For weeks now she had lived in London and in all that time the absence of certain bodily functions had not been noticed. Dear God, she thought, the idea automatically displacing her other discomforts. It couldn't be, could it? After the bland way she had spoken to Scott the night before, surely her words had not presaged the event. And yet all the signs pointed to it being so, and she sank down weakly on the side of the bath, realising that this put a whole new complexion on the situation. It was all very well for her to pretend a pregnancy to Scott, demanding Luke's address so that he might share the responsibility for what he had done, but the reality was quite different. How could she go to Luke now without feeling

180

she was obligating him somehow? What if Ella was wrong? What if she had been mistaken about Luke's feelings? To imagine Luke's dismay at her appearance if this was so did not bear thinking about. And then to confront him with his eventual fatherhood! No! She simply couldn't do it.

She got to her feet again and walked dully back into the bedroom, her fingers probing the flat muscles of her stomach. Was it true? Was she really expecting Luke's baby? If only she hadn't had to find out today of all days. In other circumstances, the knowledge would have filled her with delight. Even now, she knew she wanted Luke's child more than anything else—except Luke himself. But to confront him with the news, to put him in the position of responsibility that inevitably he would feel ... She needed time to think about that.

CHAPTER THIRTEEN

ABBY walked slowly along the loch shore, her rubber-soled shoes crunching satisfyingly among the pebbles. It was a warm evening and she had needed to get away from the presbytery for a while. Uncle Daniel was a darling, of course, but when she arrived back here several weeks ago he had been alarmed by her thin, hollow-eyed appearance, and tended to blame Luke entirely for the break-up of their marriage.

If only that was all it was, Abby thought now, running a probing hand over her thickening waistline. If she had had any doubts about her condition when she came here, they had been quickly dispersed and now she knew that sooner or later Uncle Daniel would have to be told. But goodness alone knew what he would expect her to do then.

Nevertheless, these weeks at Ardnalui had been a respite, even if she had had to prevail upon Doctor McGuire to give her something to help her to sleep. Mrs Tully had been unusually gentle with her, and had evidently decided her duty was to build up Abby's strength again, physically at least.

And Abby was feeling much better in herself. To begin with it had been difficult hiding her morning sickness from both Mrs Tully and Uncle Daniel, but that had disappeared now and she was eating quite normally again. All the same, she couldn't help feeling that in a few weeks she would be unable to hide her secret whether she liked it or not.

Returning up the slope towards the presbytery, she was lost in thought and paid little attention to the vehicle parked on the cobbled forecourt until she was almost upon it. And then, when she did look at it and recognised the familiar racing lines, she knew the almost uncontrollable desire to turn and run. But Luke must have been watching for her, and guessed what her reaction might be, because as she faltered, her lips working soundlessly, he came down the steps from the house and she knew she could never escape him.

But what she could also see brought a deepening anxiety to her dark eyes. If these weeks had served to restore her, they had had the reverse effect on Luke. He looked positively haggard, he had lost weight, and his clothes were hanging on his lean frame. He looked like a man who had been through some traumatic experience, and she could hardly believe it had to do with her.

'Abby.' He said her name hoarsely. 'I've been waiting for you.'

'Have you?' Abby ran her tongue over her upper lip. 'Where's Uncle Daniel? Have you see Mrs Tully? Has she made you a drink or something?'

'Abby, I didn't drive all this way to see your Uncle Daniel or to take tea with Mrs Tully. I've seen them, yes, and we've made our peace, I think. But you and I have yet to do that, haven't we?'

Abby passed him, realising he was steeling himself not to touch her, and ran up the steps to the door of the presbytery. 'Won't you come in again?' she invited tautly. 'We can't talk outside.'

Luke hesitated, and then bowing his head he followed her into the house. The door to Daniel McGregor's study stood wide, and guessing Uncle Daniel had left it so deliberately, Abby led the way into the booklined room. Luke came after her, closing the door behind them with a definite click, turning to regard her with shadowed eyes.

'Now ...' Abby moved her shoulders awkwardly. 'How did you know I was here——'

'How did I know you were here!' Luke repeated her words harshly, and she sensed the tenseness again. 'Abby, I didn't know you were here until three days ago!'

'Didn't you? Did you think I was at the apartment——'

'*No!*' Luke's jaw muscles were tight. 'Abby, you have no conception of the hell you've put me through!'

Abby's mouth was dry. 'I? But why? You were in Wales——'

'Abby, you said you were coming to Wales! You told Scott—God, you got my address out of him because you said you needed to see me! What in heaven's name was I supposed to think when you didn't arrive?'

Abby's face burned. 'Scott told you I'd phoned?'

'Obviously. He also told me something else, something which these weeks have made me doubt considerably!'

Abby twisted her hands together. 'He—he said he couldn't reach you. He promised me he wouldn't——'

'To hell with what he promised, Abby! Scott's no fool! He knew how I felt about you. He wanted to be sure *I* gave you the chance to tell me how *you* felt! Good God, Abby, were you lying? Don't you care about me after all?'

Abby stared at him helplessly. 'Care about you? Oh, Luke, of course I care about you. I love you——'

But her final words were stifled by the pressure of his mouth on hers, as he stepped forward, jerking her into his arms, almost knocking the breath out of her. As he kissed her, his lips hungrily covering every inch of her face, incoherently muttering protestations into her hair, she realised that he was trembling in her arms, that Luke—the man she had always imagined to be wholly in control of his emotions—was as vulnerable as she was.

With a groan, he finally sank down into her uncle's chair, pulling her with him, seemingly unwilling to let her out of his arms.

'Oh, Abby,' he breathed, his mouth against the palm of her hand, 'promise you'll never leave me again!'

Abby moved her head in a confused gesture. 'But—but if you feel like this, why did you wait so long?' she protested, stroking the curve of his cheek.

'Why did I——' He broke off, closing his eyes for a moment in remembered agony. 'Abby, don't you know?' He opened his eyes again. 'Abby, when you disappeared, this was the first place I thought about. But when I rang your uncle, he denied that you were here.'

'He what?'

'He did.' Luke's lips twisted, half humorously. 'Of course, I believed him. He's a priest, after all. How was I to know he thought he was protecting you from my brutality?'

'Your—what?'

'Well, perhaps he didn't use that word exactly,' conceded Luke dryly. 'But that was what he meant. And how could I believe he would lie to me? He must have known I was desperate. When I got back to the apartment and found you had gone ... *God!*' He expelled his breath on a heavy sigh. 'I thought I should go out of my mind.'

'Oh, Luke ...'

A dreadful feeling of responsibility was filling her, and she bent her head to his shoulder, trying to assuage some of the anxiety she had caused.

'I tried Ella first, of course. I was sure she must have said something to you—done something to make you run away like that. But of course, she didn't know where you'd gone. All she was concerned about was the scripts for the series, and I told her she could go to hell before I'd write another line for her if she showed so little concern for her own flesh and blood. Scott knew nothing either, and poor Frances! I guess I really let fly at her. I was sure somebody was hiding something, and she had seemed closest to you in London, at least.'

'I'm sorry.' Abby lifted her head to look at him.

Luke's tawny eyes flickered. 'Yes, so you should be,' he agreed, as emotion gave place to justifiable impatience. 'Abby, why did you do it?'

Abby bent her head. 'You never told me you loved me,' she murmured evasively.

'No, I didn't do that,' he said evenly. 'I didn't think I had that right.'

'*Right!*' echoed Abby disbelievingly. 'What do you mean?'

'Oh, Abby! You know what I mean. I've told you often enough. I'm almost twenty years older than you are.'

'What has age to do with anything? You married me!'

'I know that. And I lived to regret it.'

'What?' Abby stared at him, aghast.

'Oh, don't worry,' he muttered, not without some self-derision. 'I'm not regretting it now. I'm not regretting it at all. On the contrary, the way I feel right now, I don't think the presence or otherwise of a marriage licence would make the slightest bit of difference.'

Abby's legs felt weak when he lifted his head from hers, and he had to rake back his hair and force himself to go on before his need and hers got the better of them.

'You see,' he said, caressing her nape with his lips, 'you thought we were getting married because of what your uncle saw. But it wasn't exactly like that. Right from the beginning I wanted you, and it was one hell of a situation trying not to show it. Anyway, when old Daniel came upon us like that, I jumped at the chance of marrying you, of being able to take my time in proving to you how I felt. But it didn't work out that way. You were too involved with my involvement with Ella.'

'She told you about—about Daddy, didn't she?'

Amazingly, Luke shook his head. 'No, Daniel did that.'

'Uncle Daniel?'

'That's right. The night before the wedding. While Scott was trying to persuade you that you were making a terrible mistake.'

'But—but——'

'It didn't make any difference to me, Abby. As I told you, for one reason or another—where's the difference? I wanted you. And I was fool enough to believe that I could make you want me.'

'But you did . . .' she protested.

'Eventually,' he commented dryly. 'You hated me at first.'

'Only because of the power you seemed to have over me. And because I thought you were only using me.'

'Ella again,' muttered Luke impatiently. 'God, what a lot that woman has to answer for!'

'She—she did tell me that—that you loved me,' Abby murmured tentatively, and his brows drew together.

'Did she? When?'

'That—that night I phoned Scott.'

'So why didn't you come?' he demanded.

'Why did you leave?' she countered.

Luke sighed. 'That's not too difficult to explain.' He shook his head. 'Abby, I've been married before. I know how a woman can delude herself about a relationship if sexually a man can—satisfy her.' Abby coloured, and a faint smile touched his lips. 'And I did do that, didn't I?' Abby nodded vigorously, and he went on: 'I had to get away from you. I had to have time to think. You wouldn't leave, so I did.'

'But—but you were so horrible!'

'Abby, you have to understand—I'm a man in his late thirties, and you're barely twenty. I resented the way you made me feel. I didn't think it was real. I thought that once we were separated you'd realise how you felt and want to break it off. After that weekend at my mother's, I knew I couldn't kid myself any longer. I'd made you marry me, but that wasn't enough. You had to be free to choose for yourself.'

'Oh, Luke! If only you'd told me.'

'I know, I know.' He caught her chin between his fingers. 'But you still haven't told me why you ran out on me.' His eyes darkened. 'Were you afraid I'd turn you away?'

Abby pressed her lips tightly together for a moment. Then she took Luke's hand and laid it on the swelling mound of her stomach. 'This—this is why I—I ran away,' she breathed. 'I—I'm pregnant, Luke, and I was afraid you might pretend you wanted me because——'

'Oh *God*! *Abby!*' The last trace of shadow was leaving his eyes. 'Abby, Abby! You are crazy, do you know that?' And his mouth sought hers with exquisite gentleness.

'You don't mind?' she breathed, against his lips.

'Mind?' He groaned. 'Abby, apart from the fact that I hoped to have you to myself for a little longer, I can think of nothing more satisfying than knowing my child is growing inside you.' His mouth curved sensuously. 'No wonder Uncle Daniel thought it was time I came to find you.'

'But—but he doesn't know,' she protested.

'I doubt very much whether Mrs Tully is as ignorant. I

wondered why she was so vehement that I should not upset you in any way.'

Abby bit her lip. 'She has been looking at me a little strangely lately.'

'I'm not surprised.' Luke's mouth twisted. 'But when I got that phone call, I didn't stop to wonder why suddenly your uncle had decided to tell me where you were.' He sighed. 'Even then, it wasn't easy. I've been suffering from some lousy attacks of migraine, and the relief of knowing you were safe brought another one on. You can't imagine how I felt when I couldn't get in the car and drive straight here.'

'Oh, Luke ...'

There was another satisfactory interlude, and then he said gently: 'At least we have a readymade grandmother just waiting to hold her next grandchild in her arms.'

'Your mother?'

'My mother.' Luke nodded in agreement. 'I must ring her. She's been as worried about you as I have. Or almost,' he conceded dryly. 'At least if she had any doubts about my feelings for you they must have been dispersed during these last weeks.'

'Jennifer—Jennifer guessed I loved you,' Abby ventured, against his neck.

'Did she?' Luke guided her lips to his once more. 'I appear to have been singularly obtuse.' Then a frown crossed his dark features. 'But—this baby—do you mind very much? I mean, you're very young ...'

'Luke, don't be silly. Knowing I was expecting your child is all that's kept me sane these past weeks. At least I had part of you with me.'

'You shouldn't say things like that,' he muttered thickly. 'You don't know what you're doing to me.' Then he shook his head. 'But what were you going to do?'

Abby shrugged. 'I don't know. I suppose I thought that once I'd told Uncle Daniel he would contact you.'

'Well, thank God for Mrs Tully, that's all I can say,' muttered Luke, with heartfelt urgency. Then he continued: 'I'll take you back to town in a couple of days. Your uncle has invited me to stay here as long as I want, but I want you all to myself. How does Pembrokeshire strike you as a honeymoon spot?'

'I'd love to come with you to the cottage,' said Abby simply.

'And the baby? When it's born—we'll live in town, of course.'

'Is that what you want to do?' Abby asked him.

'Don't you?'

'Luke, as long as I'm with you, I don't care where I live.'

Luke pressed her close to him. 'Do you mean that? But you've lived here all your life. Don't you long for the bright lights? How can I deprive you of all the things you should be enjoying? Ella was right. London is for the young——'

'If you suggest I'm too young for you once more . . .' Abby shook his arm impatiently. 'Darling,' his mouth caressed hers, 'oh, darling, let's leave tomorrow. I want to be alone with you, too.'

Luke stared at her intently. 'Do you mean that?'

'Absolutely.' Then she smiled. 'Do you realise, when I have this baby, Aunt Ella will be a great-aunt?'

Luke's expression hardened. 'Big deal!'

'Oh, darling, don't be bitter. I don't care about Ella now. She can't hurt me.'

'I agree. Thank God I was never tempted to marry her.'

'Weren't you?'

'Abby, whatever Ella has told you, we were not lovers. Not ever. I've never loved anyone until now.'

'But'—Abby had to be generous in her happiness—'you will write for her again, won't you? I promised I'd ask you. And your books are so good! I've read them all.'

Luke's lips twitched. 'Stop flattering me, woman. It doesn't work.' Then he sighed. 'I don't know about Ella. Oh, I suppose I'll go on writing. I can't give that up now, even though I could afford to. But for the present, I have other matters to absorb me.' He smiled. 'Well, go on, absorb me, Abby.'

Also available this month
Four titles in our Mills & Boon Classics Series

Specially chosen reissues of the best in Romantic Fiction
March's titles are:

HEART OF A ROSE *by Rachel Lindsay*
Rose was just an ordinary hard-working girl who had been
lucky enough to land a job as florist in the glamorous South
of France. She had no opinion at all of the rich, idle playboy
Lance Hammond – when she gave him any thought at all,
that is. Certainly she had no idea of the far-reaching effect
he was soon to have on her life.

MASTER OF FALCON'S HEAD *by Anne Mather*
It was seven years since Tamar had left Falcon's Wherry,
her heart broken and her life in ruins. Now she was back –
and her feelings for the man who had done it all were as deep
as ever. But hadn't too much happened for either of them to
turn the clock back?

OPPORTUNE MARRIAGE *by Kay Thorpe*
Lisa admitted that she had married Brad to solve a problem
of her own – but she had thought that she also attracted him.
How was the marriage likely to work out when she discovered
that his motives for it had been as calculated as her own?

THE MAN IN COMMAND *by Anne Weale*
Sanchia had willingly taken responsibility for the orphaned
Rowland children – but that was before she realized that
their uncle Tom Bartlett, in his turn, had apparently decided
to take responsibility for her!

Mills & Boon Classics – all that's great in Romantic Reading!

BUY THEM TODAY only 40p

April Paperbacks

AEGEAN QUEST *by Elizabeth Ashton*
Who *was* Nikolaos Paleologus, Priscilla demanded, to say
that her sister couldn't marry his brother? She'd soon see
about that!

TWO PINS IN A FOUNTAIN *by Jane Arbor*
Although Paula had fallen in love with Gratien de Tourcy,
her love was plainly one-sided . . .

A MATTER OF CHANCE *by Betty Neels*
Cressida's employer was kind and friendly, but she couldn't
say the same for his partner, Giles van der Teile!

THE VILLA FAUSTINO *by Katrina Britt*
Joanna longed to visit London – but how could she leave
Ramon?

GOBLIN HILL *by Essie Summers*
Gareth Morgan couldn't forget the old family scandal – or
forgive Faith for it!

THE RIVER LORD *by Kay Thorpe*
All Keely wanted was to go on the Amazon expedition to find
the Fire Flower, but Greg Stirling refused to take her.
Would he change his mind?

A MAN OF IMPORTANCE *by Anne Hampson*
Taran's legacy had some unexpected snags – and the
biggest of all was the autocratic Armand de Courtenay.

BOUND FOR MARANDOO *by Kerry Allyne*
Jade was joking when she said she wanted a husband, but
unfortunately Tory believed her . . .

DEVIL'S GATEWAY *by Yvonne Whittal*
Her new home seemed sinister to Vicky, and so did the
near-stranger who was her husband . . .

WINDS FROM THE SEA *by Margaret Pargeter*
Sara went to the Hebrides because she wanted a change from
city life. Certainly Hugh Fraser was different from the men
she was used to!

35p net each
Available April 1977

...ills & Boon Classics Selection!

☐ ...TIME IS SHORT
...*erina Hilliard*

☐ C2
PRICE OF LOVE
Rachel Lindsay

☐ C3
THEY CAME TO VALEIRA
Rosalind Brett

☐ C4
THE PRIMROSE BRIDE
Kathryn Blair

☐ C5
TREVALLION
Sara Seale

☐ C6
THE SEA WAIF
Anne Weale

☐ C7
LOVE THIS STRANGER
Rosalind Brett

☐ C8
THREE WOMEN
Celine Conway

☐ C9
THE SCARS SHALL FADE
Nerina Hilliard

☐ C10
NEVER TO LOVE
Anne Weale

☐ C11
WINDS OF ENCHANTMENT
Rosalind Brett

☐ C12
CHILD FRIDAY
Sara Seale

☐ C 13
LOVE AND LUCY GRANGER
Rachel Lindsay

☐ C14
FLOWER FOR A BRIDE
Barbara Rowan

☐ C15
UNDER THE STARS OF PARIS
Mary Burchell

☐ C16
TO CATCH A UNICORN
Sara Seale

☐ C17
AND NO REGRETS
Rosalind Brett

☐ C18
MAYENGA FARM
Kathryn Blair

☐ C19
BRITTLE BONDAGE
Rosalind Brett

☐ C20
HOUSE OF LORRAINE
Rachel Lindsay

☐ C21
HOUSE IN THE TIMBERWOODS
Joyce Dingwell

☐ C22
FLOWER OF THE MORNING
Celine Conway

☐ C23
BARBARY MOON
Kathryn Blair

☐ C24
THE ENGLISH TUTOR
Sara Seale

☐ C25
SPRING AT THE VILLA
Rosalind Brett

☐ C26
THE HOUSE BY THE LAKE
Eleanor Farnes

☐ C27
THE GIRL AT SNOWY RIVER
Joyce Dingwell

☐ C28
DANGEROUS KIND OF LOVE
Kathryn Blair

☐ C29
THE HOUSE OF ADRIANO
Nerina Hilliard

☐ C30
FLOWER IN THE WIND
Celine Conway

All priced at 35p. Please tick your requirements and use the handy order form overleaf.